ASUNDER

A NOVEL OF THE CIVIL WAR

CURT LOCKLEAR

outskirts
press

Asunder
A Novel of the Civil War
All Rights Reserved.
Copyright © 2016 Curt Locklear
v3.0 r1.0

Cover by Karen Phillips, http://www.phillipscovers.com/

Outskirts Press, Inc.
http://www.outskirtspress.com

Paperback ISBN: 978-1-4787-6954-5
Hardback ISBN: 978-1-4787-7054-1

Outskirts Press and the "OP" logo are trademarks belonging to Outskirts Press, Inc.

PRINTED IN THE UNITED STATES OF AMERICA

ACKNOWLEDGMENT

With grateful acknowledgement to so many family members (Catherine, Nathan, Erin and cousin Jane) and friends, most particularly Sandra Timm (who has the photo credit), who helped make this publication possible, this book is dedicated to the greater glory of God.

Jane —
Welcome to
the adventure!

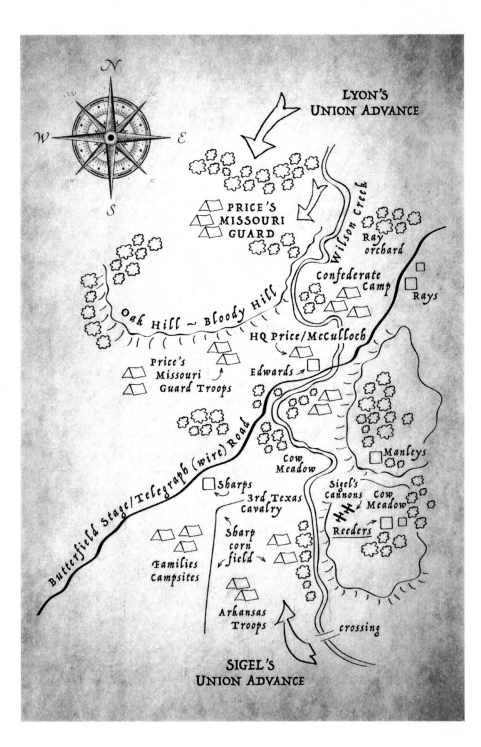

PREFACE

Fact 1. Mary Todd Lincoln, after the death of her son, Willie, held several **séances** in the White House, some of which were attended by **President Lincoln.** During the Civil War and for decades after, perhaps as much as **one-fifth of the total population,** regardless of their faith, believed in SPIRITUALISM, the capacity of conversing with spirits of the dead. **Horace Greely and A. Conan Doyle were two ardent believers.**

Fact 2. It was not unusual during the war for the combatants to change sides. Yankee to Rebel. Reb to Yank. As the war progressed, **about 200,000 Union soldiers and 140,000 Confederates deserted.** Thousands of those, often after capture, changed sides and fought for their former enemy.

Fact. 3 Heavy smoke caused by muskets and cannons often engulfed battlefields. Officers often gave conflicting orders. It is no wonder that the rank-and-file soldier became profoundly confused during battle.

Fact 4. Not all slave owners were tyrants. In many cases, the white man and the slave became good friends, fending for each other. Was slavery wrong? Without a doubt! But the culture in which slavery was allowed was complex and multifaceted. We should feel blessed that we have been freed of slavery in this country. Tragically, slavery still exists in many parts of the world.

Fact 5. More soldiers died from disease during the Civil War than from battle wounds by a ratio of two to one.

Fact 6. In Missouri, Pro-Union and Pro-Confederate marauders wreaked havoc across the state throughout the war. These were primarily gangs of men who sought to profit from the war and take revenge on anyone with whom they disagreed.

ONE

The Space between Chaos and Shape

FEBRUARY 20, 1862, WILSON CREEK, MISSOURI, 1:00 PM

"Miss Cyntha," the Negro said, "do you think we ought to be out here with the weather and all? Looks like a storm comin'." The man rolled his hat brim round and round in his gnarled hands. "And that there battle was plumb back in August, and it be February now. And that man back on the road looked he might be a marauder, and . . ."

Cyntha Anne Favor, a woman of medium stature with a serene expression, stood on a rock by a creek, her green eyes peering into a ghostlike fog floating above the water. She held up a white-gloved hand. "Shush!" She turned toward him. "I'm listening. I need to hear the battle that occurred here." She had attended a séance where the medium said it was possible to hear the anguished cries of battle.

She was dressed in the fashion of the day, and she could have easily passed as a woman of Southern nobility, having been raised in Tennessee, although her home was now in Iowa. Her upturned hands rested on her emerald skirt that was ballooned by hoops and petticoats. Her bodice was pulled tight around her chest. The dress was made of refined cloth with a delicate passementerie of Irish lace about the collar and sleeves. Her appearance, from her black hair, tied back

in a netted bun, to her Italian leather shoes, was impeccably maintained, save for the mud stains and cockleburs clinging to the bottom
of the dress. She had made her way through the ice-crusted mire of
dead, tangled weeds to the creek side. Patches of snow lay about in
shady spots.

The Negro stepped up beside her, his big shoes sinking in the muddy bank.

"I need to feel the battle, Reynolds, how it ebbed and flowed," Cyntha
said almost reverently. "So that I can hear and know where my husband
fell. I want to hear Joseph's cry when he was shot, so I may speak to his
soul. The sounds stay, you know. They linger. Most especially the sounds
of strife and of battle. It you listen hard enough, you can hear." She sought
to catch the ephemeral sounds of the battle fought months before, but she
heard only the rippling of water over smooth stones.

Reynolds stroked his salt-and-pepper beard as he leaned his head
to one side. "I reckon if we listened hard enough, we could hear the
trumpets of Jericho."

Cyntha took a deep breath and held it until she could hold it no
longer, then slowly pursed the air out. "Wilson Creek, what secrets do
you hold? Where have you hidden my husband? Awaken, spirits, and
tell me where my husband fell. Tell me where Joseph's body is buried.
Speak now. Spirits, speak to me."

She heard only the wind whistling in bare tree branches. A hawk
flew over, screeched.

"That be old Mr. Hawk, Miss Cyntha. He be a-lookin' for a meal
and knowin' they ain't none. He knows this cold means winter is gonna be a long one." The old man spoke with a voice like pouring honey.

"I know that it is cold, Reynolds." Her retort had no malice in it.
Her genteel, Southern accent revealed her upbringing in Tennessee.
She had been born into Southern gentry, a substantial business family
in Memphis, but had married a farmer boy a year her junior, and they
moved to Iowa. She cared not a jot or a tittle for highborn airs, but

she was careful never to drop a 'g' nor minimize her formal education with low banter.

"Yes'm." Reynolds hung his head, peering at the scars on his hands, half his left ring finger missing.

"And I would appreciate it, Josiah Reynolds, if you would stop behaving like a slave, with your kowtowing and subservient tone. You are free. Joseph and I purchased your freedom years ago. You're a free-man, working on our farm now for an honest wage."

"Yes'm. And I'm mighty grateful. Except that battle was way back in August of last year. This is February of sixty-two. And in this part of Missouri, there's a whole passel of Southern sympathizers and Confederate scouting parties, not to mention them marauders what don't belong to any army. It be a great deal different than our home in Iowa. We're a far piece from home. And I am a little nervous that if those scouting parties see me with you, they may start asking questions and wonder what plantation you from and why you and me are out here and..."

Cyntha smiled at Reynolds, holding her companion in the high-est regard. "Yes, Reynolds, I suppose you're right. You are so often right. Even though the captain assured us the area was well under Union control, that man on horseback we passed had no benevolence to him. I don't believe I've seen an uglier scowl. I hate to think that a criminal is lying in wait for a chance to rob us. Bring the carriage around, please, and we will depart. I have a spiritualist meeting me in Springfield, and we must return to greet her. I'm hoping she can shed light on my search for Joseph's grave."

After Reynolds left for the carriage, Cyntha turned from the creek and trod slowly up the steep, mucky bank, across patches of crunching snow. She passed through a stand of poplar trees, their white trunks stark against the dismal gray, midday sky. Most of the trees, now barren of leaves, were shredded, the inner fibers of the trunks displayed like torn and shattered bones where cannon fire had sheared the boughs from the trunks. The broken limbs lay strewn about the frozen ground. Stepping carefully around and over the debris, she noticed one oddly white branch. Moving closer, she saw, instead, a human skeleton hand and forearm sticking out from the ground. Shreds of gray cloth clung about the bones that were plucked clean by scavenger animals. She considered that the arm might be attached to a body.

"Oh dear," she said loudly, "have the spirits in their wisdom shown me my Joseph's grave?" In her deeper thoughts, she knew the odds were entirely remote, but still she held unbridled hope. Summoning her courage, she lifted the boney arm, and as soil and rotting leaves fell away, portions of a uniformed shoulder and chest were revealed. The soldier had been buried in the shallow grave, only to have his body ravaged by wild dogs or boars.

She fell to her knees. The remnants of the jacket was clearly gray, the color of the Union Iowa Volunteers when Joseph had enlisted. She brushed away the clods of dirt and leaves, lightly at first, then more vigorously. She knew in her heart that the likelihood that this was her fallen husband was near impossible, but felt she had to know. Brushing. Scraping rapidly. The rank odor of the decaying foliage and despoiled body stung her nose. Then she stopped and beheld the remnants of a checkered shirt draped on the corpse's grayish white skin, shrunk over his ribcage. Sticking out from a pocket of the shirt was a marbled parchment wrapped in wax paper. She deftly lifted the page and turned it over. It read, *Pvt. Isaac Moss, Rusk Co. Texas. Please tell my ma if I's dead.*

The corpse was of a Confederate.

Oh dear. In my zeal to find my husband's grave, I have disturbed the final resting place of someone's beloved son. I am a fool! She took a deep breath resignedly. *If only I could have said good-bye to Joseph.*

Cyntha rose unsteadily. She stumbled forward a few feet. *I feel as if I might faint. My grief has made me inconsiderate and callous.* She looked at the ragged paper in her hand and exclaimed, "At least I can try to put this letter in the hands of his mother." She thought of the plain, yet fact less, letter she had received from the regimental commander informing her of Joseph's death. Placing the page in her embroidered silk reticule, she then brushed mud off her dress and removed her soiled gloves.

The swoon passed, and she looked up at the pearl-colored sky, then at the hill across the creek. Atop the hill, she could see a portion of a house roof and chimney hidden by tall elms, boxwoods, and cedars. Lazy black smoke trickled from the chimney.

When Reynolds returned with the cabriolet, she pointed to the dwelling. "See the smoke coming from that chimney?" she said. "Perhaps that family would know where the Union soldiers are buried. Perhaps we should go up there. If I could just describe Joseph to them, they might have seen him."

"I don't know, Miss Cyntha. We've asked lots of nice families, the Rays, the Sharps. And they didn't know nothin'. I can't see us trying to find a way to climb that hill and hear them say the same thing. And we promised that captain we'd be back to Springfield before dark."

Cyntha sighed heavily and climbed into the cabriolet. "You are right. We must keep our promises." She tucked in her hooped dress. From her reticule she brought out the tintype photograph of Joseph in his uniform. She recalled observing him from the boundary of the fort grounds at Keokuk, Iowa, where he was training. He was waiting in line at a tent where a photographer was taking pictures of all the soldiers who were willing to part with a dollar for a small two-inch replica of themselves. Joseph looked up and noticed her standing just beyond the guards at the camp's periphery, then waved at her before entering the tent. In a moment, he came out and paced in a circle, his hands in his pockets. Ten minutes later, a woman, the photographer's assistant, exited the tent and handed him the metal portrait. Holding high the rendition on tin, he rushed across the yard to Cyntha, and in broad daylight and in total disregard of the guards, he grabbed her and kissed her boldly. Stepping back, yet still holding her thin waist with one hand, he handed her the tintype. She remembered looking at it, admiring his image, yet somehow saddened by its somber, amber tone.

She had smiled, though fighting back tears. She reached in her pocket and retrieved a tintype of herself. "The same fellow was in town yesterday. I'm afraid it's not a good likeness, and I would rather have——"

"It's perfect!" Joseph exclaimed. He stared at her image a long while, then placed it in his shirt pocket. "We march tomorrow to load onto transports bound for St. Louis. When I return, I shall have such a tale to tell."

"Yes." Cyntha could think of no other words to say then though her heart was about to burst, first for pride in her husband, but also for sorrow that he might be killed.

A bugler in the camp blew a few notes. "I've got to go," Joseph said. "I love you so, and I always will, even though I die. But not to worry. Beating those Rebs will be like swatting flies. You watch. This war'll be over in two months."

They kissed again, and he left. Watching him in his smart gray regimental uniform stride back to the parade grounds, Cyntha touched her lips trying to hold the memory of his kiss. The tears did not come then, but later that evening as she lay in bed in her cousin's home and listened to the steamboat whistles sounding in the night as they wafted the soldiers away.

Her daydream was broken by a sudden crackle in the bushes beside the carriage. A herd of deer trotted out of the brush and across their path.

Reynolds drew up the horse to let the deer pass, a vexed expression across his countenance. Cyntha saw his face, and a sudden realization struck her. She had been naïve to think that the man on horseback they had passed was merely a local farmer. She became aware that a band of men like the one they had passed might take their lives. Fear surged through her, and she desired to somehow hasten the horse's stride back to the Union army encampment at Springfield, Missouri.

Her eyes darted about the tangled foliage that crowded the road. "I hope I haven't put our lives in danger coming out here, Reynolds." She bit her lip. Her heart raced.

Reynolds shook the reins, then placed a hand under his coat and thumbed the hammer of a long revolver. The little cabriolet topped a rise, and, at the hollow of the road, they beheld the sour-faced rider they had witnessed earlier astride his horse standing perpendicular to the side of the road. Reynolds slowed the carriage, keeping his hand hidden and on the gun.

"What shall we do?" Cyntha whispered.

"We'll just ride on by. Try not to look at him. Peel your eyes on the brush to see if there's more of his sort hid out."

Drawing closer to the man, Cyntha could not help but behold the man's countenance. A long scar ran across his forehead and the bridge of his nose. Coarse black hair shoved out from under a filthy bowler hat. When the carriage passed, the man spat a stream of tobacco juice on the road before their horse, then stared bald-faced at them. He said no word. He made no move.

Over the next rise, with the rider out of sight, Cyntha said, "Hurry, Reynolds, hurry!"

TWO

Blood and the Hunger

Six months earlier

August 9, 1861, a hill above Wilson Creek Valley, Missouri, 6 pm

"There's to be a battle soon," the gentleman farmer spoke in a dry, matter-of-fact manner. He wore a dark, coarse, wool jacket over his shoulders. It was too heavy for the sweltering August heat, but he wore it as an impediment against the light shower drifting in on a darkening sky. The brim of his cavalry officer's hat kept the upper half of his face in shadow. He stood beside his daughter, his only child still alive, near the edge of a rocky escarpment thirty feet above a valley of rusty beige cornfields. In the valley, an army was encamped.

Below the bluish-gray cloudbank and just above the horizon of the low, corrugated hills that were fading to grayish purple, the setting sun threw spears of light through the trees that danced across the soldiers who hurried about the camp.

"How do you know that, Papa?" His daughter was a petite blond a week shy of seventeen years. She wore a calico bonnet with a long bill and seemed to care not that her clothes were getting wet from the drizzle. Shading her eyes, she peered down at the soldiers rushing about, often colliding with each other.

Many wore various tones of gray uniforms, others sported blue frock coats, and a few had black jackets with gold braiding on the cuffs. Most wore overalls and homespun shirts. A few were decked out in Sunday suits and top hats, and others wore checkered shirts and slouch hats. Many walked barefoot.

Lucas Reeder, two years short of fifty and retired from the cavalry was as robust as a lumberjack. He removed his hat and ran his hand through wavy, black hair. Replacing his hat, he lifted a conical listening device to his ear. "Say again, darlin' daughter."

"I said, how do you know there's to be a battle? Those soldiers look to be doing about the same as they have for the past six days. Some comin', some goin'; nothing special. Not much different than watchin' an ant mound." She fluffed her dress and raised it above the tall, moist blades of grass, black-eyed Susans, beard tongue, and chicory, burned brown by the August sun.

Lucas pointed toward several spots where the soldiers, many who were shirtless, moved with purposefulness among tents and lean-tos. "See those soldiers there, Sara," he said. "They've been molding bullets at that fire faster than anything. And those sergeants strutting about shouting orders. In the rear, the sutlers are packing up their wares to get a considerable distance from any battle."

At the trailing end of the camp, a half-dozen peddlers were hitching their mule teams to modest carts and storing away sundry goods: newspapers, blankets, pots, shoes, plugs of tobacco, and canned fruit.

Lucas said, "Soon, the entire army'll be striking tents and marching to battle."

To himself he said, "And many will die." He had read newspaper reports of battles back east and how the Rebel army had chased the retreating Federals to the outskirts of Washington. The entourage of civilians who had gone out in their carriages and their finery to watch what they deemed would be a magnificent victory party at Bull Run became caught up in the melee, and some of them died as well.

Sara caught sight of cavalrymen in dusty black jackets charging across the muddy fields in mock duels, their sabers clanging. She was enamored by such drama. It reminded her of Alexander Dumas's novels. She thought of a brave D'Artagnan in their midst.

"Isn't this war *glorious?*" she announced. "All our fine soldiers. I just know we'll be victorious. And Missouri will be *rid* of the Yankees. Too bad you can't hear well enough to fight any more, Papa."

A sudden commotion arose in the camp, and Sara rushed closer to the edge of the escarpment to watch. Confederate cavalrymen with hawk feathers in their hats galloped out of the dense trees and crossed the creek.

"Come here! Look what we caught!" the lead cavalryman yelled.

"We got us some Yankee spies," hollered another. "They thought they could outrun us!"

Dressed in a florid red shirt, he held the reins of a horse on which two soldiers in blue-tinted gray uniforms sat in tandem with their hands tied.

The Confederates dismounted and dragged the Yankees from the saddle and sat them down hard in the clearing. The jubilant cavalrymen, joined by other Confederates from the camp, crowded in a circle around the prisoners. The obstreperous captors tossed gibes and insults at the unfortunate pair. A few booted their captives in the buttocks. Lucas knew that any given crowd of men on one occasion could be as amiable as elderly madams at a quilting bee, and the same group turn as savage and lethal as a tangled nest of cottonmouths. This troop's activity comprised less of the acrimonious of embattled soldiers and more of the joviality of a capture in a game of hide-and-seek. The prisoners, their heads hung on their chests, offered no real sport, and, after a few minutes, the assembly fell silent and merely stared solemnly at the captives. Lucas, though he heard none of their words, sensed that the merriment had gone out of their escapade. A captain arrived and directed the prisoners be hauled out of sight under the poplars.

"You see, Sara, the Federal army is encroaching, else they would not be spying our Confederates so recklessly. A battle is forthcoming, probably quite near. We need make haste to gather our belongings and head as far away as——"

"If you were leading our soldiers," Sara interrupted, smiling broadly, "the war'd be over in no time." She walked away again.

Lucas smiled at her confidence in him. For a moment, he wished he could lead again like he had in the Mexican War, imagining himself once more astride a gallant stallion leading his troops.

His thoughts plied their way into his past to the war with Mexico. He winced when he remembered the shriek of his horse, impaled by a Mexican lance, and the horse going down and him thrown hard to the ground. He fired his first pistol point-blank at the Mexican soldier who was trying in vain to dislodge his weapon that had thrust through the steed's chest. Then he aimed at the head of his screaming horse and fired. In the engulfing smoke, with the whine of cannon shot streaking overhead, musket fire clattering all about him, he waved his troops forward. They marched over the piled corpses of the Mexicans in their soft, blue and white uniforms stained red. Then he called up the artillery, and when the cannoneers rolled the heavy cannon wheels over the limp Mexican bodies, he heard their bones crack. That sound was about the last he had heard clearly for years, for when a cannon exploded, it sent him flying and demolished his eardrums, ending his career.

Now, he looked at the thrown-together, ragtag army of Southerners in the valley. The officers were the benighted royalty because of their wealth, while most of the enlisted were hard-scrabble farmers and shopkeepers, and many were the off-scourings of Southern society, hoping for a chance to redeem their sorry situations through some act of bravery. He knew most were merely itching for glory, for a brag to tell family and friends or anyone who would listen. *If only they could foretell the toll a battle would take.* Lucas knew that what the raw recruits were hungry for – a sort of fisticuffs with ornery neighbors. It would be no such thing—instead, an anguished melee of blood, madness, and untimely oblivion.

His heart ached, too, for the Union soldiers somewhere to the north. When General Lyon's Union troops retreated through the same valley a week earlier, he had marveled at the irregularity and flamboyance of the army. Each regiment had fashioned for itself its own distinct regalia—various shades of gray as well as blue or taupe; some uniforms sported red, ballooned pants—quite a parade. He chuckled at the circuslike appearance of both armies. *We all adhere to the same lunacy . . . rushing like a startled flock of starlings straight into the lion's jaws.*

The war had been avoidable. Lucas knew this. For him, the root cause of the war, the useless waste of life, was neither slavery, nor state's rights, but the person of President Lincoln. He deemed the man abominable. It was *that* lawyer's treachery that had split the country apart. He knew Lincoln personally and despised him for a deed Lincoln had perpetrated on a dear friend years before.

Now the war which that bastard wrought is in my valley.

Of a sudden, mellow harmonica tones accompanying a striking tenor voice rose from the valley. "Papa, music!" Sara applauded. "Oh, I wish you could hear it." She leaned out and caught sight of a young cavalryman perched in a wagon bed, singing some maudlin, ill-fashioned words to match the tune. His ballad of a love lost on account of battle hung like a gossamer on the breeze. When the song crafter quit his tune, Sara said, "I wonder if the boy singin' is the one who sang 'Aura Lee' for me the other day. He was a handsome fella."

The singer, joined by fiddle, concertina, and tin whistle players, broke into "The Arkansas Traveler." Sara stepped back from the edge and sashayed to the music, holding up her dress hem, spun, and curtsied, dancing a made-up reel. Finishing with a pirouette, she set to humming the melody. Her father heard nothing, but his eyes watched, in the shadow-laden valley, cook fires and torches beginning to light up the camps like fireflies.

Sara laced her arm through Lucas's. "I hope all these boys come back from the battle in their glory. Maybe I'll marry one of them; that is, as long as he measures up. I won't be marryin' a man just because he wears a uniform. He'll have to earn my hand."

Lucas nodded. Sara was as hardworking as his three sons had been, but he did not quite know what to do about her budding interest in men. To him, she had seemed to emerge from her chrysalis of a dutiful child into a woman with a mind of her own almost overnight. Now she appeared to be so smitten with an unnamed blond soldier who sang to her. He worried that her lack of circumspection would bring her to ruin.

In the valley, a half-dozen soldiers hurried back from the brown-stalked cornfield. They hollered as joyously about the sacks of corn they had scoured from the field as if they had found a buried treasure.

"Mr. Sharp let our boys have their fill of his corn," Sara said, her lips close to her father's ear. "Helping the *cause*. Wasn't that considerate, Papa?"

"The Sharps had little choice. Both armies just helped themselves. We're fortunate that General McCulloch is an old friend, or we might have found ourselves short of some pigs, chickens, and maybe our milk cows."

"I should like to meet General McCulloch someday," Sara said. "I don't know what I'd do if I met a real general."

Thunder grumbled, and the rain splatted bulbous drops. Lucas and Sara retreated under the wide branches of a live oak. The soil under the tree was dry silt. Occasionally, errant drips of water broke through the canopy and punched little wells in the dirt. The two maintained a view of the Rebel army spread along both sides of the Wilson Creek that flowed like a slithering snake.

First, only slightly, then like a percussion symphony, Sara heard the clang of metal plates and spoons and the thud of cleavers on tables. The soldiers designated as cooks stoked the fires and set about rendering suppers of pork, pinto beans, and corn bread. The soldiers propped up blankets across trimmed tree branches over the fires to keep the drizzle away. Soon, the spicy effluvium of onions, garlic, and fried pork wafted into the air.

"Sara, it's getting dark," Lucas said, "and if there's to be a battle anywhere near here, we need to be far away. Let us to home. We'll pack necessities and head far south."

"Wait a moment. Look yonder, Papa." Sara tugged at her father's sleeve and pointed down at a circle of troops with their caps removed. In the center of them, a narrow man in his mid twenties stood, stiff as an iron rod. "Our dear Reverend Felder is rendering an invocation," Sara called out. "His is a powerful voice. He's asking almighty God to keep our boys in a safe harbor. He says that our righteous cause must in truth be esteemed by our Father in heaven. Now he's asking God to let whatever blood is spilt on the field of battle be a sin offering to Him so that our just cause may claim victory."

Lucas, though anxious to leave, listened intently through his trumpet to his daughter's retelling of the sermon. Lightning crackled and thunder roared like cannons, and the soldiers flinched and ducked. Reverend Felder never stirred from his prayer.

"And he's pleading to God," Sara continued, "to smite those from the North who would dare to take our lands from us, our inheritance for all our hard labors." Then, in an aside, she said, "Those Yankees aren't going to take our land. I'll fight 'em for it." She set her fists up and punched at imaginary villain soldiers.

"You're a fighter like your dear mama was. She would've been proud of you." He acknowledged that Sara was like his wife who had died of typhus when Sara was a child. Sara emulated her in appearance and in gumption. She had freckles across her nose and cheeks, a rosy complexion, full lips, and her hair shone golden. And, though often given to chimerical ideas based on her reading of romantic novels like *Ivanhoe*, she was headstrong. *Sometimes*, he thought, *too headstrong.*

Sara beamed at Lucas's compliment. Then she pointed. "Look there. Let's ask this soldier when the army's marchin' out to fight."

A gray-clad sergeant struggled up the hill toward them, huffing and cursing. His beard, almost the color of his uniform, hung down on a bulging belly, quite to his belt. He wore a dark blue kepi cocked a little to the side, and his face was ruddy with a raised purplish weal at his temple. He struggled to keep from tumbling down the slope, grabbing onto saplings and bushes that protruded out of the hillside.

When he came nearer to the Reeders, Lucas called out, "Is the army marching to battle?"

The sergeant plodded up beside them and spoke congenially into Lucas's ear trumpet, "We're gettin' ready to strike out and get 'em, sir. McCulloch's done called in his pickets. That's what I'm doing now, retrievin' our pickets. Soon as all the soldiers have 'et, we're to make a night march. After them pickets, I have to order them families camped in old man Sharp's cornfields to stay put. Damned shame. They've no business following the army anyway, to my way of thinking. This close to the army, they're in danger of being killed."

"An army camp is no place for women and children," Lucas agreed, "but they came so they would have food."

The three of them looked out to the western edge of the cornfield at a number of piteous campsites where soldiers' wives tended cook fires while children gamboled and chased amidst bent, dried cornstalks. In the twilight gloom and smoke, they looked akin to specters.

"Do you think the battle could work its way here?" Lucas asked.

"There's a high potential," the sergeant said. "Even though we outnumber the Yanks, the North's General Lyon's is itching for a fight. Word is he thinks this war is a big cockfight, and he's the meanest rooster. I just hope we get to the Yanks and whip them first. As it is, McCulloch's scouts don't know what Lyon's up to, but that he's holed up somewhere nearby. Us troops are pretty confident, but we're a 'feared, too. And what troubles most of us is that only about half the army even possesses a weapon. Not many guns. Too few bullets. We ain't been fully equipped to fight. But I best be on my way. I'd encourage you to get somewhere far away. Unless Providence smiles on us, there's to be a reckoning. Good evenin' to you, sir, miss." He tapped a finger to his kepi and treaded further up the hill.

"Come, Sara," Lucas demanded. "Even if the armies fight further north, the battle could spill over to here. With this many soldiers, a battle could spread many miles. We'll need to hide the valuables, and head south tonight."

"But, Papa—"

"Listen to me. War is at our doorstep. We've much to do."

Sara hurried to keep pace with Lucas. In a moment, the sergeant trudged past them on the way back to the camp accompanied by three young privates, the pickets. Sara turned her head to watch the four soldiers negotiate the steep hill. They sometimes leaped from boulder to boulder like goats, and used their rifles as walking sticks.

The rain had ceased, but the night was gathering around them like a cloak of black velvet.

Following a cow path through a dark phalanx of cedars and elms, they stepped with caution around the patties strewn about.

A sudden movement in the trees caught Lucas's eye. Several dark forms rushed along in the black woods. He squeezed Sara's arm and held her still. He pointed into the shadows. "Look!" he whispered. "Do you see anything?"

Sara peered into the inky smudge of trees and brush. Whispering. "No, Papa."

"Do *you* hear anything? Rustling of leaves? Anything?"

She cocked her head to listen. "No, Papa."

Lucas scanned the woods. Seeing no further movement, he sighed. "I hope that's just more pickets returning. Maybe it was some deer."

"Maybe your eyes're playing tricks on you."

Continuing to watch the dark trees and not wishing to frighten his daughter, he said, "Let us proceed to home. Probably only some deer."

THREE

Pale Death, with Impartial Step, Knocks at Every Door

Seven hours later

August 10, 1861, north of the Confederate encampment
on Wilson Creek, Missouri, 4 am

Battle was imminent. Whether it would be in a few minutes or in an hour, Private Joseph Favor, a soldier in the Union army for only two months, sensed the impending fight. He had no idea where the army had ceased its tedious night march, but figured that the Rebel army must be near. He stood in line with the Union's First Iowa Volunteers, leaning against a white oak tree.

The soldiers, gloomy shadows in the early, lightless morning had halted a full hour earlier. Up and down the regiment, he heard the soldiers' mutterings, many grumbling about the smothering heat. Some of the First Iowans had blue-tinted uniforms, but his company wore gray uniforms with a hint of blue. Their uniforms were soggy from the rain that had come and gone throughout the night. Sweat was beaded on Joseph's forehead, and the odor of musty wool and perspiration prickled his nostrils.

He tried to envision the looming battle. The drill at camp had

given him only an inkling of what to expect. How a battle would tran-
spire, what it would look like and sound like and feel like, remained
a conundrum. He was not unnerved by this but frustrated. He was
more bothered by a recent dream in which he witnessed his own body
laid out cold and gray on a slab of marble.

He forced himself to think on something else. Thinking about
death, he decided, might actually bring it about.

He patted his jacket pocket where he kept two newspaper clip-
pings, one headlining Lincoln's presidential victory, the other about
the Rebels' firing on Fort Sumter. He was glad Lincoln had called for
volunteers to put down the rebellion. Though every other soldier in
the regiment Joseph had queried told him they had joined explicitly to
"preserve the Union," or "whip the Rebs," for him, this war meant the
possibility of freeing the Negroes from their bondage. *Damn preserving
the Union*, he thought. *Just let our victory set the Negro free.* He thought
of Reynolds in highest regard, the former slave whom he and his wife
had purchased, then given freedom and a paying job on their farm.
"God bless you, Reynolds," he said under his breath. "Take good care
of Cyntha."

In his left shirt pocket, he kept a tintype photograph of his wife,
Cyntha Anne, and her most recent letter; her other letters bound with
twine in his tent back at camp in Springfield. He missed her to the
point of lament. In his mind, he beheld her calm, gentle face always
with a hint of an admiring smile when she listened to him speak, and
how her cheek felt when cupped in his hand, and the smell of her
hair, and the glow of her flushed cheeks after she had returned from a
walk on a brisk, snowy morning. A sadder thought entered his mind.
The day when he joined the army, how she melted into his embrace,
clutching tight to the lapels of his jacket. He remembered as he was
walking away of glancing down at his lapels to see tear stains there.
Turning the corner of the street, he stopped and felt the wetness. He
held his head up to diminish his own tears.

He touched his shirt pocket. He felt assured that nothing, especially no bullet from a Rebel gun, could keep him from returning to Cyntha. In his mind, the war would end soon after this battle, and the rebels would be sent scampering all the way to Alabama.

The sweat from Joseph's forehead trickled down his straight nose, across his narrow lips and onto his angular chin. His eyes were bright blue with a light in them like the fire of a minister bent on preaching the Word. His sandy blond hair hung shaggy over his ears, and a short beard bristled from his jaw.

His regiment was butted up next to other regiments, some dressed in blue uniforms, others in gray, one regiment in brown. The regiments formed the brigades of General Lyon's Union Army of the West. Behind them, the path they had marched upon meandered amongst the trees. Before them, a long, narrow meadow with tall, Bluestem grass extended far to the left and right. Beyond that lay a much denser clump of sycamores, oaks, and blackjacks.

Overhead, rainclouds had rolled away, revealing a full moon hung low on the horizon, and the stars were little lanterns. Joseph strained his tanned neck to watch the stars flicker in and out of view as the tops of the trees swept back and forth in the wind. Leaning akimbo against the white oak with his rifle held in the crook of his arm, Joseph recalled sitting with Cyntha observing the constellations above their Iowa farm.

His back aching some from standing so long, he mildly regretted joining the volunteers, though he did not feel afraid. He had succeeded in squelching any anxiety of impending death and assured himself daily that only the enemy would die, and that he was immune from harm. His camp mates spoke mostly of the glory they were sure to attain, seldom of death. Only when the order came down that they were going to the front did some fear rise in him. His sense of foreboding had abated on the wearisome night march, and now he felt dog-tired.

The rumble of horses' hooves snapped Joseph from his boredom.

The regiment had been lulled into torpor from the all-night march in the bothersome drizzle, but instantly became alert. A group of officers galloped into the clearing and halted just in front of Joseph, drawing up beside his own commanding officer, Colonel Merritt.

"That's General Lyon in the center." A lanky, older soldier with a bushy mustache and moles on his face was standing opposite the tree from Joseph. The soldier was named Dred Workman, but Joseph barely knew him. He continued, "I'd recognize that bearded scowl anywhere. I served with him in California when he ordered them Indian villages cleaned out. He carved 'em up bad. Killed every one he could. He's a mean bastard."

Other soldiers whispered comments up and down the line, creating a steady hiss. Joseph leaned forward to grasp the officers' comments.

"Maybe," the same tall, string bean of a soldier continued, "he's here to tell us what the hell we're doing out here in the dead of night. We can't even see the Rebs, much less shoot at 'em." When Workman talked, his pronounced Adam's apple bobbed up and down, and his broad mustache fluttered with each word. His pale eyes reflected the moonlight and looked like stars fallen from the sky. Well over six feet tall, he was about the tallest man Joseph had ever seen, yet the Iowa Gray uniform fit him fine.

"Colonel Merritt will tell the general a thing or two," said another soldier on the other side of Joseph.

"Quiet in the ranks," a lieutenant called in a hoarse whisper. He walked along behind the men, slapping the broad of his sword on the backsides of certain hapless soldiers.

Joseph strained to hear the officers, a mere thirty feet in front of him, but the abundant noise of stretching leather, clanking of guns and canteens, and soldiers' coughs made comprehension difficult. The general, a short, stout man wearing a wide-brimmed hat, was gesturing to the left, then to the right, then back to the left. Colonel Merritt also gestured left and right and toward his own line of troops. A third rider approached, dressed in dark clothing and riding a black horse. He spoke in hushed tones to the officers. He wore no insignia.

"That's a scout," Workman commented. "He's been inspecting the Rebel position, I'll warrant." Joseph looked at his companion soldier with greasy black hair who was at least ten years his senior. He chuckled inwardly at his companion's skinny neck with the bulbous Adam's apple.

After the officers' conversation and animated gestures had gone on for some minutes, Joseph heard Colonel Merritt say a few sentences that included the words "strong" and "ready." Joseph stood taller, knowing that his regiment, the First Iowa Volunteers, was recognized and would soon be seeing action.

Joseph had never encountered anything close to a battle, but he figured himself a good marksman, having won shooting contests in his original home state of Tennessee. He spoke with such a strong Southern accent that he had been accused of spying for the Confederates. Nothing could be further from the truth for him. He and Cyntha had once attended a debate between Abraham Lincoln and Stephen Douglas. By the force of Lincoln's arguments, the two of them became firmly convinced of the need to free the slaves. Their later involvement in a fledgling abolitionist group increased their fervency. He felt no allegiance to Tennessee. He considered the state of his youth traitorous for seceding.

He peered down the regiment's line at men he had come to know. The faces of the two to his right resembled pale dish plates in the moonlight. He detected some fear in their look. Though unsure of whether the Union Kansas and Missouri soldiers would fight well, he believed like a matter of religious faith that the First Iowa Grays would fight hard, no matter what.

"What's he saying, the general, that is?" asked Workman.

"I think we're to march again somewhere else."

"That figures," Workman said.

"What do you mean?"

"It's the same ol' thing. I'm regular army. Marched many a mile, only to turn around and march back to where we started."

"Are you scared of the fight that's about to ensue?"

"Ensue? That's a fine word. No, I ain't a sceared of any fight."

"Me neither. I volunteered for this army just two months ago. I'm fighting to set the slaves free. How about you?"

"Well, I ain't fightin' to set no slaves free. I'm here because they said they'd let me out of prison if I fought for a year."

"Why were you in prison?"

"Stole from the captain's larder. They put me in the stockade and said they threw away the key. But I guess I deserved it. Ain't the first time I stole somethin'."

"What else did you steal?"

Workman snickered. "Stole a young girl's heart." He commenced to laughing.

Joseph smiled, but was not sure how to take this new acquaintance.

"You sure you ain't a rebel?" The tall soldier fixed his gaze squarely on Joseph. "You sound like you're from the South."

"I grew up in Tennessee, but I moved to Iowa four years ago. I take no allegiance to those Philistines who would divide the Union for the sake of preserving slavery."

Joseph's ardent remark gained no response from the tall soldier. He whistled a low tune through his sagging mustache.

With all the immediacy of men fleeing from flood waters, General Lyon and his entourage galloped back the way they had come. Colonel Merritt issued some whispered orders to his captains and lieutenants. The soldiers began to murmur again. The young soldier on the other side of Joseph suddenly doubled over to the ground and threw up.

Joseph bent down. "Are you all right?"

The teenage boy was as pale as a white-washed fence. He wiped his mouth and looked up. "No," he said. "I don't want to die. I don't know why I ever volunteered."

Joseph rubbed the soldier's back and offered him water from his canteen. The young man declined and sat back on his haunches, head down. He continued to make puking sounds. A knot twisted Joseph's stomach, but he steeled his resolve and stood erect. Then, by an irritated compunction, he kicked the sick soldier in the flank. "Get up!" he whispered harshly. "You're an embarrassment to us all. Coward, stand up!" When it became clear that the soldier was not going to rise, Joseph moved away from him. "Stinking coward," he said to Workman.

Workman glanced down at the sick soldier and blew through his mustache. "Likely to see more o' that." He drew a long breath. "Likely to see a lot of dyin', too."

At the rear of the regiment, Joseph heard the drummer youths clattering their drums against their legs as they jogged back to the cow path. He knew that the regiment had new orders. Arriving at the site where they now stood had involved at least three direction changes. Now the regiment would move again.

"Company C, attention!" the sergeant called. "The captain's got something to say."

Captain Mason, his face in shadows, strutted up before Joseph's company. "Gentlemen, we are not in an advantageous position for battle. We are to retire to the rear and march back down that path to a new position. We are to arrive there and prepare for battle in one-half hour. Before we march, I need volunteers for a skirmish line. You will go forward before the line and engage the pickets with haste to give us a better idea of the Rebels' position and strength. I want no one under the age of twenty. Any seasoned soldiers and good marksmen would be best."

Joseph felt his arm going up. He was twenty years old, and he considered himself a good marksman.

The sergeant beckoned the volunteers step forward. He sent three back, leaving himself, Joseph, Workman, and five others. "You men come with me," he said.

Joseph and his fellow volunteers lurched forward across the meadow and halted beside other skirmishers from different companies in a broken line formed in the trees. Joseph glanced backward to the regiment that had done an about-face and was trooping toward the cow path. He could not tell what had become of the fearful, sick soldier.

Then the realization sank in. He would be one of the first wading into the battle. He felt a measure of guilt for his treatment of the frightened soldier. How many others sensed death knocking at their door? Now he realized he faced his own personal eternity, perhaps in the immediacy of moments. His own emotions were a blur—a blending of exhilaration of his assured personal bravery, wonder about the great beast of war, and an increasing, all-consuming dread. His feet felt like they were fettered with iron.

FOUR

How Does One Prepare for Onslaught?

AUGUST 9, 1861, THE REEDER FARM, WILSON CREEK, MISSOURI, 8 PM

Striding at a rapid pace through a column of trees that crowded the path, Sara clung to her father's arm, smiling. "Why are we rushing so, Papa?"

She had instantly forgotten about the shadowy figures her father had seen. Her entire being was filled with pride and abject confidence in the Confederate cause, a mood of elation unlike any she had felt before. Her fervor for the Southern cause masked any misgivings of the imminent deaths of the soldiers she so admired. Not having experienced war, she knew only of the colorful uniforms, the refined manner of the officers, the bands playing, the spectacle of soldiers marching, or the saber-flashing cavalrymen dashing across a field. The soldiers acted in gentleman fashion and were grateful for the tin cups of milk that Sara and Lucas divvyed among them, and they paid liberally in new-minted Confederation coins. She enjoyed the admiring looks from the soldiers each day when she delivered a bottle of milk to an officer's wife with a baby. The woman was exceedingly thankful.

On Sara's first visit, a Kansas Confederate of about twenty years and dressed in a flowered shirt stepped forward and sang "Aura Lee" for her. She felt certain in that moment that he must have fallen in love with her. A mere wisp of a boy with long, soft, whitish blond hair, he held a book in his hand, so she was sure he was book learned. At the song's end, he smiled at her, drank the cup of milk she offered, then slipped away while she dipped out servings of milk to other soldiers.

Sara and her father walked out of the tree line into a logged-over meadow filled with moonlight. The rainclouds were rolling sleepily away, revealing a sort of lacework of mares' tails. The full moon's gleam overhead colored the trees cobalt blue. The honeysuckle that crowded both sides of the path shimmered gold and translucent with raindrops. The vibrantly sweet aroma of the honeysuckle, enhanced by the rain, hung propitiously in the air. Sara plucked a blossom and licked the honey of the stamen. She smacked her lips. Just then, she was startled when a mother possum, packing baby possums on her back, crossed their path and scuttled underneath the bushes.

"I have decided," Sara said, laughing, "that when I marry one of those soldiers that we will have as many babies as that possum mama."

"And will you carry them all on your back, just like her?" Lucas teased, hoping to lighten his own mood. He did not mind that Sara was proud of the cause, but he wished he could illuminate her thoughts to their danger in the ensuing hours. He knew the rushing forms in the woods were not deer, but Union scouts. He also hoped that those scouts would not accost them in the house with the lamps turned up. As long as the scouts believed they were not found out, they would leave Lucas and Sara alone. Looking ahead, Lucas detected their house lights flickering through the trees.

Nearer the house, a barred owl hooted a doleful tone near their small family graveyard behind a white picket fence. The graves of Sara's mother and three older brothers, marked by simple board crosses, lay under a spread oak. Sara halted. "Papa, we must stop to pray for Mama and my brothers."

Reluctantly, Lucas stopped, and the two stood perfectly still in silent supplication, such that a passerby might have mistook them in the moonlight for well-made statues. Lucas still studied the shadows for movement.

After the prayer, Sara picked up a stick and ran it along the picket fence, making a tick-tick sound. "Our life is so good, isn't it, Papa?"

"The good Lord provideth."

They crossed the yard of their warmly lit house. A mulatto slave with freckles about his cheeks sat on a rocker on the front porch, humming a hymn. He waved a hello to them and continued to rock and hum.

Lucas called loudly to him, "Abram, you may be more'n seventy, but I see some youthful larceny in your face." His jocularity was calculated for any scouts nearby to presume they had not been seen.

Abram, a slave of the Reeder family since before Lucas was born, had passed the point in his life where he could help much with physical labor for any extended period. He cooked and did small chores about the house, and occasionally helped with the milking. He slept on a corn husk mattress bed in a small room behind the kitchen.

Abram's dark eyes, whitened by cataracts, twinkled above a dense, gray beard. He rose slowly and tottered over to join them on the long porch steps. Sara, Lucas, and he turned to feel a warm wind that came up from the south sending the tree branches fluttering. The moon shone on them and transformed their white-washed porch silvery. "I turned the house lamps up so you all could find yor way home in the dark," Abram spoke into Lucas's trumpet.

"Thank you," Lucas said. Then he whispered, "Abram, other than the Confederate pickets, have you seen any other men moving about?"

"No, suh, it's been mighty quiet," Abram wagged his head back and forth.

"I'll explain shortly."

Turning north, the three gazed for a moment over the verdant pasture of silver grasses bowing in the breeze. The mountaintop was dotted with burned, goblin-shaped remnants of trees from the decades-old fire that had cleared the mountaintop and become an ample meadow for their milk cows to graze. From the porch, they had an unobstructed view of the valley where the Confederate campfires glowed, and the waters of Wilson Creek glimmered. In the distance, the lights of their neighbors' homes, the Ray and Manley families, looked like low-slung stars. Lucas wondered if his neighbors had any inkling of the considerable danger of the battle brewing.

His knowledge of the unpredictability of battle, coupled with the sergeant's warning and the clandestine soldiers traversing the woods, wore on his mind. Union soldiers doing some nighttime scouting of the Rebels was one thing, but his real concern was of how immense an engagement could become, in many cases, spreading over miles. Sara, Abram, and he would *have* to get far away.

Lucas spoke in a whisper to Sara and Abram. "There will be a battle very near here by tomorrow. I saw Union scouts in the woods a few minutes ago. Tonight, McCulloch is marching the army to attack the Yankees, but I don't believe they're going to have to travel very far. The Union army is nearer than they think. Any battle could spread far and wide. Cavalry raids. Retreating soldiers. Tonight, we're going to stow the food and valuables in that small cave out in the cedar grove. You know the one I mean."

"Yes, suh," Abram whispered.

Sara's face showed alarm, her father's warnings finally settling in. Her eyes groped the black forest. Her convictions waning, she trained her ears for the sound of footsteps.

"We'll load the wagon with only what we need," Lucas said, "and head south on the Telegraph Road this evening. We'll tie the cows to the back of the wagon. It'll be slow going, but if a battle comes, I want us nowhere near. I'm sure our friends, the Martins, will take us in. It's a day's journey to their farm."

"Yes, Papa," Sara said.

"Yes, suh," Abram said, "but before we start packin', take a minute. I got a surprise for you both."

The three entered the house, passed through the great room, replete with stuffed furniture, a piano, and tall bookcases festooned with books. The great room blended into the kitchen with no partition. Lucas and Sara came to the kitchen table. They smiled to find that Abram had left slices of a fresh-baked apple pie on china plates for them. He strode chuckling into his bedroom off the back of the kitchen and began gathering some of his sparse belongings into a flour sack, preparing for their departure.

"Thank you, Abram," Sara called after him.

Lucas took the plate and ate standing. Brushing a fly off her pie slice, Sara sat at the table. "Papa, do you think we are bound to win this war? I look at our soldiers with their sharp uniforms, their eyes full of purpose, and their bravery, and I know that there's no way under heaven that we can lose this war."

In the quiet of their home with only the crickets keening their tune in the night breeze, Lucas could catch enough of her remarks without his trumpet. "Have you seen their bravery, darlin'?"

"Well, no. But I sense it. I'm certain we have the bravest soldiers that ever lived."

"And tomorrow they'll have marched into battle . . . and many of them will die. Bravery doesn't stop bullets. There'll be many more widows in this land."

"Papa, you almost sound like you're against this war. You know if the Yankees win, they'll take Abram from us." She paused to let her words sink in. "What will he do if they steal him from us? How will he live?" A tear rolled down her cheek. "What will we do without our dear Abram?"

"Darlin', I don't know the answers to those questions, but I feel that Abram would rather be free to decide for himself . . . for his own life." Lucas had been considering granting Abram his freedom for some time even before the war and had broached the subject circuitously with Abram, never quite stating his ultimate desire.

Sara finished her pie quickly, rose from the table, and set her dish and fork in a wash pan on the sideboard. She inhaled the stiff breeze that blew through the open windows fluttering the pale blue curtains. With her back turned to Lucas, she said, "Abram don't want to be free. How would he survive? Become a wandering tinker, fixing old pots?" She washed her plate. "And our Confederate boys are the bravest. Tomorrow, they'll set those Yankee boys to runnin.' And I will *not* let the Yankees take Abram! I will fight them with all that I am!"

Thunder from a new, fast-approaching storm cloud shuddered loud and long, sending tremors along the walls of the house

"All right, you two, rain's coming." Lucas swallowed the last bite of pie. Reverting in manner to his days of ordering soldiers, his tone was demanding. "Get moving. Load the wagon with as much as we can. We'll tarp it from the rain. We need to leave within the hour."

Sara, still nursing her hurt and fears of losing Abram, began gathering their china, pots, blankets, and food into wooden boxes. If heading south meant keeping Abram from the Yankees, she was for it.

Abram hobbled out into the dark, lantern in hand, carrying a box of canned vegetables to the cave.

With the storm's rapid approach, Lucas's anxiety increased. His partial deafness was so ubiquitous, he felt impotent to protect his daughter and their slave. He walked out onto the front porch, lit a cigar, and scanned the woods again, silently cursing his impairment.

He was proud of the life he had built on the hill overlooking Wilson Creek. The Reeder family had moved there shortly after his military discharge, and lived in the large, clapboard house for most of Sara's life. Behind it, a tall barn housed the milk cows and their two horses. A hog sty squatted behind the barn. Lucas and his young sons had completed the house and outlying buildings a year before Sara's mother succumbed to typhus. Abram had tended to her all day and late into the nights. Her last words were neither to Lucas nor her children. "I love you, Abram. Watch after my little Sara," she whispered, then passed.

The Reeders' small herd of dairy cattle provided a modest income. A neighbor boy used to carry a five-gallon tin can of milk in a cart every day to sell to the folks who lived nearby. It had been a good arrangement until the boy joined the Confederate Missouri Guards. For five days now, the Reeders had been selling or giving away milk to the soldiers.

Lucas looked up. Coal-black clouds roiled, and lightning fingers scratched the sky. He felt he might as well be blind, for he could see nothing beyond the porch except, when the lightning flashed, the white picket fence around the graves. His memories of his wife and three sons suddenly flooded his thoughts and played havoc on his soul. *Sometimes, I wish I had no memory.*

The rain began beating like a thousand snare drums on the roof, and fierce gusts of winds slammed against the house.

Lucas knew he could not chance taking Sara and Abram into the dark storm. They would have to wait until daylight He hoped their departure would not be too late. "Damn Lincoln for bringing this war!" He flung his words into the darkness. "And damn this war coming to our home, and there's not a thing I can do to stop it!" He went inside and helped gather their belongings. Later, he loaded both of his rifles.

FIVE

Battle—How Few There Are That See It Clear

AUGUST 10, NORTH OF THE CONFEDERATE CAMP ON WILSON CREEK, 4:30 AM

The mugginess in the crowded trees was like a choke hold. Joseph struggled to catch his breath. A tangle of briars tugged at his legs like hands of a drowning man. He stood with the other First Iowan skirmishers in the pitch-black pre-morning. Presently, a lieutenant of one of the companies stalked up and down the line, his saber drawn, perhaps to tout his rank. Joseph could not see the young man's face and just the glint of the moon on the saber. The lieutenant lit a match and held it by his pocket watch. He barked out whispered orders that Joseph only heard parts of: "Keep close . . . retire . . . commence . . . no . . . stay at all times . . ."

Then the lieutenant was past him, and he had no idea what he or any one of them was supposed to do.

In a jerking fashion of brisk walks, then halts, then scrambling, the line of men moved forward. Joseph was not tall and had to raise his legs quite high in the dense, tall grasses strewn with low bushes just to walk in a relatively straight line. His older companion, Workman, appeared beside him. "Keep up!"

"Where are we going?" Joseph asked.

"We're heading west through these trees to a more advantageous attack position. The lieutenant said it's nigh on a hundred yards off. We're to look for the Iowa field battery, then advance in front of it."

The little company plunged headlong down a steep embankment brimming with tangled brush. Branches, wet from the night's rain, slapped Joseph's shoulders and arms repeatedly. Gossamer spider filaments tickled his face. He took off his kepi cap for fear of losing it to a low-hanging branch. He reached down to his cartridge box on his belt. It was still there, not knocked loose in their rapid pace. Then the troop was splashing through knee-deep water—the creek. Once across, Joseph's water-logged brogans felt heavy, but the coolness of the water on his legs was a relief.

"Damn it, damn it, damn it," the lieutenant bellowed from ahead.

The strung-out line shuttered to a stop just as they reached the creek bank.

"Sergeant," the lieutenant was no longer whispering, "we're out of position. Go up that embankment yonder. See if there's anything."

The sergeant disappeared into the foliage. The men stood gasping for breath in the oppressive humidity. Joseph could not make out a single face. All were a tableau of shadows. He took a step backward and collided with a man standing behind him.

"Oof," the man expelled his breath.

Joseph heard the labored breathing of the soldiers, the occasional crackle of twigs, and an owl hooting somewhere above him. Sweat was pouring down his back, and he yearned for a drink from his canteen.

The lieutenant paced rapidly back and forth in front of the line, swearing. He stopped and said, "Load your rifles. Do that now. Quiet. Quiet."

The soldiers set about loading their guns in the dark. The First Iowa soldiers had an array of guns—from Prussian muskets to Belgian rifles, though most held rusty, flintlock muskets, late delivered from the St. Louis armory. A few had enlisted with newer rifles, but most had brought no weapons, expecting the army to provide their needs. Clatter and clicks of ball and powder horn and ramrod blended with cricket chirps as the men rammed home their shot loads. Joseph loaded his own personal Enfield rifle.

He followed the maneuvers taught him at camp in drill after drill. He took hold of the firelock with his right hand, pinning it back, then changed the hold to the left hand. He used his left hand to glide the butt to the ground. With his right hand, he took a cartridge from the box on his hip, brought it to his mouth, and bit the paper cartridge end. He poured the powder in, then placed the ball just in the barrel. He removed the ramrod from its loops and rammed the ball home. He returned the ramrod to its loops, grabbed a firing cap as he swung to the right on his heels, brought the gun up, then placed the cap on the nipple. He lowered the hammer slowly to a closed position. He was ready in seconds while many soldiers still labored at the task.

While some were still loading their weapon, the sergeant returned. "The battery is up there," he said. "About a hundred yards."

"Well done, Sergeant." the lieutenant said. "Skirmishers, follow me, on the double quick."

He drew his sword again and lurched up the embankment through the brush as if he were charging the enemy. Joseph and the skirmishers struggled after him. Mud caked upon Joseph's boots, making his legs heavy. His nostrils filled with the aroma of wet trees and grass, men's sweat, and, for a moment, lilac. His mind drifted to a remembrance of lilac bushes in bloom, but he wondered how, in all this mad rush to battle, his mind could consider the subject of a bush.

In a moment, they had gained a flat meadow at the bottom of a broad hill and quickly crossed the almost-level ground, knee high in moonlit, silver grass. The panoply of the heavens spread in a cloudless sky. Joseph observed a shooting star streak its brief life. Looking ahead, he saw some muted lanterns and heard the clank and the grinding of the artillery being hauled into place paired with the whinnies and snorts of horses and mules.

In what seemed to Joseph to be less than a minute, they arrived at the artillery battery. The cannons were shiny new. He conjectured for a moment of how it would feel to have cannon shot rip through his body. He shuddered. He had only heard the cannon in the distance at camp and had no idea how loud the cannons would be up close. The six cannons, as yet unlimbered, their caissons, the cannon shot boxes, and the crew of each cannon were all arrayed as if posing for a photograph, clean and orderly. The cannon wheels were still wrapped in blankets. He knew that the blankets were used to muffle the noise. The lieutenant stepped forward and spoke a few words to an artillery officer. With the help of a lantern with but one open pane to allow the light, he again checked his pocket watch.

He strutted back to the skirmishers gathered in a tight group. "Soldiers," he barked, "spread out in a line about ten paces apart across the front of this battery. Be ready to fire. You need not wait for my order, but be sure of your target. You don't want to shoot one of our own."

Joseph had never thought of the possibility of shooting a fellow Iowan in error. He imagined the credibility of such an event, especially in the dark, and he suddenly had an impression of one of his gray-clad Iowan comrades with blood pouring crimson over a white shirt.

"Make no mistake," the lieutenant continued, "the pickets will see you first and shoot first. Then they will run back, reload, and fire again. Most likely, they will not see you any better than you them, so use your rounds judiciously. Now, spread out. Wait for my orders."

Joseph did not know the name of the lieutenant, but he admired him for what he appeared to know about battle tactics.

The skirmishers filtered out in the field in a wavy line. They faced a mass of darkness about a hundred yards ahead, a gloomy, seemingly impenetrable forest of oak and scrub brush. He pondered how different this skirmisher arrangement was than the parade marches back at the training grounds.

Suddenly, the sounds of night, the crickets, and a soft breeze, were drowned by the cacophony of regiment after regiment mounting the wide hill behind Joseph. Stretching as far as he could see, hundreds and hundreds, now a thousand of dark forms packed tight, shoulder to shoulder in three lines deep. Clatter and clank of rifles, and stomps of feet, and hushed orders rose like a percussion symphony. Joseph was astounded at how quickly the Union army had assembled. Far to his left, what he believed was his Iowa regiment extended almost into the brush lining the creek. The army that he had observed in marching drills and in parades through cheering crowds, and in endless days of camps, was now battle bound. He and every other soldier were no longer an individual, but part of a great clockwork about to be set in motion.

Off to his right, he heard a series of sharp pops of rifle fire followed by the hollow pounding of horse hooves rushing away to the south. A feeling of dread nudged its way forward into his mind. He realized he had no idea of what he was to face. This was no target shooting at a fair. He could be firing at shadows, and the shadows would be firing back. He worried about when the skirmishers would be expected to stop. Would they not stop until they ran into the entire Rebel army? His curiosity that he had held for many months about what a battle might entail now deflated into something akin to panic.

He became aware that far to the left, and to the right, other skirmish lines had formed. Shadowy clumps of Iowan gray and the blue-black uniforms of other state regiments flowed over the open field. The skirmishers to the left were almost thirty yards ahead of them. Of a sudden, that skirmish group advanced.

The lieutenant raised his sword and pointed at the dark forest. "Forward. March."

For a moment, pacing toward the unknown, Joseph wondered

how the other general, Sigel, and his Germans were faring south of the Rebel force. Were they in position? He was aware by way of idle talk in camp of only a little of the strategy General Lyon had laid out—that the army was split in two to attempt to smash the Confederates from both ends. He had no idea of how large the Rebel army was, but he knew enough about war from reading Caesar and other tomes that, in a battle, only one side wins.

Joseph and the skirmishers trudged along at an agonizingly slow pace. They were entirely out in the open. A good marksman might pick off any one of them.

"Where are the pickets?" the lieutenant grumbled. "Where are their pickets?"

No shots were fired anywhere.

A rage came over Joseph. It occurred to him that they were marching into a trap. He felt like a pestered animal surrounded by other bedeviled animals. He was being forced to face ravenous wolves. Not wolves, but cannibals. He became angry with his rifle, because it could only shoot one enemy at a time. His agitation grew as he trudged across the muddy field, the deep wet soil sucking his feet down. He wanted to rush forward and take on the enemy with his bare hands. His head grew hot as a stove, and he sweated profusely. With his sleeve, he wiped his brow. He wanted to cock his rifle, but with the moisture in the air, he dared not, lest the firing cap become too wet to fire.

Without warning, he heard rifles popping in the distance to his left. Then, thuds of galloping horse hooves, followed by more pops and snaps echoed far to his right. He could just hear smothered orders coming from somewhere in the thicket to his left and in front of him. The enemy was before them, but hidden in the dark foliage.

Finally, the dark monolith, the dense thicket, loomed up before him like a wretched beast, menacing and terrible. In a moment more, they were surrounded by the knotted, vine-covered trees. Each man dashed, crouching and twisting from tree to tree, waiting for the bullets that would come. The lieutenant strutted in front several paces, sword still raised. Joseph felt a modicum of relief that they no longer walked in the open.

After three more steps, rifle shots cracked not thirty paces in front of him. Puffs of smoke drifted up in the brush. Like an over-wound clock, the Iowans dived and fell like broken springs sprung from their case. They leapt behind trees and rolled into ditches. Only Workman stood erect, a few feet from Joseph. His rifle raised, he fired. Joseph heard the sound of a body fall, crashing against bushes and leaves.

"Forward, men," the lieutenant ordered. The soldiers crept forward, but each man alone in his own world. Joseph's mouth felt like cotton. He found it hard to breathe. His first battle was nothing like he imagined. In the trees, despite the rising sun to their left, dark shadows and forms pervaded.

The floating line of skirmishers moved in a faltering fashion. Suddenly, shots came at them from all quarters. Bullets clipped tree branches, and leaves tumbled down around the skirmishers. Two Iowans fell backward. Joseph heard the bullets hit them, and, to him, it sounded like hammers hitting an anvil. Those around him leapt for cover and fired at the darkness. Joseph fired at a puff of smoke, but he could see no target. Then he dived behind a tree.

"I will return, Cyntha. I will survive. Survive!" Joseph murmured, his heart racing.

———»((●))«———

FEBRUARY 20, 1862, TELEGRAPH ROAD, MISSOURI, 3 PM

The late-afternoon sun flashed in and out of ragged clouds. Cyntha watched the sun's flickers glimmering on the hide of the horse pulling the carriage. Having ridden several miles, she began to feel more re-lieved since the scar-faced rider had not followed them. She gathered a satchel from the floorboard, removed a handful of papers, and tried to read from her notes she had written when she had attended spiritual-ism events. She thumbed through some newspaper articles and found the one she sought, a story from the *Banner of Light* newspaper. She said, "Reynolds, let me read this to you."

Reynolds nodded.

"This past evening, at Corliss Hall," she read, "renowned spiritual-ist, Cora Weiberg, summoned the spirits of a sum total of fourteen fall-en soldiers and one matron who had passed away in London, England. To the amazement of the audience observing the séance, not a single question or entreaty asked of the medium was found to be inaccurate." Cyntha paused from reading. "See there, Reynolds. Fourteen. This ar-ticle goes on about how the spirit of one fallen soldier tells all the details of his death, lists his friends from his company, and . . . I only wish I had that gift to contact the spirit world."

"Yes'm. My old granny could speak to the dead. At least she said she could."

"Well, there's further proof. So much of this world is beyond our ability to fathom. I know that this cold winter is God's way of remind-ing us that we all go to the grave." She paused, reflecting. "And God gave us the sun in the sky to remind us each day of the warmth and joy that awaits us. And He gave us minds to study and be curious, and we learned to write books to spread the knowledge. And now, God, in His wisdom, is helping us learn about the world beyond the grave. Not to all of us. But to a few who are willing to share it. The evidence is there, Reynolds. It is becoming common knowledge now that the spirit world runs parallel to ours. Here . . ." she said pointing at an ar-ticle, "here is a listing of the messages received from dead soldiers who contacted the newspaper's medium, Fanny Conant. It's all in black and white."

"Are you sayin' all this the more to convince me, Miss Cyntha, or convince yourself?"

Cyntha's eyes widened. She knew Reynolds meant no malice in his question. Yet, his point showed her the need to be prudent in assessing a person's touted access to the spirit world. She sighed and turned her head to look out at the trees and fallow fields of deep southern Missouri. For a moment she was in a faraway haven of five years ago; she thought of the first time Joseph and she had thrown off the bindings of propriety a week before their marriage. He had been such a gentleman for so many months and had restrained himself always, but while strolling in a meadow of golden grass on the bluffs above the Mississippi outside of Memphis, it was she who had forgotten her modesty. "I am brazen," she had told herself, but could not halt the inexorable tide of her desire. They had kissed twice before, but at this moment, far from sight of her parents' home, she turned to him and lifted his hand, placing it on her breast, then pleaded with her eyes. Joseph looked at first confused, but pulled her to him forcefully, and their passion blossomed.

She remembered the tangy smell of the grass as he took her slowly to the soft earth. She remembered the warmth, indeed, the fire, in her inner self. He kissed her lips, then the nape of her neck. He pressed his body against hers, and they writhed in ecstasy. She felt herself quivering like cottonwood tree leaves in the wind. She loved Joseph so.

A blast of icy air tore her from the remembering. She looked up and saw that the once-clear sky had rapidly become a low-slung drapery of foreboding, gray snow clouds. The storm gusts felt wet against her cheek. She pulled her coat hood tighter over her head.

"Reynolds," she said, "are we close to Springfield at all?"

"Not yet." Reynolds shook the reins and said, "Git up, there, horse. We don't intend to be caught in no storm." The horse's stride hastened.

At first, neither Reynolds nor Cyntha saw the rider in shabby clothes who had come up out of the brush and was keeping pace with them in the field well off to their right, and slightly behind, not ever quite catching up. The rider had a rifle in the saddle scabbard. He rode hunched over, his fierce face turned toward their carriage. When Cyntha turned to watch some crows take flight from a tree, she caught sight of the rider. She clutched Reynold's arm. "He's back."

SIX

The Enemy Has a Face

AUGUST 10, 1861, THE REEDER FARM, 5:30 AM

Sara awoke to fretful mooing from the barn. Something had disturbed the cows' sleep. She rushed to the window, pulled back indigo curtains, and looked out expecting to see a coyote or maybe a cougar near the barn. Instead, she saw shadowy blue-clad soldiers rushing through the yard. Behind them, mules strained in their harnesses pulling cannons. Horses whinnied, and officers whispered raspy orders all around the house, and in an instant, the yard was overrun with Yankee soldiers.

She ran to her father's room. "Papa!" she called directly into his ear. "Papa, wake up. There are Yankees in our yard! A whole army!"

Lucas awoke, threw back his sheet, and rushed past Sara to the window and peered out. "Quick," he said. "Get dressed. They'll be in our home in a moment. I'll not let them have you. Get dressed now, and get in the cellar." He spoke of the shallow underground room, its door hidden beneath the kitchen rug.

Lucas dressed himself quickly, grabbed his loaded rifle from the pegs above the fireplace, cocked it, and set the firing cap in place.

Sara threw on a camisole and pantaloons, bound her corset, then donned her homespun dress and her work boots, but she had no intention of hiding. For her, the Confederate army had to be warned. She determined that if she hurried she could reach her fine soldiers to warn them in time.

She inched into the great room and strode up to Abram who was standing in his bedroom doorway rubbing his eyes. She pushed him toward the hidden cellar entrance, threw up the rug, then the hinged floor door, and whispered forcefully, "Get in there. The Yankees are here to steal you."

The old man picked his way down the steep stairs, and Sara closed the door and drew the rug over it. She considered for a moment trying to explain to her father what she planned to do, but he would not have let her go. She was determined to warn *her* soldiers in the valley. Bursting out the back door, she almost collided with three blue-clad men.

"Hold on, missy," one of them said. "There's about to be a big fight here. You best stay in the house!"

She paid him no heed but raced past their packed wagon and across the back of the property to the barn.

"Is there anyone else in the house?" The soldier called after her.

On the run, she yelled back, "Just my papa, and you leave him be." She did not mention Abram, determined that he would not be robbed from them.

She dodged through the tangle of soldiers rushing past the house in the dark. Officers on horses shouted orders in English and in a foreign tongue she did not recognize. Mules pulled cannon after cannon, rolling along through an ashen fog past the house. Soldiers pushed hard against the muddy wheels.

When Sara reached the barn, she swung open one of the double doors and darted inside. Her heart racing, she closed the door, then felt along the wall and found the lantern. On a shelf, she located the metal box of matches. She lit the lantern, then strode quickly past the line of moaning cows, the fluttering and cackling chickens, and to the stable alongside her father's black gelding. She grabbed saddle, blanket, and bridle, and saddled her brown mare, Esther. She took the hem of her skirt in her teeth and, just as she rose in the stirrup, a group of Yankees flung wide the doors.

Sara dug her heels into the side of her mare and bolted past the soldiers, knocking one to the ground, and sped out the door.

"Stop!" one of them demanded. "Get back here, you Rebel hussy."

They kept calling after her, but she was not stopping. The mare galloped across the farm yard, into the grove of trees behind the barn, and negotiated the steep descent down the back of the hill. If she could reach the bottom safely, Sara knew she could round the hill and cross the creek. She hoped she would be in time to sound the alarm to *her* Confederates. She thought fondly of the young soldier who had sung to her, of the officer's wife and baby and of Reverend Felder. Her mind was set. *They must be warned!*

"Come on, Esther!" She encouraged her mare onward, twisting side to side through the trees in their downhill surge, her long blond hair flowing behind her.

Esther picked up speed in their downward rush. She leaped over a fallen log and landed in deep mud. She slipped and pitched wildly onto her side, sliding down the hillside. Sara flew off, slamming hard to the ground, knocking the wind from her. Esther recovered, but continued to slide and lunge down the slippery embankment. Sara gained her footing and called after her mare, "Esther, I'm coming! Oh God! I hope you're not hurt!" She chased after her, grasping tree branches to keep from tumbling headfirst. Finally, the two of them slowed to a halt at the bottom.

Mud clinging to her clothing, Sara checked Esther for injuries, running her hands along all four legs and across the big mare's neck and back. She looked in the horse's bright eyes, and Esther, appearing unscathed by the fall, snorted, as if to say, "Let's go." Patting the mare's neck, Sara leaped into the saddle. Horse and rider inched along a ravine and forward through a rocky, ankle-deep rivulet. On flatter ground, she galloped Esther around the hill. At one point, she passed within yards of a squad of Yankees. They yelled at her, but she steeled her resolve even more and pushed Esther faster.

When she reached Wilson Creek, she urged her mare forward into the deep, dark water, startling the thrushes nesting in the tall water willows and sedgy grasses that surrounded the banks. The rain-fed current rose to the horse's withers. Sara clung tight to the mane, praying, "Dear God, give me time to warn the soldiers and the families."

Exiting the creek, she suddenly remembered what the sergeant the night before had told her father and her about the Rebels planned night march to attack the Yankees at Springfield. She let out a sigh and slowed Esther to a walk. "Our army has gone and headed north. The Yankees are too late," she smiled to herself. "The foolish Yanks are *too late*." Relief flowed through her.

Alongside the creek, she was about to turn around when she caught sight of the moonlit cornfield with lanterns and glowing campfires. Rows of tents and lean-tos were still positioned neat and tidy. She saw shadowy figures moving. Her fine fighting boys had *not* marched after all. She realized why she had never heard warning shots from guards. *There were no pickets.* She remembered the old sergeant bringing in the pickets. "The army's still here. Why didn't they repost the pickets?" Her heart sank. She knew enough from the war tales her father had told that the waking Rebel army was about to be showered with iron and lead from the Yankee cannons. Her mind flew to the young soldier-singer and to the officer's wife and child who were living in the camp. She dug her heels into Esther's sides.

Racing toward the camp, she saw campfires flickering up and smelled pork frying. The camp cooks were at work, for them, just another morning in camp.

When she reached the southernmost tents, several loud shrieks split the air. The first shots from the cannons on the Reeder farm hill flew overhead and crashed into the poplar trees, sending limbs hurling to the ground. Hundreds of bewildered soldiers spilled from their tents, rushing to throw on clothes and boots and to grab their guns; yelling, falling, colliding in their confusion. More cannonballs exploded in the trees, splitting the limbs and showering canister pellets and balls over the camp. Other cannonballs landed with a thud, rolled along, and exploded. Sara watched a tent burst into flame. One soldier, his clothes on fire, fell and rolled in the dirt, screaming in agony while fellow soldiers fled past him.

Sara raced her horse into the melee. "Get out!" she yelled, "The Yankee cannons are all over that hill." An explosion drowned out her words. She prodded Esther onward through panicked soldiers, but was forced to draw up, because the throng of running men was too dense. These were the Texas and Kansas cavalry. Most ran to their mounts and were doing the best they could to saddle the frightened beasts that reared and sprang side to side. Other Confederates fled through the trees. Some, scattering in a fashion akin to chickens in flight, splashed across the creek directly toward the hill where the Yankees were positioned. The oratory of fire swept the Rebel campsite. A single bugler stood, half-dressed, blowing his horn, turning first in one direction than another. Sara thought, *Blowing that horn is of no more use than my shouting. The Yankees have already attacked!*

A new sound erupted from behind Sara, back beyond the cornfield. She turned to see a deep mass of black—the Yankee army rolling like an immense wave. She made out flags—the Stars and Stripes of the nation she used to adore—amid sabers and bayonets, twinkling in the moonlight. The faceless dark army rendered a guttural growl more horrid than her imagined dragons from her books of medieval lore. No longer did she feel the earnestness of her naïve bullheadedness, but felt dread for the loss of her own life, almost succumbing to a faint.

She heard the roll of drums and blaring bugles amidst the yells of the charging soldiers. Officers called orders in a strange tongue. *What are they saying? Are they foreigners?*

In front of the dark mass of soldiers, women and children and slaves still in nightclothes hurtled along, tripping, falling, and screaming. The family camps lay directly in the path of the onslaught of horse and man and steel.

"There are so many! I have no way back. I'm trapped here." Sara's heart pounded like a hammer. Unable to decide to rush to the aid of the terror-stricken families or pursue her original course, she turned the horse first one way, then another, then spun in a circle, finally facing away from the Yankee charge. Straight in front of her, an officer of the Texas regiment gathered a line of his soldiers. They knelt, shouldering a mishmash of armaments from flintlock muskets to shotguns to revolvers and rifles. She galloped hard past them and reined her steed to a halt. Their rifles cracked. In the glow of the campfires, she saw several Yankees fall, but nowhere near enough of them to stop their charge.

Sara turned her mare again in her original direction and dug her heels into the horse's sides. The mare sprang forward through running men, past campfires, collapsed tents, crates, barrels, sacks of food, and discarded rifles. Terrified, riderless horses shrieked, dashing all about her like the zigzag of lightning strikes. She passed almost all of the fleeing Rebels and pulled Esther to a halt. Her dress, soaked from her ride through the creek, clung to her body, chafing her. Scanning the men rushing from the Yankee onslaught, she did not see the young singer, nor the officer's wife. "I have to find them!" she yelled. She called to one soldier, "Have you seen a woman and a child?"

The soldier paid her no heed, but kept running.

Out of the trees, Rebels in large number were moving forward a dozen yards in front of her. "Form up here! Make a line here," a hoarse voice ordered. The wavy line extended behind a rail fence, stretching on the edge of an oval-shaped grazing meadow, bounded by the cornfields to the south and trees to the north.

The morning sky was turning violet and pink, revealing patches of bright yellow and orange flowers that dotted the bucolic setting. A small herd of cattle, spooked by the battle noise, huddled, bawling in a back corner adjacent to the forest.

Officers, half-dressed, trotted up and down the line, rallying the men. They faced a barren field. Beyond, stretched a narrow row of hackberries, crabapples, and smaller hawthorn trees with their white and pink flowers clinging to the branches. The trees marked the edge of the Sharp cornfield. The Yankees would have to charge across open land. At a break in the Confederate's formation, Sara jumped Esther over the fence and stopped, yanking on the reins to turn her horse toward the oncoming Yankee army. Her curiosity outweighed her sense. Fear coursing through her like a flood, still, she felt she had to watch.

The hurried orders of officers ceased, and, save the occasional click of metal hammers of the rifles being cocked, a smothering silence ensued.

The growing sunlight revealed vapor rising from the sweating soldiers, their shirts and jackets steaming like their souls were already escaping them before death.

"Steady, steady," one officer kept repeating. More gray-clad soldiers raced toward them out of the trees and across the field. Those with rifles jumped down beside the formed line, those without a weapon continued to run. One soldier, terror in his eyes, passed Sara screaming in a loud voice, "They're comin'!"

A half-dozen Yankees, yards ahead of the main assault, burst from the trees, spilling into the meadow like bats from a cave. At first, they raced toward the Rebel line. Sara saw their shocked expressions when they drew up quickly, then attempted to run back. They did not reach the trees. A volley dropped four of them. They fell, their bodies immediately hidden in the tall grass. The others escaped to the tree line.

The Yankee mass arrived just inside the edge of the trees. Their officers shouted in the foreign tongue. One Rebel officer exclaimed,

"They're jabbering in German. They don't even know English. Give 'em hell, boys!"

Sara's eyes widened. In her rush to give warning, she had not considered the collision of the armies, each bent on destroying the other.

Now, Yankee officers shouted in English, and, with a rush, the line poured out into the field, running halfway across it before stopping to form a firing line. Before they could aim, the Rebels fired first, the rifles and muskets bucking and smoking. Dozens of Yankees fell to the ground. A horse screamed, falling under its officer. The Yankees fired a volley. Two Rebels, struck as they were reloading, tumbled over, clutching their wounds. Sara, only a few feet from them, saw their blood spilling and the terror across the men's visages. This image in no way matched her idealized version of battle wrought from the chivalric tales she had read.

Like an angry wasp, a bullet shot past Sara's ear and knocked a branch loose from the tree above her. The branch tumbled onto Esther's neck. Just as her horse reared, Sara felt a hand grab her arm, and she was yanked from her mount. Ester galloped into the forest behind the Confederates.

"You best get down, little lady," a young soldier with a strained voice and a bulbous, wide-brimmed hat pulled down to his ears said. "What're you doing here anyway?"

Bullets whizzed overhead, thudding into the elms directly behind where Sara had been seated on Esther. Her knees on the ground, she looked up at a face of a man not more than twenty leaning over her. His chin was angular, and his flushed cheeks bore the pockmarks from smallpox. A long, white scar ran across his forehead, his light brown hair ducked out from under his overlarge hat. He barked at her, "Like I said, why're you here? You need to hide!"

Sara was barely listening. She watched after her horse, growing smaller and smaller, racing away.

Several loud shrieks filled the sky above the Confederates, and

Sara watched two cannonballs bounce and bound along the ground many yards before the line, then explode, sending dirt and flames flying.

She turned back to the soldier who had kept her from harm. Angry, she shouted, "Don't ask me why I'm here. Why is the army still here? You all were supposed to march last night. You would not have been here, and the Yankees would not have found you, and they're running right over our fine army . . . and . . ."

Above the rattle of bullets, the young man, trying to remain calm, yelled, "We didn't march because General McCulloch thought the rain might ruin the powder for our guns, so he called it off till morning. And those Yankees may have got the jump on us, but we ain't licked yet. Now you best keep your head down." He tugged her downward until her chin was buried in grass.

The Yankees marched closer, officers in front walking backward and keeping their arms outstretched attempting to keep the line straight. The line creased here and there when the soldiers trod around their fallen comrades. Methodically, they prepared to shoot a second time. The Rebels beat them again, fire leaping from their guns like a lightning strike hurled sideways. Even more blue-clad soldiers flopped to the meadow grass amidst the dainty wildflowers. Sara watched one soldier grab his arm and shriek.

The Yankees fired again, but too high, for not one Rebel fell. Sara heard the balls thud into the trees behind her. One whistled by her ear. The young soldier pushed her body flat to the earth. She struggled to raise her head to see, but he pinned her with a knee in her back. "Get off me!" His weight held her prone.

Yelling like screeching train wheels, the Yankees charged, shoulder to shoulder, bayonets flashing in the new sunlight. Sara twisted her body in a futile effort to free herself from the young private's firm hold. Peering under the fence railing, she could make out the faces of some of the Yankee soldiers. They looked determined. They looked intelligent. They did not look like the cruel, stolid faces she had imagined all Yankees had.

Directly, the Yankees were cut down by more fire from the Rebel line. Far to Sara's left, a host of gray-clad Texan cavalry charged, flanking the Yankee line. They fired pistols and sliced with swords, driving back the attacking force. One Yankee bludgeoned by a charging horse flew backward some dozen feet, his rifle spinning through the air like a whirligig before colliding with a fellow soldier's head. The formerly pristine Union line buckled from the onslaught. Smoke enveloped riders and infantry, concealing them totally, but their cries of agony and anger passed through it, like the voices of ghosts.

"That be Colonel Greer's Texas Cavalry, I'll warrant," said her captor. "We've been spoiling for a fight. Now we got one." He seemed to be filled with glee.

The world slowed for Sara. Her ears were filled with the crackle of rifle fire and fallen men's cries of pain. The acrid smoke burned her eyes and nose. Wiping her eyes, as the smoke ebbed, she beheld, just a few yards from the Rebel line, a soldier with his face half missing, the body kneeling, already dead, before slumping into a heap. Another soldier fell with the blood from his neck spurting like a red fountain. A third soldier sat in a puddle fingering the wound in his arm.

When a small number of the Yankees collided with the Rebels at the fence, the Confederates had no trouble driving them back. "Retreat!" the Yankees called, "*Ruckzug!*" The Germans in Union blue fell back in disorder, reaching the safety of the tree line. Wounded soldiers crawled on hands and knees in the field. Others rolled or doubled over, calling prayers mixed with curses and begging for help.

More Rebel soldiers emerged through the trees behind Sara to join their counterparts, bolstering the line. More cavalry rode out from the trees to take position on the Rebel left. The sun melted away the darkness, and Sara stared at the field where the Yankees had fallen.

The grass was so tall that the wounded soldiers, crawling back to their line, looked to Sara like the field was alive with snakes. A couple of Rebels marched a half-dozen Union prisoners with crestfallen faces to the rear past Sara and her captor.

The Rebels let out long hoots and hollers. "Run, you Yanks, run!"

"Run back to your mamas!"

"Damn you, Yanks. You done spoiled my breakfast, but we got ya!"

"Go back and tell Abe Lincoln to leave Missouri alone. This is our state, not yor'n."

The young soldier who had held her pinned, let her sit, yet still held her arm firm.

"Let me go. You've no right! I've got to find someone." For her, just seeing the man who had sung her the song would somehow set things right.

"You stay put, little lady. The battle is on. They surprised us, but we've held 'em so far. Is there a particular fellow you're lookin' for? Maybe I know him."

"Well, yes. Well . . . no. I don't actually know his name. I just met him the other day . . ." Sara made a hard realization. Having seen the dark color of war, the finding and warning of a single individual within an army of thousands no longer meant what it once had. A new conviction began to sink into her. *I will stay alive*, she thought. *I will find my horse and return to Papa and Abram . . . and, by the grace of God, save any soldier that I can.*

From behind them, a voice yelled, "Back in line, soldier. They're getting ready to charge again, and they've been reinforced!"

When the young soldier turned, Sara freed herself and ran pell-mell in the direction her horse had run. Forcing up her courage, she searched the face of every soldier hiding in a ditch or behind a tree. "If he's fine, then I'll be fine," she said over and over.

Behind her, she heard the cannons spewing their missiles amidst volleys of rifle fire. But she also heard shots far to her left and to the right. The battle expanded so much wider than she could imagine. On she ran, calling for Esther and looking for a soldier whose face she barely remembered and for Reverend Felder and for a woman with a child.

SEVEN

The Odd Arithmetic of War

AUGUST 10, 1861, REEDER FARM, 6 AM

Lucas Reeder stood by a window where the early-morning light spilled through and across the floor. His rifle leaned in the corner beside a soldier who had wrested it from him, and his house was filled with Union officers and their aides. Abram ladled water from a wooden bucket to any soldier who asked while the cannons roared not fifty yards from the house. The windows rattled, and the walls trembled. Lucas could only watch as the officers perused maps, paced back and forth, and passed orders to waiting dispatch carriers. Other messengers from the battle waded in among the throng to deliver updates. Some of the talk was in English; some Lucas recognized as German.

Abram walked over and lifted the trumpet to Lucas's ear, "They done marched their muddy boots all over the floor. And look at the hook rug your mother made. It's most ruined."

"No point in worrying about the trivial. What's done is done. At least, we're alive, and there's not a window, nor plate broken. This is Missouri, so they didn't know if we were friend or foe. I thought I was through with warring, but the war came to my home. Old friend, please pray that Sara returns. I am undone for worrying."

Standing against the wall with heads bowed, the two men prayed silently while all around them earnest men said urgent words, and the cannons growled outside.

The soldiers in the room talked and cursed with great alacrity. "Where is that other damn map?" bellowed one. "Hold that lantern closer!" yelled another. "We should put the artillery here," said a third, pointing a stubby finger at a crude, muddy map. Soldiers came and went. They handed scraps of papers to officers who took other scraps of papers and scribbled their orders with stubs of pencils. They shoved the papers to the messengers who, with great purposefulness, rushed from the house.

Observing the feverish gestures and animated discussion of the Union officers, Lucas's thoughts again drifted to the war with Mexico. A deep inner part of him yearned to be part of a great battle once more. His mind looked through a knothole in a tall fence. Through this narrow opening, he saw the jubilant American armies waving their caps in victory, the American flag flapping atop the Mexican government building, and the hearty slaps on the backs he received from fellow officers. Then the wall collapsed, and his thoughts were flooded with the bloody carnage of beast and man in that war, the despairing Mexican prisoners, and the little Mexican girl whimpering over her mother killed by American cannon fire. His ambivalence toward his army service led his thoughts to and fro, and he could not auger his own feelings.

After another half hour, without a good-bye or a thank-you, the entire staff hurried from the room, maps under their arms. Abram and Lucas looked in awe at an empty house. The officers mounted their horses and galloped away. The infantry fell in behind them. Presently, the cannons were limbered and hauled past the house and down through the meadows and trees to somewhere neither Lucas nor Abram could guess. Lucas fell to his knees. "Dear Lord, keep my Sara safe. Why'd she have to grow up so bullheaded? Bring her back to me."

━━➤«◈»⟵━━

Joseph ducked behind a boulder. Bullets flew about him. He bent low, huddled beside two other Iowan skirmishers. One of them rubbed blood from his hand onto his jacket. "Durned if one of them winged me," he said rather calmly, though his face showed concern. The other soldier wore a bright red scarf about his neck. Joseph wondered if he wore it to be more readily recognized, or maybe that he just liked it.

"What's the red kerchief for?" Joseph asked. The man did not answer but stared with a blank expression away from the Rebels at the forest they had just traversed, now with a few errant sunbeams blinking through the trees.

Bullets clipped off chunks of the boulder. Joseph finished loading his rifle, leaned around, and fired a shot toward the Confederates. With the sun at the horizon now, he had just a moment before he fired to assess the movement of a multitude of gray forms weaving among the trees. He had no idea if he hit anyone. Down deep, he hoped he had not.

Most of the skirmishers from the Iowa regiment had gathered close together, using trees and rocks as cover. Joseph recognized many of his comrades. He observed the lieutenant wincing while he bound a cloth around his knee. He wondered how long they were supposed to stay here. Fear broke upon him, his stomach churning. He felt a sudden urge to run away, back to his regiment, but with the fire being poured at them, he deemed that a sure way to get shot.

The firing abated for a few minutes, and he thought of Cyntha's letter in his pocket. With the cessation, he felt safe enough to draw the letter out. A modicum of just-born daylight allowed him to survey the words, though he had it mostly memorized.

Dearest Joseph,

I am at pins, waiting for your safe return. You are my light
and my joy. I feel as we are bound by a tether, a golden
rope, not of this world. When a breeze comes by and
brushes my cheek, I feel it is your spirit that you have
sent me across the miles.

His reading was broken when, about fifteen yards away, an Iowan
jumped up to flee. Joseph watched the man as a bullet hit him square
in the back and passed through him, taking bits of clothing with it. He
fell, crawled a little, then collapsed. For Joseph, staring at the prone
body, the war took on a different, and now, wretched meaning. He
wanted to see the face of the dead Iowan, wondering if he had ever
met him, but tall grass hid his face. Another soldier rose to help the
fallen comrade, but was forced by the hail of bullets to return to hiding. Joseph folded the letter and replaced it in his shirt pocket.

Dear Cyntha, if I could but send my thoughts to you, my love.
I vow I will return to you.

"Hold on, boys!" the lieutenant shouted. "We're about to get help."
Joseph then witnessed the spectacle of the Union army, a vast blue
and gray mob, approaching in a rush through the trees. One advance
squad reached the Iowans first, and they came up on him so fast, it
sounded like thunder.

A blue-clad soldier with furious red curls spilling out below his
kepi and a sharp, red beard surrounding his round face, raced ahead of
the line. He stopped and aimed his rifle at Joseph and his comrades.
"Surrender," he barked, "ye lousy Rebs." Several other Yanks stormed
up beside him, bayoneted rifles pointed at Joseph and his companions.

In a discordant chorus, the Iowans called out, "We're not Rebs!"

"We're Iowans. We're Union!"

Joseph's heart sank. His own army had just accused him of being the enemy. "I'm Union, damn you," he said, his face flushed in anger.

Bullets whizzed around them, so the accusers lowered their guns and knelt behind the cover of trees and boulders. A moment later, the rest of the great Union army arrived, so many soldiers that the color of the wild thicket transformed from brown and green into deep indigo. The Rebels ceased firing, and Joseph became aware of the clamor of feet in hasty retreat through the brush. Joseph and the rest of the skirmishers rose. They formed up within the line of blue, assimilated like a spill soaked up with a cloth.

"Where's this regiment from?" Joseph asked the man with the crimson curls.

"Missouri," the man replied. He spoke with an Irish brogue. "We be taking the state back from those maraudin' Rebels. That we be."

"Do you know where the First Iowa Grays are?"

"No, I dunnot. But ye be fine right here with us Missouri lads. We'll take good care of ye."

He had no sooner spoken than officers pranced their horses up and down the line, shouting orders. Joseph, taking a quick swig from his canteen, could only make out that they were to advance on the enemy on the double quick. Then he heard the call he had imagined hearing over and over. Buglers blared their horns.

Hundreds of Union soldiers raced forward, burst from the trees, and arrived at a wide field dotted with bushes that spread up a sloping hill. A small Confederate campground—tents, a wagon, bedrolls, and crates—was abandoned. Joseph and his companions slowed as they approached a handful of bloody, lifeless bodies in farm clothes lying about the camp. None wore anything resembling a uniform. A few wounded Rebels lay in the grass, moaning.

"For God's sake," one boy about twelve with a little drum by his side pleaded, "please don't kill me."

Joseph thought to say something consoling to the little fellow, but the line pressed forward, and the opportunity passed. *Stay safe, little one*, he prayed.

Beyond the Union advance, a few Confederates scampered away up the hill. Joseph saw them join hundreds of motley-dressed Rebels massing at the hill's crest. Various Confederate flags fluttered along their line. As best he could tell, his army outnumbered the enemy. He sensed imminent victory and felt a gladness and pride. *I will be part of a great victory to tell Cyntha*, he thought.

A Union battery opened up on the right. Explosions threw fire and dirt into the air of the hilltop. Joseph felt his confidence in victory rising. Having slowed while passing through the Confederate camp, the long line of mostly blue, with some gray-clad Iowans interspersed, moved doggedly up the long, steep hill.

In a move that was baffling to Joseph, the officers in front of the regiment pointed their swords and called for the men to continue their advance but angle to the left.

"What are we doing?" Joseph asked the burly Irishman.

He shrugged his shoulders. "Most likely we be flankin' Johnny Reb."

Joseph figured the Irishman was correct in the assumption. He wondered, "Why'd he call the rebels Johnny? Why that name?"

In another hundred paces, the officers called for a halt of the Missourians and Iowans in a glade. A major walked up to Joseph. "You Iowans," he said, "move down the line and join your regiment. On the double quick, soldiers."

Joseph fell out and scrambled to the left. Other Iowans joined him, and they ran together, about fifty of them, along the front of the Missourians. Just ahead of him, Workman ran with his arms and legs perambulating like a scarecrow in a gale.

In a few minutes, Joseph stood beside Workman with his fellows in Company C. He joined in laughing and back-slapping, but soon they fell silent. Then, for several minutes, all of them could hear, off to the right, the noise of battle—volleys of rifle fire, shrieking cannon-balls followed by explosions, guttural yells, screams of agony, and the clank of iron and lead. Their portion of the line stood hidden from the Rebels, but hidden also from their own troops at their far right who were charging the hill.

Unable to ascertain the progression of the battle, the soldiers be-gan to fidget, some squatted down, while others leaned left and right attempting to gather a glimpse through the trees. One slight soldier with an untidy thicket of hair swung lithely up onto a low pine branch and, in short order, gained a high limb. He called out, "We're on the hill. Our boys are on the hill!"

"Are we winning?" Workman called up to him.

"I can't see. There's too much smoke. Wait. I see our colors. They're up there all right. We're on the hill!" His voice fell silent, peering into the battle smoke in the distance.

"Well, dang it, boy," said Workman, "tell us what's happenin'."

"I can barely see!" the lookout shouted, "There's just smoke and bodies. But the Rebs ain't givin'. They're holdin'."

A gray-haired major galloped up and dismounted. "Get down here, soldier!" The major's tone was vehement. The young fellow scrambled down, leaping from the last limb. The major walked up to him and cuffed him full in the face, knocking him to the ground. The private held his cheek. The major turned to the regiment. "Stand to, soldiers. I'll not have insubordination. We have orders to wait here, and *wait* we will until orders come." He mounted his horse and rode out into the trees and was gone from sight.

Sergeants up and down the line called, "At ease."

The young lookout moved back into line beside Joseph, still hold-ing his jaw.

Joseph thought he should say something to him, but chose not to. *This is war*, he thought. *No time for sentimentality*. Within his heart, however, he felt ambivalence for he had seen white masters treat black slaves in such a manner, and he hated that.

The men of Company C and the remainder of the regiment had to be content with only hearing the battle. Joseph reached to his pocket. He took out the letter, opened it, and as he read it, his breathing relaxed. The letter continued,

> You are my streak of gold running through a coarse mountain. All golden, all precious. You are with me and I with you, but the months of your absence tell on me. My brother came from Minnesota to visit, and all I could talk of was you. I feel I quite bored him with the way I was going on. But I cannot forget you nor have a single moment that I do not think of you. Know that our spirits are joined. Should you die in this war, this travesty that must be fought to free the Negroes, you will be a hero always to me and my family.
>
> Your ever faithful,
> Cyntha

Joseph looked up from the letter into the bright clear sky, interspersed with puffs of gray smoke. *Cyntha, I will return to you.*

Colonel Merritt, the mutton-chopped, regimental commander, rode up on his stallion and danced it back and forth before his troops, standing in the stirrups. He spoke in a gruff, demanding manner. "Men, we are going to take this hill. We are going to charge up there and take this hill from the Rebels. They do not own Missouri. *We* do. Let's show them our valor!"

A hundred voices shouted, "Huzzah!"

"Can we take this hill and give it as a gift to the great state of Missouri?"

"Huzzah! Huzzah!" came the reply, over and over.

Joseph was caught up in the colonel's impassioned speech. His face flushed. His throat grew hoarse from yelling.

Other officers strutted on foot up and down the line, sabers drawn. Sergeants relayed orders. Joseph became aware that not only his own company, but those of the entire Iowa regiment and another state's regiment were preparing to charge the enemy.

Colonel Merritt raised his sword. Joseph hurriedly wrapped the letter around the tintype and shoved both in his pocket, leaving the pocket unbuttoned.

EIGHT

The Dew of Compassion Is a Tear

AUGUST 10, 1861, WILSON CREEK, 9 AM

Sara, winded from running and despaired of ever finding her run-away mare, waded across Wilson Creek and collapsed in a verdant clearing. The battle rattled in the distance like rocks in a tin can. Here and there, vestiges of the erratic flight of soldiers lay—haversacks, rifles, and hats. She heard the battle behind her, but standing in the warm sun amidst oaks and hawthorns, she considered the portent of what sounded like a battle in a circle. The battle sounds echoed through the valley.

For a moment, all cannonading ceased, as did the gunfire. Sunlight twinkling on the still-moist tree leaves evoked for Sara a remembrance of the stained glass windows in Reverend Felder's church in Springfield. In that brief spell, she thought of a Bible verse and said it aloud, "Their hearts are set upon the pilgrimage; when they pass through the valley of majestic trees, they make a spring of it; the early rain clothes it with generous growth." Closing her eyes, she tried to see pages of her Bible in her mind. She prayed, "Dear Lord, help these men quit fighting. May they eschew all war."

Her respite ended in a moment. From every direction, war roared like great beasts set loose upon the world. She hung her head. Her horse was lost, perhaps dead. The young singer could be dead as well, not to mention the officer's wife and child.

"This is not what I thought. Dear God, please let the battle end soon. Let our boys *stay alive!*" Her strident call, made in a break of the battle clattering, sounded loud in the chamber of trees. She fell to her knees and dug her fingers deep into the soil, grasping handfuls of grass. She sought to reclaim the assurance of her heretofore gentle farm life to replace the reality now surrounding her.

Her throat felt like she had swallowed dry cornmeal. She remembered a shallow stream that fed into the creek a few yards back. She rose, and, retracing her steps, she found the stream. She sank to her knees and cupped several mouthfuls of water to her lips. It tasted coppery and salty. Then, she recoiled—the water was colored pink. A sort of calligraphy of red lines swirled about in the slow-moving eddies of the stream. She looked up and saw, just a dozen yards from her, a Confederate lying lifeless across the stream, his jacket stained crimson. Horrified, she spit out the water. Still kneeling, she lowered her head. She dared not look again in the direction of the dead soldier. She crawled over to a vast fallen trunk, bent over it, coughing.

Before she could stand she heard crashing and yelling in the trees to her right. She turned to see several Confederates running down an incline just beyond the clearing. Behind them, not one hundred paces, charged a dozen Union cavalry, sabers raised.

Sara dove behind the fallen tree trunk. The Rebels raced by her across the clearing, then leaped into a dense thicket. She stared at the array of scrabbly undergrowth and trees, for the soldiers had vanished as if the thicket wall had swallowed them. The Union cavalry thundered past, and drew up abruptly before the thicket. As they turned their horses this way and that, a volley erupted from the thicket. Some bushes burst into flame from the gunfire. Screaming horses and soldiers fell like heavy stones. Sara covered her ears. When the smoke had cleared, only two of the cavalry raced away. Those same Rebel soldiers plus many more emerged from the trees, dodging the burning undergrowth, cheering.

"Run, you yellow dogs!" called one.

"Run back to your mamas," another shouted gleefully.

"Boy, we sure put the slick on 'em. They fell for it," an officer wearing a gold, silk-lined cape stated, thrusting his saber into its scabbard.

Sara stepped from her hiding place, pleased at first with what seemed like a small victory for her Rebel soldiers and shouted, "Hurrah . . ." but her voice sank as she took in the dismal sight before her. A line from a poem fell into her thoughts. *War has come. The carnal has prevailed against peace. Man is killing man for glory.* She held her hands to her cheeks.

The Confederates, ignoring the moans of the wounded around them, were startled to see a woman in the midst of the battle, and stood stock-still, gawking.

Sara smiled at their incredulous looks, then put her hands with a firm motion on her hips. "Either you boys go back to finish whipping those Yankees or help me with these here wounded."

The Rebels, clad like a troop of cavaliers with pheasant and peacock feathers in their wide-brimmed hats, stared with mixed expressions at the carnage they had wrought.

A gray-bearded sergeant in a red shirt, his suspenders hanging down, said, "I don't know what you're doin' out here, missy, but we aim to kill Yanks, not save 'em." The rest of the soldiers voiced aggravated agreement.

Sara did not know what came over her to suddenly care for the soldiers of the enemy, but, when she looked at their faces, they looked like kind men, and her heart was aggrieved hearing them moan so. Her previous perception of Yankees had slid away like film washed from her eyes.

"Here," she pointed at the wounded men. "They're hurt. And this one is bleedin' like a gutted goat." No sooner had she said the words than the bleeding cavalryman, trapped under his dead horse, let out a gurgling gasp and died. A surge of nausea came upon Sara. Forcing herself to relax, she looked away from the corpse. She again turned to the Confederates, "Go on, now. Divvy up your canteens for these boys. They are human, after all."

The lieutenant stepped before his troop and commanded, "Look lively now, lads. If they're well enough, we must take them as prisoners. They may tell us valuable information about the enemy. And we have here a woman . . ." He turned and eyed Sara up and down, then looked again at his troops and continued sarcastically, "who appears to have the spirit to save a few." Then in a more somber tone, he said, "It is our Christian duty, despite our abhorrence of these pig swill."

The soldiers began to grumble, but he put his hand on his sword hilt, and they quieted. Sara wondered if he was threatening to cut them if they did not obey. *This is not at all what I thought about our soldiers. Where is their compassion?*

The lieutenant pointed to a half-dozen soldiers nearest Sara. "You men help with the wounded. Sergeant, make sure these men assist this woman. Send the wounded under guard back to our lines. The rest of you, come with me. Get the lead out of your britches." The lieutenant and the majority of the men plunged into the same thicket and disappeared once more.

The cadre of men left to help, all of them about her age, gathered near this new female commander to do her bidding. Sara, not sure of what to say, pointed one by one at the soldiers lying about.

Four of the band lifted the wounded soldiers and lay them nearer the stream. One private set about beating out the small brushfire with a Union soldier's jacket. The sergeant drew his pistol and began shooting the downed horses in the head. Slow and measured, he fired, the sound piercing the air. Sara cringed at each shot. He came up to one standing horse with a destroyed leg, bent at an angle and bleeding.

He grabbed the horse's reins, aimed his pistol straight between the animal's eyes, and fired. The horse crashed to the earth. The sergeant calmly walked over to help his companions.

While two privates attempted to tourniquet one Yankee's bleeding leg, Sara bent to another who was holding his stomach and grimacing. She smiled while giving him a sip of water from a canteen taken from a Yankee's saddle. The young teen's face was as pale as a scaled trout.

"Am I going to die?" he asked. He seemed less anxious and more curious.

She had seen death before when a cow or calf had died. She had helped with the slaughtering of pigs, goats, and chickens. She had attended funerals of friends and, when she was young, of her brothers and seen the bodies stiff in coffins, but she had not seen this. She felt she could only dissuade him from the truth. She stroked his brow, "Of course not. You're just a little hurt. You'll get better."

"How come I can't feel my legs?" he asked.

When Sara knelt, she saw blood spilling from the soldier's back and spreading, turning the grass russet. The blood had spread to stain her skirt as well. She struggled to hide her horror. Without thinking, and more to just be doing something, she set about rubbing his legs.

"I'm kind of cold, miss," he whispered, "Is there a blanket?"

Sara bit her lip to hold back her tears. He had a face not unlike her youngest brother.

Then his eyes seemed to look delightedly upon some sight not of this world. A moment more and the pupils dilated and fixed.

She stopped rubbing his legs and set her hands in her lap. Her mind refused to believe the young man had died. Time froze. Once again, she felt the pinch of nausea, but it was mixed with a deep sadness. Trying not to look at the peaceful expression on the lifeless face, she closed his eyes.

With a deep breath, Sara rose and walked to the next wounded soldier. She tore a strip of cloth from her skirt hem and bound his bloody shoulder. Three Rebel soldiers bent over the remaining wounded, staunching one soldier's bleeding foot and binding the head wound of another. The sergeant and a private gathered the remaining weapons from the dead and wounded soldiers and stacked them against a tree.

In their little shaded forest hospital ward, the battle seemed far away. The deep forest muffled the sounds of battle which, once more, momentarily dwindled to almost nothing.

One of the Confederates said, "I wonder if we won this fight, or if the Yanks did."

No one answered him. The battle no longer mattered to them, only the wounded.

Sara continued to give directions, though she did not need to, for the soldiers bound the wounds with torn shirts taken from the dead and offered swigs of liquor from an earthenware jug that one of the Confederates had carried with him all through the battle. They labored in general silence. A slight-built one said to her, "I was wondering, are you the general's daughter?"

"No," Sara, taken aback, laughed nervously. "I'm just here to help you in your fight and make these Yanks go home."

A private, dressed in a smart gray jacket that hung open and a shirt with a dainty flowered pattern, approached Sara and offered a weak smile. "Miss, would it be okay if you take a look at me, too?" He lifted his hand from his stomach, revealing a blossoming red stain, then he slumped backward.

Sara rushed to him, caught his arm, and slowed his fall. This soldier, with long, tangled, blond locks spilling over his eyes, looked familiar, and she at once thought perhaps he was the one who had sung to her. With her hand behind his head, she helped him lie on the ground. "Give me some help here. One of ours is sure enough hurt."

Sara brushed the hair from over his eyes and beheld a face, though begrimed with gunpowder, she was sure was too familiar. Her mind raced, and her heart felt like it would burst from her chest. Breathing came hard for her, but she forced herself to ask the young, fair-skinned man lying cradled in her arms, "Did you three days ago sing a song for me in camp?"

The soldier looked puzzled, then stared off in the distance as if recollecting. He coughed a rattling cough, then whispered, "I do like to sing." Then he said something else, too soft for Sara to hear.

She bent closer to his lips, tears pooling in her eyes. "Please, say that again. I couldn't understand." She looked into his eyes that seemed to hold no fear, but a sort of quiet resignation. His clean-shaven face was bluish pale though his cheeks were peeling from sunburn, his thin lips chapped.

In a whisper she could barely hear, he breathed out, "Yes, I sang to you, and you gave me a tin of milk." He smiled, the lids of his eyes fluttering to close. "It was good milk. Reminded me of home."

The other Confederates gathered around Sara and their fallen comrade. The sergeant lifted the boy's shirt, coated in blood. A jagged wound oozed dark maroon. The sergeant looked up at Sara. His face said it all. The young soldier had no hope.

Sara's eyes flooded with tears, and she began shaking uncontrollably and wailing. "No!" she screamed between heaving gasps. "This is not what war is supposed to be!"

The old, gray sergeant gently took her arms and lifted her to her feet. She stumbled away with him supporting her. Sobbing and laboring to catch her breath, she collapsed to the ground.

Somewhere in the caverns of her ears she heard one of the Confederates say, "Sergeant, he's passed to the further shore."

NINE

Things Done in Desperation

August 10, 1861, Bloody Hill at Wilson Creek, 6:00 am

Joseph and Workman, along with the First Iowa and a regiment of Missouri Union, emerged from the dense cover that had hidden them and sped on the double quick up the hill. They were met by a hail of bullets from the Rebel soldiers dug in behind boulders and a tight mesh of vine-covered trees. Joseph hurried to keep step with Workman. The steep upgrade of the hill surprised Joseph. His footsteps faltered. Some forty yards beyond them, Rebel Missouri Guardsmen did not hesitate, their guns belching fire. To Joseph, in his alert condition, he seemed to be witnessing the spectacle as if watching from above, seeing himself among a melee of blue and gray goblins under a black canopy of smoke.

Shaking off the vision, he trudged crouching up the muddy slope. Iowan soldiers fell about him, some emitting a harsh scream of pain, others a mere waft of a last breath as they died. Interspersed in the cacophony of gunfire, he heard the prevarications of the Union officers, encouraging the soldiers forward. A belligerent lieutenant yelled epithets and pushed Joseph and Workman in the back.

"He pushes me one more time," Workman called to Joseph, "I'm gonna throttle 'im."

Joseph did not feel fear, but wonder. In this wretched struggle against death, he felt instead a heightened intensity. When one of the gray-clad Iowans that he recognized collapsed to the rocky ground, arching his back and twisting in agony, his astonishment turned to rage. He wanted revenge.

To his right, the flag-bearer was struck square in the chest and toppled backward, dead before he hit the ground. Two others beside him crumpled, wounded. The flag drifted almost to the ground before a fourth soldier snatched it up.

The new color-bearer waved the flag back and forth and yelled, "Come on, boys! The hill is ours!" Their courage galvanized by the admonition of their comrade, Joseph, Workman, and the Iowans charged at a full trot, growling like animals. They stopped in a jagged line when the Rebels came into view. The Iowans' rifles released a horrendous volley. Several Rebels fell. Joseph felt certain that his bullet had found its mark. The remaining Southerners fled.

Then, like a wind had blown them away, the defenders ceased firing across the entire hilltop. Joseph's regiment and the Union Missourians crested the hill and stared down at the Rebels retreating, running, sliding and tumbling down the hill. Many on horseback were coaxing their mounts into the trees below. Joseph joined his fellow Iowans in exuberant cheering.

One plump soldier, his shirt soaked in sweat, went around asking, "Did we win? Did we win? Is it over?"

Joseph and the other soldiers ignored the fellow while he whirled around looking for anyone to answer him. When the cheering stopped, the utterances of the wounded rose to Joseph's ears. Officers ordered various soldiers to tend to those struck down, both Yankee and Confederate. For the most part, the wounded soldiers were hoisted by three or four men and carried back down the hill far enough so that Joseph could no longer hear their moans.

Workman made his way next to Joseph and stated flatly, "Most likely, they're gathering up to charge us, but with more of 'em." Workman's words landed like an avalanche on Joseph's joy. This was war. The enemy had run for now, but they would return.

Joseph touched his pocket where the tintype and letter perched. *Cyntha, I send my soul to you, so you know that I am safe so far. The Rebels have retreated. When this battle is over, I shall write you such a letter of love.*

Presently, a captain and several lieutenants made their way among the mixed groups of Iowans and Missourians calling for the men to form up. Grumbling, they complied. Dirty, sweating privates, corporals, and sergeants piled rocks, small and large, in a patchwork fashion of pitiful parapets. At length, the men developed an undulating defense along the brim of the hill. Some companies were moved to the rear as reserve. Joseph's Company C was posted on the far left where the hill fell at a slant toward Wilson Creek. A captain came along, grabbed a few individual soldiers by their collars, and ordered them back down the hill. They followed him into the trees. Joseph did not know why. He pondered for a while the odd goings-on of an army. Officers seemed to give orders just for the sake of giving them.

A captain roared, "You men, move forward. Even up the line!" Two dozen soldiers moved ahead several yards.

A minute later, Colonel Merrill noticed the advanced men. "Get back here where there's cover. Are you *trying* to get yourself picked off by their sharpshooters?" The group slunk back to their original position, looking like whipped dogs.

Most of the soldiers appeared to Joseph to be as bewildered as he at the conflicting orders from competing officers, yet they dutifully complied with each command. Joseph wondered how many soldiers just like him remained confused as to their intent in this battle.

"Workman," he said.

"Yeah?" Workman was sitting on a tree stump, his eyes squinted against the now bright sunrise, swabbing out his rifle barrel with a small cotton cloth on the end of his ramrod. He held up the rifle and aimed down the hill, then cocked the hammer and pulled the trigger. "She's sound." He seemed almost to be avoiding Joseph.

"Do you know what we're supposed to do?" Joseph asked. "Are we to hold the hill, or . . ."

"Or charge? Not likely. The sun's up, and I've a notion that them Rebs are pullin' together from all over, gettin' ready to give us a dandy time."

"Dandy time?" Joseph did not grasp the sarcasm.

Workman smiled deviously. "If I know anything about these Southern boys, they're gonna work themselves up for a fight. Just watch."

Joseph lifted his forage cap and wiped his tanned forehead with his kerchief. A whiter skin tone was evidenced below the hairline, marking where his cap sat day in, day out. His blond hair was soaking wet.

"I don't see why we don't move to that ledge below us," Workman remarked, pointing his long arm. "When them Rebs come back, they'll be hidden from our view until they top that ledge. We won't be able to shoot 'em until they're almost on us. That'd make more sense to me, but then, I'm just a private."

Joseph inched forward in a crouch, enough to peer at the lower ledge. It appeared to be a more defensible, tactical position. "You're right, Dred." Turning, he spied a Colt revolver covered in dust. He picked it up and examined the chamber. Not a bullet had been fired. He swept the pistol left and right, feeling its weight. He aimed at a distant tree at the bottom of the hill. He thought to himself that that tree might be hiding a Rebel. He looked up at the Iowans. No one seemed interested in his find. All were hurriedly pitching soil with their drinking cups into small mounds, or running hither and thither in search of large enough rocks, then prying them from the soil to carry back to their spot in the line. Others worked in teams dragging fallen tree limbs into a makeshift redoubt. Joseph and Workman were well situated behind a fallen tree trunk.

With the morning brightening, Rebel cannonading began. Cannonballs burst over their heads, showering canister, tearing the flesh of many Iowans. The Union line dove for cover at each explosion. Joseph noticed a private begin to look about wild-eyed. He broke and raced away. A sergeant intervened with his rifle pointed straight at the soldier's stomach. The soldier turned around, and the sergeant swatted him on the rear with the rifle butt. The frightened private took his place back in line, then wept.

Joseph felt both anger at the timid soldier and a sort of grief for him. *It's hard enough not to just turn around and walk away without that fellow doing that. If he got away with running, I fear a number of these boys would run, leaving just a few of us to fight.*

Joseph knew that were he to run, it would be the height of ignominy. *God, give me courage today*, he prayed. *Please don't let me falter in my duty.*

The cannon fire continued to crash about them. The Union battery roared back at the Confederate artillery position, so that the air was filled with shrieking and fire and smoke.

The morning grew humid, and many of the soldiers took off their coats and rolled up their shirt sleeves. Joseph did the same, folding his jacket and setting it beside some others tossed in a heap. He could see masses of Confederates assembling at the bottom of the hill, too hidden by brush and trees for him to shoot at them.

A few soldiers fired desultory shots down into the forest vale, wasting their bullets on shadows. Occasional shots from the Rebels pinged off rocks, but none struck a human form.

Word came down the line that they were waiting for further orders. Joseph wondered whether his army would be called to charge again, or would they be reinforced to hold the hill. Would they be told to retreat? At the pinnacle of the hill, he recognized General Lyon and a few other officers on horseback. They pointed in all directions and looked through field glasses. He wished he had the field glasses Cyntha had given him for his birthday. He imagined that if he could but look at the enemy and see the face of the one ordained by fate to kill him, then he could dispatch that Rebel before he ever fired a shot. He extended his hand. It was trembling.

He fumbled for Cyntha's tintype and letter. He deeply desired the comfort of her embrace. He wanted a sense of purpose, beyond this reality. He and his wife had adopted spiritualism into their faith and saw no discordance with it and their Methodist religion. They had read the scientific treatises and listened to lectures of renowned spiritualist leaders. They, like millions of others, believed unabashedly that the spirits of the dead were nearby, and that the souls of those alive could communicate across an ethereal distance, that the spiritual and mortal planes were closer than had been previously believed. He wished to know what she was doing at this moment. Was she thinking of him as he was of her?

He would not have his questions answered, for from the bottom of the hill came a deep, aggressive growl from a thousand Rebels that rose to a high-pitched shriek. They charged along the entire Union line, hundreds of them running at the beleaguered Iowans who were crouching and still trying to construct cover. Joseph began shivering with fear.

"That's Price's Missourians," called a captain. "They wanna drive us from the hill!" His voice sounded as shrill as a woman's. "Give 'em hell, men. We'll stop 'em here."

"Ready!" the captain shouted. Rifles raised in unison up to a hundred shoulders. A hundred hammers cocked. "Fire!" The rifles erupted in flame and smoke. Rebels fell.

In automatic motion, Joseph began reloading. Powder, ball, ramrod, grope for the firing cap, cock the hammer. Hands shaking, eyes squinting, mouths dry, lips praying. Joseph had his Enfield ready in seconds, but was unnerved seeing his comrades struggling to reload their guns.

"Steady!" called the captain. The Rebels, who at the beginning of their assault charged through sparse bushes and trees on the hillside, became, for a moment, lost from sight, hidden by the lower ledge. Workman had been right. The firing stopped, followed by abject silence along the entire line. Joseph heard only the Rebels yelling, and the tread of hundreds of feet, loud as a rushing locomotive. The erratic smoke drifted higher. Joseph saw each man in the regiment lean forward in anticipation, and, like him, unsure of what to expect.

First, a Confederate Missouri Guard flag appeared above the ledge. Then, like a wave breaking over a shoal, the Rebels topped the ledge in a run, yelling, rifles held in all manner, pointed down, pointed up, held across the chest, and held by the barrel like a club. The Guard did not stop to line up and shoot, but charged with a galvanic, hysterical fury. They fired on the run with no apparent formation at all. Two Iowans pitched backward, pierced by bullets.

The Iowa captain called, "Fire!" Rifles and muskets blazed. Joseph took careful aim at a man holding a shotgun and shot him in the chest while gaining footing on the ledge. The dying Confederate's arms flailed in the air as he fell. Joseph drew the pistol and fired at the center of a mob of men that looked like a great octopus of arms and legs. He did not consider the form as men, but as an indiscriminate figure, like the rendition of men in a painting, resembling human form, but in no way real beings. One of the mob toppled backward. Dozens of Rebels were felled by the Union rifles, but still they charged, screaming maniacally. Then, the distance between the two armies collapsed like a musician's accordion, and the Rebels were in the midst of them. Soldiers of both armies clubbed with rifle butts, sliced with sabers, and grappled hand to hand. Joseph fired the pistol again at one Rebel about to bayonet an Iowan. The man tilted a little, propped against his rifle as it stuck in the ground bayonet first, then he slid to the ground like a sheet drifting from a clothesline. Joseph fired again in the general direction of several Rebels. The smoke was so dense it hid the sun. Faces and bodies passed by him in a rush.

Like a phantom emerging from a dark cemetery, a hefty gray-bearded Rebel with officer's insignia on his uniform collar hobbled toward Joseph, his sword raised. Joseph shot the man point-blank in the stomach. Dropping his sword, the man collapsed to his knees, then struggled to un-holster his pistol. Joseph reached out for the officer's hand, hoping the officer would surrender, but he fought against Joseph. When the man freed the revolver, Joseph fired into the man's neck. He toppled backward, his blood spraying out onto Joseph's shirt and face. Joseph picked up the officer's sword and turned toward his fellow Iowans.

Amidst billowing black smoke, a young Iowan raced toward him, his gun butt raised high. The Iowan's face showed animal terror. Joseph raised his hands to ward off the blow, but before he could say, "I'm Union," the rifle butt hammered his forehead. Splotches of light in deep darkness sprang to his eyes, and he fell backward to the ground, hitting his head again on a protruding tree root. He tumbled down the hill, over and over, his body finally coming to rest under some crepe myrtle bushes. In one hand, Joseph clutched the sword; in the other, lay the revolver. The battle raged around him. Several feet from him, fallen from his pocket, lay his wife's tintype. The letter, lifted from the tintype by the retreating Rebels' trampling feet, floated away on the breeze.

TEN

A Cold Loneliness

Sara gave over the care of the wounded Yankees to the Confederates. She tried to wash the blood from her hands in the small stream, but the stains remained. Turning to the sergeant, she said, "Sir, I can do no more."

He responded with a nod. "You've done your part, little lady."

"Yes." She gazed for a moment at the little churchlike glen, then turned south toward home, retracing her steps as best she could. Crossing Wilson Creek, it now flowed parallel to her left, muttering over the rocks. She passed the Edwards' home, a crass shack surrounded by tents. The door of the house swung back and forth on its hinges, clattering. Before the war, the Edwards had been friends, but they bore allegiance to the old states, and they fled with the arrival of the Southern army. The war had broken their family friendship. Sara felt a pang of remorse.

The sounds of guns had dwindled to almost nothing. Single, almost imperceptible, rifle shots sounded both behind her to the north and far, far in front of her. Her thoughts of the frightful battle wore on her. Though filled with grief over the carnage, she considered now how she must have caused deep concern for her father and Abram.

It occurred to her that her father may have been killed and Abram hauled away in chains, and she felt the urgency to race home, but could barely force her exhausted body forward.

She drifted through the battlefield, halfheartedly looking for the officer's wife and child. She mulled over the realization that her perceived paramour, the singer, was dead, and the shock of his death had caused the contours of his face to wane in her mind. She could no longer quite recall his appearance. Forcing herself to set his memory aside, she became driven by the greater need to find her horse and return to the arms of her father.

Ultimately, she could see in the distance the Sharp home with gaping holes in the walls. She saw no evidence that the Sharps were anywhere near. She arrived at the meadow where the young soldier had saved her life when he pulled her off Esther. She climbed the low fence and found it rough going, stepping through mud and knee-high grass. The cattle had spread out and were grazing. All about her, Confederates carried wounded from the field, a few on stretchers or blankets; but more often, one man gathered a bloodied comrade under the arms, while another took him by the legs, and they strained awkwardly with their burden toward the camps. She passed a half-dozen pairs of soldiers where one leaned on another, and half of those were Union soldiers leaning on a Confederate. She found herself drawn to these suffering men. The bloody wounds, the pained faces, and the shortage of care being afforded them amazed and sobered her. She felt useless and found herself repeatedly looking down at her bloodstained hands, cursing them, for there were *so many* in need. Once, she rushed toward a soldier with a destroyed arm being carried away on a stretcher, yet stopped short, for she had no means to help. She raised her hands toward heaven but no prayer came to her lips.

At the southern end of the meadow she noticed a bullet-ridden cow's body and four horse carcasses, still saddled, covered with flies. The meadow was littered with lifeless blue-clad soldiers, half-hidden in the grass. The dead bodies lay stiffening in rigor mortis like grotesque statues. As she entered the cornfield at the farther edge of the meadow, a group of slaves passed her carrying shovels and small harrows. She looked back and watched them begin digging.

She reached the northern edge of the Texan-Kansan cavalry camp and at last could see her home. She yearned to run there but felt it incumbent upon her to find her horse if it was alive. She continued crossing back and forth through the shambled encampment.

In this camp where the Union cannonballs had first showered down, she saw soldiers celebrating outside their flattened tents and lean-tos, their faces still streaked with grime and gunpowder. Several of the Rebels dipped mugs into some homemade corn-squeezings in a large wooden washtub. They drank great draughts, much of the liquor pouring down their cheeks. Other soldiers lit up their carved wooden or corncob pipes. Sara appreciated the aroma of the potent tobacco, an odor so much more pleasant than the foul battle smoke.

Her legs tired beyond measure, and her thoughts so muddled, Sara collapsed onto a vacant camp chair. She realized she had no saliva; her mouth felt powdery dry. She looked around in search of water. Throughout the camp, many soldiers were laughing and slapping each other on the back. Others slumped on camp chairs or on the ground in various degrees of dishevelment. Some nursed minor wounds. A lieutenant rode a sweaty horse back and forth through the camp issuing orders to soldiers, some who complied, and others who did not. Those who did what they were ordered went about the chore in a dilatory fashion. *What is this bedevilment?* she thought. She saw a soldier washing plates in a tub. She gathered her strength to stagger to the tub and, to the astonishment of the soldier, cupped her hands and drank of the soapy water. She stood, wiped her mouth with her sleeve, spitting the soapy taste. "Thank you," she said and continued her search for Esther.

A few yards further on, Sara witnessed a soldier with gunpowder-stained palms digging in his reddened eyes as if he was trying to pry them loose.

Another soldier seated on a camp stool, surrounded by consoling friends, sobbed, "They killed my brother!" At his feet, a dead soldier was laid. She halted. She remembered the hollowness she had felt when all three brothers died when she was but six years old. She looked for a moment at the fallen soldier and marveled at the face, devoid of expression. *Was he happy in paradise now?* she thought.

Near an adjacent tent, Sara spotted Reverend Edward Felder, his knee bent beside an ashen-faced soldier lying on a cot. She could not tell if the prone soldier was alive or dead. The reverend clinched his hands together, and his eyes were turned in supplication toward heaven. The dark haired reverend was gaunt with deep set eyes. He had a high forehead divided by a widow's peak. He rose from the man's cot, placed his black, wide-brimmed hat on his head, and shook hands with the man's companions. The prone soldier then raised a hand wearily and clutched the forearm of the man nearest. Sara sighed in relief.

Reverend Felder suddenly brushed past her, shouting and shaking his fist. He rushed upon the men drinking the brew, knocked the tankard from one man's hands, and railed against them. "How dare thee take the devil's brew when all about you men have died! Have you no respect?" He glared at them.

The cadre of soldiers appeared at first surprised, then burst into guffaws and began hoisting their mugs again. The reverend stormed away. The moment he departed, a major rode up to the liquor-sodden group. "Grab shovels, men, we've got bodies to bury!" he shouted. "That's an order." The soldiers drained their mugs, trudged to a wagon, and retrieved shovels. They followed the major. With the sodden drinkers gone, Sara's thirst was too overwhelming. She grabbed a mug and dipped into the brew and downed the full mug.

Her thirst somewhat quenched, she became aware of the smell of cornmeal in pork grease and boiling beans. Camp cooks were preparing an afternoon meal, for the Confederates had not eaten since the night before. One camp gourmand pulled forth steaming biscuits from a heavy Dutch oven. Lifting the biscuits with a fork, he flipped them one by one to hungry soldiers who grabbed them eagerly, then tossed them from hand to hand and blew on their fingers. Sara became aware of her own hunger. The pungent, savory smells made her think of Abram's delicious fried fish and hush puppies. Then of how much she loved him. "Dear Lord, please keep my dear Abram safe. I beg you. Don't let him be stolen by the Yankees."

At the tail of the tents, and directly below the ridge where she and her father had stood the day before, the officer's wife knelt beside a cradle, comforting her crying child, wiping the tears with her apron. In front of the tent, a rough table was bedecked with a tablecloth, blue and white platters, and crystal glasses. Two slaves carried armloads of firewood and set them beside the cook fire. Sara came up to the woman, whose face was set like stone, but tears sat on her eyelids. Sara dared not ask her about her husband, but stroked the small child's hair. The woman did not speak. She rose for a minute and looked around the camp, her expression like a trapped animal. At last, she sat painstakingly slow on a campstool. Sara took a seat beside her, placing her hand on the woman's shoulder. Sara saw in the woman's eyes what she had seen before in the eyes of neighbors who had lost a spouse or a child. She knew the woman needed to express her grief, but not in front of a thousand strangers. However short a time her now-disaffected, wretched life would allow, she needed one small moment. Surrounded by an army of men, she had no one who could console her. Sara, in bringing milk to the woman those few days, had developed a modicum of friendship.

Sara picked up the baby, set it on her lap, and soothed it. The baby relaxed.

"Shoo!" Sara said to the two slaves, waving at them to depart. Their faces seeming to reflect the officer's wife's sorrow, they slipped away well beyond the tent. The woman rose and stepped into her tent while Sara tended the child. From the tent, Sara heard gentle sobs.

Several yards across from the tent, a young soldier seated on an overturned bucket, his cherubic face beaming as he watched a soaring hawk, struck up a raucous tune on a banjo. A bearded comrade with raw-skinned cheeks added rhythm to the melody beating on a coffeepot with a spoon. Where only hours before, terror and death had reigned, the humdrum of the camp life returned. Sara thought, *Why are they so happy? Their friends died today.* She was disturbed by what seemed like callous disregard by the soldiers and felt a little antagonistic toward them. "Were I their commanding officer, I would have a word with them," she said under her breath while rocking the baby. "No reverence. No taking a moment to honor the dead."

In a few minutes, the woman emerged from the tent and took the baby from Sara.

"Thank you," the woman said. "If you've milk tomorrow, I could use some . . ." Her voice trailed off, and she seemed to look off into infinity.

Sara stroked the baby's fine hair. "Good-bye. I'll see about getting you some milk."

Sara trudged on, her heart as heavy as lead. Her legs hurt, her neck felt knotted, and she had bruises and scratches on her arms.

In a small grove of poplars, nearest the creek, she came close to a number of Yankee prisoners walking listlessly about an enclosure made of a few ropes tied from tree to tree. Two Rebels with rifles in their hands and pistols in their belts stood guard. All the prisoners appeared morose, save one. She could not help but notice him. He was so tall, all bone and angle with a droopy mustache, moles across his face, and a bulging Adam's apple. He was dressed in a dirty blue-gray uniform, and he spoke adamantly to his captors. "Look, I ain't no real Yank. I don't care to be with 'em. I want to join up with you gents. I've had my fill of Yankee officers and Yankee drills, and I'm ready to fight for ye. I will. I'll fight for ye."

Sara was too drained to continue listening to the ranting prisoner.

After a while, his voice, switching from pleading with to chastisement of his captors, faded behind her.

She walked to the tree line by the creek where the soldiers had kept their mounts tied to the long staked rope. Interspersed in the line, five horses, destroyed by the morning cannon fire and still tethered to the stringer, lay bent, gnarled, and blackened like heated metal. Then she saw Esther alive, tied to a tree. She felt joy akin to finding a treasure. She rushed to her mare, untied the reins and stroked its neck, and the mare tossed its head in acknowledgment. Sara jumped in the saddle. "This one's mine!"

A few soldiers lay on blankets in the shade. Though most paid her no heed, a stocky soldier with yellow, twisted teeth rose to stop her. She kicked him in the chest. "I said, this one's mine."

He grappled at the saddle and yanked on her dress. "The army needs that horse," he said, "ya bald-faced plunderer."

Turning Esther in circles, Sara tried to free herself from the man's meaty hands. Finally, she managed one swift kick to the man's jaw. He flopped to the ground. Sara galloped Esther away. "She's mine!" she called over her shoulder.

She rode out of the grove and onto the cart path called Dixon Road. Here and there, she saw corpses, mostly Yankees, blowflies buzzing about them. One dead soldier's body had a green and violet dragonfly perched on his nose. Sara noticed that the sun shining through the insects wings like a prism spilled little rainbows of light on his face.

A Confederate doctor, stripped to the waist and covered with sweat, was accompanied by a couple of soldier nurses—husky men with brawny arms. They walked from body to body, checking for signs of life. When they would find one alive, the doctor ordered them to carry each to a ragged cart, from which a tangle of arms and legs protruded. The attendants flippantly hoisted the bodies on top of other wounded. Sara again felt a surge of remorse at the treatment for the wounded.

A handful of Rebel soldiers with a lieutenant barking at their backs were casually picking up the dead bodies and laying them alongside the ditch that ran beside the road. Sara hoped that the bodies they intended to bury were indeed dead.

A single soldier jigged from one corpse to the next, gathering various items—watches, coins, rings—and pocketing them in his haversack and tittering in a silly fashion. Sara's shook her head in disgust.

When she rode past him, he turned a dark eye on her. He pointed at her a finger with an overlong, torn nail. He smirked. "Don't you tell no one, little girl. Don't you tell my sister!" He suddenly ran at her. She dug her heels into Esther and trotted away. The man returned to his looting.

At the far end of the cornfield, she saw the women and children who had accompanied their husbands to war. Their tents were flattened, and their wagons overturned by the morning onslaught of Union troops. A few spots of the cornfield bore small, dying fires, and little flaming embers dangled about in the wind. The families labored to raise the tents and put some semblance of order to their excoriated campsites. Scorched soil and burned cornstalks, punctuated by small, smoldering fires with drifting smoke, covered much of the Sharps' field.

Sara at last reached the crossing at Wilson Creek to the cow path that meandered up the ridge toward home. At the top, she passed the site where her father and she had their picnic the day before and where the sergeant had met them on his way to call in the pickets. Deep wheel ruts crisscrossing the area indicated the route the Yankees had pulled their cannons after their initial bombardment from the Reeder yard. She passed through the corridor of trees, then the family graveyard, and the vegetable garden. Her father, standing on the porch, saw her and raced to meet her. Abram hobbled along behind. She dismounted, and hugged her father for a long time. Stepping back, yet still holding each other, Sara could feel her father trembling and saw little pools of tears in his eyes. Tears spilled down her face. She kissed him on the cheek, then hugged him again. Next, she held Abram by the shoulders, hugged him, then kissed him several times on both cheeks and his forehead. The old man looked befuddled at first, then smiled.

"Dearest Abram," Sara said, "I was so afraid the Yankees would steal you. And yet they did not. Praise God. I should've stayed here to ensure your protection. You are so dear to me."

Abram nodded his head knowingly. "You, too, are dear to me, child. But you needn't have worried. The soldiers came in the house and ignored me, even when I came up out of the cellar."

Sara was surprised.

"Yes, dear child, I came up. It was too dank in that old cellar. They could not have cared less about me."

"But I thought, Pa...how could he..."

"Before you say another word, Sara," Lucas sighed. Sara attempted to speak, but, without his trumpet, he waved her off. Abram led Esther back to the barn while Lucas and Sara strode arm in arm inside. In the great room, Lucas again hugged his daughter.

He had her sit on their flowered sofa, and, taking his trumpet from a lamp stand, he sat beside her. Sara could see he was struggling with his next words.

"I am deeply disappointed in you," he said, punctuating each word. "I know I raised you better. Running off into certain danger! You could've been killed. I've never struck you, but I'm angry enough now I almost could, except that I'm so glad you're safe." He stroked her matted hair, then blotted his eyes with a handkerchief.

Sara bowed her head for a moment, then raised it. "Would I have been safer here with the Yanks in our yard and in our house, Papa? I'm duly sorry to have worried you, even to the point of throwing myself down a well for ever doing such a thing. In my heart I am chastising myself. I shall pray tonight for forgiveness for my thoughtlessness." She took his rough hand and kissed it. "Still . . . I did what I had to do."

"Very well." Lucas grasped her hands tight. "See that you speak with me first before doing something like that again. You're all I have left."

They hugged once more.

Releasing her embrace, Sara pleaded, "Papa, someone must help the wounded. They are lyin' in the sun all throughout the valley. I worry they may be buryin' some who aren't yet dead."

"I fear that you may be right about the wounded," he replied. "I followed after the Yanks' cannons out to the ridge where you and I stood but yesterday. I brought my telescope and watched when McCulloch's Louisiana boys—I recognized them by their flags—swept up the road. The Yanks had no chance. They ran. It would've been a slaughter had McCulloch pursued them, but I think he must've been aware of the fight on the northern flank, so he rushed his troops there. As best I can tell, Lyon split his army and attacked from the north and the south."

"There was fighting *most everywhere*, Papa. North, south, east, west. I was surrounded by war. I had no idea there could be so much fightin' . . . and so much death." Her lips trembled, but her resolve remained firm.

"The battle was indeed horrid. All battles are. You've heard my retelling of battles. Whatever took hold of you to go out into it? I was beside myself with worry."

"I had to warn our boys. I just had to . . . But I was too late. I guess they turned back the Yanks though."

"Our soldiers did. The Secessionists won this battle."

"Do you remember that kind boy that sang 'Aura Lee' to me a few days back?"

"Yes, a little."

"Well, I watched him die!" The weight of her words coming from her own mouth felt like heavy stones.

Lucas at first looked incredulous of this heavy burden thrust upon his daughter, then he took her hand. They sat for a moment in silence. Abram came in from the barn and was about to speak, but, seeing them, he held his tongue, wondering what dire news had been wrought on the people he held most dear.

"Is all the fighting over now?" Sara's blue eyes burned. The tears that had welled up in her eyes glided down her freckled face. "Is the war finished? Are the Yankees done fighting? Will they go back North and leave us alone?"

Lucas drew a deep breath. He looked over at Abram standing by the fireplace. "I'm afraid, darlin' daughter, that this is just the beginning. From what I've read in the papers, there are armies formed up all across this country—North and South. And until they've all had their fill of fighting and dying, the war could go on a long time."

"How long, Papa?" Her voice strained.

"Months, maybe years. It all depends."

Sara rose and tightened her fists by her side. She looked to the open window and observed that the sun shone lower in the sky. Long shadows extended across the floor. She knew the cows would need milking and that chores about the house needed attention, but she could not tear her mind from the suffering soldiers. She stood there for a long time, the muscles of her jaws working, her eyes shining fierce as a wolf. "Very well, then. Whether this war goes on or not is something I can't control. But I can do something about helping the ones who are hurt. At least we can try to save their lives. We'll carry them from the field to where a surgeon can help. Would that there were a kinder hand to offer aid, I would leave it be, but I cannot. I cannot!"

Lucas and Abram eyed each other.

"We must go now, Papa!" she demanded.

Lucas saw in Sara what he loved so much about his wife—the ardent heart, the initiative, and, despite her naïveté of the immenseness of the situation, the absolute self-assurance of her course of action. He had fallen in love with his wife for that same character, which was both

a blessing and a flaw, and he loved his daughter more for it. He nodded and said, "I will do this because I raised you to do the right thing.
Abram, can you . . ."

"I'll fetch up the wagon and see you out front," Abram said.

ELEVEN

Those that Sow in Tears

AUGUST 10, 1861, THE REEDER HOME, 3 PM

Within an hour of Sara's arrival home, Lucas, Abram, and she rode in the buckboard wagon to the battlefield. She had changed her soiled, torn dress. She sat munching on a sandwich. Crossing the ford at Wilson Creek, they drove onto the Dixon Road and headed north through the Sharps' cornfield, passing the Arkansans. A few soldiers peered curiously at the threesome, but kept busy resetting tents and trying to restore order to their demolished camp.

They drove past a long line of Confederates walking abreast across the field. When the soldiers came upon a prone man, alive or not, they loaded the body in a mule-drawn dray, then restarted their search.

Just past the camp, Abram spotted a Yankee with a torn leg crawling through the grass. Sara and Lucas climbed down and gave him a few ladles of water and tied a bandage around the wound, then carefully lifted him into the back of the buckboard. They zigzagged northward across the battleground, and, in the space of an hour, found five soldiers down and suffering in the heat—four Union, one Confederate.

They came upon a makeshift Confederate field hospital, and Lucas asked some soldiers nearby to unload the wounded. The heat was withering, so the soldiers laid the wounded in the scant shade of some skinny blackjack trees. Most of the wounded lying about the area had only the shade of shirts stretched across sticks to cover their faces. They called and moaned for aid, for prayers, and even for death, and Sara could not count how many times in their short stay she heard them calling for water. Two Negroes, carrying buckets, passed among the lines of tortured men, ladling water to those that were conscious.

Under a large tarp, two surgeons worked feverously. Each stood at an operating table made of a dismantled wagon laid across large crates. A dozen "soldier nurses" rushed from one moaning man to the next, tying bandages, offering whiskey or brandy, and applying powdered opium to wounds. Under shade trees, about twenty or so soldiers with less worrisome wounds sat on the ground. Their wounds were wrapped with cornhusks. Slaves boiled water, cut bandages from tent fabric, and tossed bloodied garments in a ditch.

Sara and her father approached a surgeon wearing a blood-spattered apron laboring at his operating table. Using a pestle, he was pushing pulverized opium into a young soldier's bloody arm where a splintered piece of bone pierced the skin. He called to a nurse, "Hurry up with that enaculum. I've got to ligate the artery before I begin the cut, or we'll have a bloody mess here and a dead soldier. And bring the gnawing forceps and bone file—quickly."

A boy of about fifteen, the nurse, rushed up with the surgery tools clasped in his bloody hands. He placed the tools on a barrel near the table. The surgeon poured ether from a brown bottle into a white cloth set in a small copper funnel. The wounded soldier begged, his face expectant, "Can you save me, sir?"

The surgeon replied, "We're going to try." He held the ether laden funnel above the soldier's face.

Just then, the patient arched his back. "Save me, please!" His entreaty escalated into a long keening like a rabbit stuck in a trap.

The surgeon dripped additional ether into the funnel, and the soldier's screaming abated, then stopped. The surgeon took a long knife and carved skin away from the muscle around the torn arm. He laid the flesh to the side. He told the nurse nearest him, "I'll need that piece to stitch to the stump when I'm done with the bone. So don't let it fall off the table."

Even under the anesthetic, the soldier's body thrashed about again. "Secure him!" the surgeon called to the aides.

The nurses, spattered with blood from head to knee, held the soldier down. One pulled the jaw shut. Another lay across the body. A third one held the legs that dangled off the table. The surgeon again dripped a modicum of ether, and the patient finally lay still.

Once the enaculum clamp was secured to a main artery, the surgeon tightened a tourniquet near the shoulder, then turning to grab his bone saw, he saw Sara and Lucas waiting, "Yes. What do you want?"

"We found more wounded," Sara replied, "and brought them here."

"Am I to be grateful?" the doctor growled over his shoulder, his eyebrows pinched as he checked that he had stopped the blood flow.

"They're lyin' there in that grove," she said.

The doctor, evidencing a distracted and weary nature, nodded. "There's too many wounded now," he told them. "We'll be working on them until daybreak already." He picked up the bloody saw, wiped it on his apron, and took hold of the young man's torn arm. "You'll excuse me."

Sara glanced at the patient's face and recognized him—the young man who had pulled her from Esther and saved her life. His sandy hair matted with mud, his uniform blackish purple from blood, his smallpox-scarred face ashen in color.

In a moment, the surgeon was sawing on the limb creating a noise more execrable than scraping on a metal pipe, the bone squeaking in a high pitch.

Sara stepped back, pale and rigid. Lucas moved around in front of her to block her view and facing her, he spoke soothingly. "Hold steady, darlin' daughter."

After she slowed her breathing and regained her color, she tightened her fists, fighting against the faint.

"You can't do anything here, Sara," Lucas said. "Let the surgeon do his job."

Sara managed to nod, then wobbled like a drunkard to the buckboard.

Abram helped her climb to the seat. Lucas gained his seat, and Abram shook the reins. The lathered horses pulled doggedly on the wagon, creaking and slamming over the ragged terrain. Sara looked across the creek at the little glen where she had succored the wounded Union soldiers, where she watched the young soldier die. The glen was calm and empty of men, though the dead horses were still there. The little stream flowed crystal clear, but the blood had turned the grass rusty brown.

They passed the Louisiana troop camps in various stages of disarray. Some soldiers stood in tight groups, talking and smoking, but the majority had collapsed in some shady spot, and most were sleeping. A few soldiers re-erected tents or stacked crates. She watched one thin soldier with a stovepipe hat practicing steps to a reel, spinning, stomping his feet, and traipsing around with his arms in the air. Another shaved his face while a third carved at his toenails with a broad knife.

"Is this the way war was for you, Papa?" Sara asked, exasperated. "Do men go to war and kill each other, and then go back to their daily routines like nothing even happened? Is war just one more chore to do? It seems like they have no sense, like their heads are full of pumpkin seed. I'm so confused."

Lucas lowered the trumpet from his ear. "You are seeing men *surviving*. If they thought too much about what just happened, they'd lose their minds. By some grace, they put the horror of it away in some dark room of their minds, and only bring it out a long time hence. Now, they're just glad to be alive."

Further on, they found two more severely injured Yankees. After loading them in the wagon, they hastened to yet another thrown-to-gether hospital. When the nurses, stripped of their shirts, and their skin so covered with blood that they looked like reddlemen, stepped up to the wagon, they found that both the soldiers from the field had died. "It's just as well," one nurse said. "We're taking care of our own before we even look at the Yanks. We won't get to some until late to-morrow. They'd just have suffered and died anyway."

Sara and Lucas helped the nurses in unloading the corpses. Sara took a moment to take a cloth and wipe crusted blood from the face of one of the dead. She could not help but notice the way the inert, dead flesh felt, like bedsheets left on the line on a cold day. The nurses carried the corpses to a long ditch being dug by a sweating, weary company of Confederates. They laid the bodies beside a line of other deceased soldiers, both Confederate and Union.

Sara, Lucas, and Abram bowed their heads in prayer. After the pause, they recommenced their sojourn.

The afternoon wore into evening, and the muggy air felt suffocat-ing. Lucas, his dark hair as wet as rain, guzzled a ladle of water from the crock stowed under the wagon seat. He gave the ladle to Sara, who drank a draught. Abram drank last. Sara took another and poured it on her head. The water trickled over her sunburnt cheeks.

"Ready to quit, Sara?" Lucas asked.

"No! Not until we have covered the whole of it. I don't care if they're ours or theirs. They deserve a chance to live."

"I can't argue. I would hope that, if I was lying hurt, someone would do the same for me."

Abram turned onto Telegraph Road, then, at Lucas's direction, turned northwest onto a rough path that angled toward the flat-topped, expansive ridge the valley residents called Oak Hill. Approaching the hill, they stared in shock. The hill was littered bottom to top with dead bodies, contorted and often piled together in heaps. Buzzards hopped from corpse to corpse, plucking at exposed flesh. Another twenty of the birds perched like gargoyles on nearby trees. Even more of their ilk circled above. A single shoeless Confederate walked back and forth waving at the birds. They flew away briefly, only to return after he passed.

Searching the hill as far up as the crown, the Reeders found no more wounded, just the dead. At the bottom of Oak Hill, where the soil was less rocky, soldiers toiled vigorously digging graves. A few gathered from the dead bodies anything from shoes and boots to cartridge boxes to wedding rings.

"It looks as though General McCulloch ordered the dead buried as soon as possible. Good," Lucas said. "If the bodies aren't interred soon, they'll have a disease problem too large to handle."

The sun began to set, and the sky glowed crimson, and in the darkening fields and trees, the colors faded into muted grays and blacks. Fireflies jiggered in the grass, and nighthawks swooped about the sky.

Sara and Lucas walked east toward Wilson Creek along the bottom of the hill and ahead of the wagon driven by Abram. Looking out beyond the trees, they saw pinpoints of light flickering from the Rays' house on the hill across the creek. "I'm quite certain," Lucas said, "the Rays' place has been turned into a hospital."

From somewhere nearby, they heard a voice crying like the wail of a lost soul. "Matthew!" The voice called again and again, echoing across the hill. Sara turned slowly, searching for the source of the call. Then out from an arbor, a young Confederate, short in stature and with vacant eyes under sweaty black hair, rushed toward her. His pants were torn, and his jacket was in shreds. Dried blood stained his arms. Coming at her with such fury, she stumbled back against the wheel of the wagon. He grabbed her by the shoulders, but his grip was weak, and he shook with uncontrolled tremors. "Have you seen Matthew? Have you seen my brother?" He spat his words as if heaven itself needed to hear him.

Before Sara could respond, Lucas stepped forward and cuffed the man, who tumbled backward. He sprang up again, not to fight, but his eyes pleading. He turned his head upward and screamed, "Ahhhh!" He once more looked piercingly at the Reeders. "Have you seen my brother?"

"What regiment was he with?" Lucas asked, extending his hand to calm the man.

"What?"

"What regiment was he with? Was he with Price's volunteers or McCulloch's army?"

"What? What? He wasn't with our army. He was with the Yankees. I think we killed him. Someone said they saw his body. Is he dead? Who shot him? Oh, please, Lord, don't let it be me who shot him!"

Before Lucas or Sara could ask him what his brother looked like, the little soldier ran off crying his brother's name again and again until it was but a faint call in the night.

Sara looked into her father's eyes and wept. Her heart had been torn, as if she again was witnessing the slow death of her own brothers. She leaned into her father's chest. Lucas held her tight, his own heart heavy with a weight that he had not chosen, but had been thrust upon him this day. *That man's burden is mine as well,* he thought. *Everyone in this nation—every officer and soldier, every farmer and politician, every widow and orphan, every heart that beats for another—bears the same burden.* Then he cried out, "We've been torn asunder!"

TWELVE

The Immense Burden of Mercy

AUGUST 10, 1861, BLOODY HILL, WILSON CREEK, 9 PM

After the sun had melted into the hills like butter in a hot pan, the Reeders came upon blue-clad soldiers digging graves by lantern light. Near them, Yankee corpses were stacked like cordwood. A white flag tied to a pole stuck in the ground near where they labored. Sara paused, listening to the sordid symphony of picks and shovels landing with thuds and clinks against the dirt clods and rocks. The air smelled rank, like spoiled meat.

"McCulloch's allowing the Yankees to bury their own and find belongings to send to loved ones," Lucas said. "They'll be working way into tomorrow."

A few grim-faced Union grave diggers nodded at them while relentlessly digging.

The Reeders reached a point filled with boulders, smashed trees, and stumps past which they could not drive the wagon. Abram pulled to a stop. Stepping down, Sara proceeded into the gloom. "Let's continue around the bottom of the hill. Perhaps we can find more wounded."

"All right, Sara, for ten minutes, but this is the last for tonight." Lucas turned to Abram. "Stay here. We'll be back soon."

"Yes, suh. But I'll bet it's more than ten minutes. I know that daughter of yors." The aged Negro stepped tenuously down from the wagon, his muscles aching, and lay on a grassy spot. He put his hat over his freckled face and was soon asleep.

Sara, lantern in hand, trudged along, determined to search the entire field. She repeated her previous question. "It's such a big battle, Papa. Surely, this is all the fighting we'll see. Won't the Yanks go home?"

Lucas did not hear her. Holding his own lantern, he scanned the bushes and hollows of the hillside. Sara walked faster than he and was soon several yards ahead of him. Suddenly, she cried out. "I found one alive, Papa. Come quick. He's one of ours, and he's breathing."

The young, blond soldier in gray pants and blood-speckled white shirt drew short, labored breaths. He lay hidden under a crepe myrtle bush, its blossoms radiant scarlet in the lantern light. In one hand, the soldier loosely clasped a sword. A revolver lay in the palm of the other. Sara knelt when her father approached. "Papa," she whispered. "He's for sure alive!" She checked his pulse. "Hurry, Papa, fetch Abram."

Lucas looked up close at the soldier. Then he turned and ran for Abram.

Brushing away the petals, Sara leaned closer and examined the body thoroughly and found no bullet wound. Then she discovered the lump across his forehead with an ugly, scabbed brown gash. She leaned nearer his face and felt his breath, warm against her cheek. She examined his smooth features and soft blond hair. She placed her hand on his chest, feeling his steady heartbeat. She was as sure of her next course of action as of anything she had ever believed.

Lucas and Abram returned. Abram carried a ladle of water. Sara took it and attempted to pour the liquid into the young man's mouth. He choked, but did not awaken.

"Let's get him to the field hospital," Lucas said.

"No! Not this one!" Sara raged. "You heard those nurses. They can't help all the wounded. We're taking this one home with us. He's ours to care for. Papa, you've cared for enough wounded in your day, and Abram knows all kinds of remedies. We're going to save at least one."

In that moment in the lantern's glow, her expression filled with fierce determination, Lucas beamed with pride at her strong will.

Seeing the smile and nod of her father, Sara hugged him. "Thank you, Papa."

———— ((O)) ————

At their home, Lucas and Abram laid the comatose soldier in gray trousers onto Lucas's bed. Lucas leaned the sword found in his hand in the corner. Sara hid the revolver in the cupboard.

Abram and Lucas stripped Joseph of his clothes and put a night-gown on him. Sara returned with a water basin and cloth. She cleaned the dried blood of the head wound, then washed his face, her hands gently bathing his skin. Abram then covered the wound with a dark salve of his own making—congealed grease, vinegar, and pokeroot. He wrapped a clean bandage around Joseph's head.

"Papa, do you think he's a Confederate or Yankee soldier?"

"To hazard a guess, I would say, with those gray paints, he's a Confederate."

No sooner had Lucas spoken than Sara and Abram heard worried mooing of the cows in the barn, then the rapid approach of horses and wagons, followed by a fierce knocking at their rear door, loud enough for even Lucas to hear. Lucas, with Sara at his side holding a lamp, opened the door.

"Begging your pardon, sir." A tall, clean-shaven officer in his late thirties stood below the porch steps in the light of a lantern extended on a hooked staff. He was backed by a handful of cavalrymen in gray trousers and a motley assortment of shirts. They had dismounted and stood holding the reins of their horses. Seeing Sara, the officer doffed his hat, revealing his haggard, begrimed face. Despite his weary appearance, he spoke in a thunderous Southern drawl as if he were speaking for a seat in the legislature. "Good evening, sir and miss. If y'all will forgive my calling at this late hour, my name is Elkanah Greer, colonel of the Texan-Kansan cavalry under General McCulloch, and I urgently request your aid."

Coming down from the porch, Lucas shook the colonel's hand. "My name is Lucas Reeder. This is my daughter, Sara. We have observed your cavalry before and during the battle. It is an honor to meet the officer in charge of such gallant men."

Sara curtsied. "I, too, am honored."

Colonel Greer gave a weak smile. "I am pleased to meet you both. As you are aware, we have fought a terrible battle from which our stalwart soldiers have emerged victorious. However, many valiant men are wounded. Too many for our surgeons to administer to adequately. Our army is endeavoring to place some of the wounded in surrounding homes for the time being in order to assist in their convalescence." He paused, and the flickering lantern light danced shadows across the cavalrymen's wan, smoke-stained faces. Several of their horses were so tired, they slept in their traces.

Gaining no response from Lucas, Colonel Greer, his shiny forehead reflecting the lantern light, continued. "I have been told by soldiers who served their picket duty about your home that you are supporters of our illustrious Southern cause, and *our cause* is in great need of houses to allow these wounded soldiers to rest and repair." In a sweeping motion, the imperious colonel pointed back beyond his cavalry squad at two buckboards which held moaning men. "May we use your home, Mr. Reeder, to keep them out of the sun for a few days? Not for long, mind you, just for a spell. And we will provide nurses, soldiers who are experienced in the care of the injured. For our part, my Texan-Kansan regiment must ride out before sunup to pursue the enemy and drive them from Springfield."

"Say yes, Papa," Sara said to her father, "for that is my wish and our Christian duty."

"We would be honored, Colonel Greer. As it is, we are already caring for a wounded Confederate."

Sara looked beyond the loquacious colonel whose voice rose in his encomium to the valiant Southern army, and her eyes fell upon a bulky silhouette of a man on a horse well behind the rest of the cavalry troop, his scarred face revealed in thin, slanting moonlight. The sinister figure never moved. She wondered if he was even a Confederate, and she sensed a foreboding about the solitary rider. Suddenly, he guided his horse away toward the trees. In a moment, farther away, that rider was joined by a dozen more horsemen, a featureless mob. Then they vanished into the woods. No one else seemed to notice, Colonel Greer's men too weary to even look. When Sara pointed and attempted to call attention to them, Colonel Greer's voice rose again like an exuberant volcano detailing the bravery of his Southerners.

When he finished his speech, the exhausted cavalrymen unloaded the cots, blankets, medicines and, finally, the wounded, taking them into the house.

The presence of the shadowy figure elicited in Sara a severe dread, and she sought to share her concern with her father, but she found herself bustling about the wounded. Five soldier nurses rolled out mats and propped up cots throughout their great room, kitchen, and the unused bedroom. Sara, her thoughts still festering over the dark figures, and though exhausted from the day, found new strength to offer consoling words and ladles of cool water to the wounded. Among them, two had saber wounds. One soldier's head was bound with a blood-soaked cloth, a great shock of hair sticking out above the wrapping. He had a weeping eye wound as well. Five suffered with amputations of arms and legs, and one, his skin as white as rice, breathed heavily with a hip wound. Save for one with a bruised and purpled face who chewed at the bill of his kepi, the men groaned without ceasing.

When Sara gave each some water, she saw up close their faces filled with anguish and confusion. One soldier, his leg gone below the knee, rubbed feverishly at his thigh, then wiggled his fingers in the vacant air where his leg used to be, then laughed pitifully.

The last one, a tall, brown-bearded private with half an arm and the opposite leg removed near the hip, said, "I never thought my death would be in a stranger's house." Sara could think of nothing to say. To console him, she patted his hand. It felt as dry as an autumn leaf.

The nurses broke out laudanum for each of the wounded. Then Colonel Greer and the remainder of his squad departed.

Abram called from the bedroom where he had been sitting beside Joseph. "I'm still unable to wake this man."

Sara's concerns about the disconcerting, shadowy troop that had ridden into the trees fell away, and she came to Joseph's bedside and looked at the face of a man whose name she did not know, and her thoughts drifted toward seeing him as possibly the one with whom she would share her future life. His face seemed kind. His hands were calloused, so he was no stranger to hard work. His stature was lean; his chest, partially revealed in the nightshirt neck opening, appeared strong. For a brief moment, she imagined him unclothed, then blushed that her passions had been so aroused. She pulled the sheet up to his chin.

THIRTEEN

No Other Medicine but Hope

February 20, 1862, just south of Springfield, Missouri, 3 pm

Cyntha and Reynolds bumped along the rough road heading northward toward Springfield. A line of telegraph poles extended along the road, the wires cut and dangling in many places. The rider who had followed them for some distance until about a mile back suddenly galloped away in the opposite direction. No sooner had he departed than a troop of a half-dozen cavalry trotted past the carriage headed in the same direction as the rider. The troop seemed oblivious to the two travelers in the carriage.

Cyntha pulled a coarse blanket tight around her against a sharp winter storm wind. Trying to keep from worrying that their pursuer would return, she read intermittently from a book on spiritualism by the renowned Andrew Jackson Davis—*The Divine Principles of Nature*. The road being so rough, she put it away and asked Reynolds to tell her one of his folksy tales.

"That big, old tree there," he said, pointing, "that be an elm. That be the favorite of the possum. We know that and so do the hound dogs.

They find brother possum, and we have some good stew." He pretended to be lighthearted, but glanced behind to ascertain the whereabouts of the rider who had been shadowing them, hoping he would not reappear.

"Tell me again about your escape from the plantation," Cyntha said, pulling the hood of her cape over her netted black hair. "I never tire of hearing it."

Reynolds shook the reins and settled back in the seat, pondering. He wore a soft, glossy overcoat, a gift to him from Cyntha and Joseph, bestowed to him just before Joseph enlisted in the First Iowa Volunteers. The former slave, now freeman, was skinny with knobby knees and sharp elbows, and his face was swarthy with a large nose and lips. His eyes shone like wells of gold, gentle, wise, and kind. Having spent most of his life as a slave, he guessed that he was fifty years old. "Well, Miss Cyntha, let me see." He tugged at his salt-and-pepper beard. "I guess you knew old Mr. Fox was a sly little fellow, and I had to be like a fox. My old Master Snodgrass was mean, but he was slow. So I asked Lady Abagail, the finest slave cook ever, if'n she'd sorta make a big fire in the kitchen and cause such a commotion that I could slip away. Well, everyone come running across the yard because of the ruckus, and no one knew I was escaping like a fox. Then, when I reached the deep woods, I cut across . . ."

Reynolds drew up the team. He and Cyntha heard the rumble of horses ahead and saw the dust rising like a cloud of yellow smoke above the crest of a deep dip in the road. Then as fast as a flock of doves startled to flight, a team of six horses drawing a cannon raced over the hill toward them. The Yankee driver seated on the two-wheeled limber carriage seat cracked his whip. Two cannoneer soldiers rode on the lead horses and clung tight to the harnesses. A cavalry escort kept apace alongside. Behind the first cannon, a second team of horses pulled a caisson; a third pulled a battery wagon filled with tools, leather, and cloth. A fourth wagon carried a mobile forge. Reynolds barely had time to move the carriage out of the road.

The horses and cannons and wagons flashed by, the drivers whistling and shouting at their horses. Cyntha and Reynolds sat cornered by the onrush against a wall of scrub bushes. After they passed, Cyntha brushed away the dust that had swept onto her clothes. Reynolds removed his floppy hat and batted the dust from his coat.

"Well, lookie there," Reynolds said. "Springfield, must be just over this next hill. See the smoke from the chimneys. We be there soon. Be a shade warmer inside. And them clouds comin' up be snow clouds." He clucked at the horses to continue down the road, but Cyntha stayed his hand.

"Hold," she said. "Those soldiers have too much urgency. I believe they're heading to battle." Just as she spoke, topping the same rise the cannons had roared over, a column of soldiers in heavy blue overcoats marched, the thousand feet rumbling like a bison herd. The regimental flags and guidons and the flags of the Stars and Stripes fluttered briskly. The column stirred the clay into a billowing mustard-colored cloud, contrasted to the charcoal storm clouds.

A colonel with icy-white hair and bushy sideburns was leading the column. He drew his horse to a halt beside the carriage.

Cyntha called out, "Sir, could you be so kind as to tell me if the First Iowa Volunteers are nearby? I wish to inquire of Colonel Merritt, their commander."

The colonel, his shoulders hunched against the wind, motioned for the column to continue marching. He was joined by a major and a captain. The colonel spoke in a gruff, condescending voice. "Ma'am, I am fully amazed that you are on this road. It is restricted to all travel except to the armies of the United States. How is it that you came to be here?"

"My companion, Mr. Reynolds, here, and I traveled by rail from St. Louis to Rolla, then rented this carriage to Springfield. From there, we received permission to travel in order to ascertain the whereabouts of my dear husband's grave somewhere around where the battle of Wilson's Creek, as some call it, was fought."

"And have you evidence of this permission?"

"I do have a letter of permission. I had hoped to go as far as Elk Horn Tavern on the Butterfield Stage Road. I have cousins there. But the captain said that would not be possible." She retrieved a folded paper from the reticule tied on her wrist and handed it to the colonel who handed it to the major. "Captain Dawes vouched for me. I came to look for the grave of my husband, Private Joseph Favor, and perhaps lay some flowers there."

"You would be hard-pressed finding flowers this time of year, madam. And does this slave have leave as well?"

"Reynolds is a freeman." Cyntha, so used to Reynolds as an employee, companion, and confidant, often assumed that everyone understood he was a freeman. "He works for me for pay."

"You'll forgive me, ma'am," the colonel said, "but in this part of the country, the chances of finding a freed slave accompanying a woman is almost zero, and your Southern accent belies that presumption. Spies come in both genders."

"But I assure you——" Cyntha attempted to respond.

The major, a gaunt fellow with a narrow clean-shaven and bespectacled face with gray, short-cropped hair, interrupted her. "Everything is in order, Colonel Buescher. The letter says this is Mrs. Cyntha Favor and her companion, a freeman, Josiah Reynolds. It further states that they hail from Iowa, and Captain Dawes knows them personally. I recognize his signature." He returned the paper to Cyntha.

The colonel remonstrated his second in command. "Major Reid, you were to have made it understood by all personnel that no one travels on this road. General Curtis made that quite clear. Write to Sheridan ordering him to desist allowing anyone who is not on army business to travel this road either north or south of Springfield. That means anyone."

"Yes sir," the major gathered paper and a pencil from a saddlebag and began scribbling a dispatch.

"Now, Mrs. Favor," the colonel's voice turned somewhat kind, yet reprimanding. "Have you no idea of the marauding gangs roaming these woods and hills? Be they northern jayhawkers or southern bushwhackers, you are in peril. The jayhawkers would see you with this colored man, steal him from you to save him from Secessionists, and pack both him and you off as contraband of their own, and one can only guess for what purposes. The bushwhackers would take the man to force him back into slavery on some plantation, and perhaps kill you for having a freed black man in your company."

"Captain Dawes warned of as much, but he also said that the army had cleared the area sufficiently as far as the Arkansas border and only bade us return before sundown." Cyntha crossed her arms over her chest in defiance. "And that is precisely what we are doing. Captain Dawes obtained permission from Quartermaster Sheridan to retain a room for us at a Springfield boarding house."

Colonel Buescher motioned to the captain. "Ma'am, this is my adjutant, Captain Corkrell."

The captain, a young man with a kind, serious face, was impeccably dressed, every button on his coat polished. He tipped his kepi. "Ma'am."

"Captain," Colonel Buescher said, "escort this woman and the Negro to Springfield and ensure that they are sequestered in the boarding house. Deliver the dispatch personally to Quartermaster Sheridan. From now on, no plain citizen is to leave the confines of Springfield."

Captain Corkrell saluted, took the dispatch from Major Reid, and laid his hand on the harness of the carriage horses and guided the carriage onto the road.

The colonel returned the salute, touched a forefinger to his hat. "Good afternoon, ma'am." He and the major galloped to the head of the column.

Cyntha called after him, "But what about the First Iowa and Colonel Merritt?"

She received no response.

Cyntha stomped her foot. "I can't understand why I could not get a simple answer. I don't mean to hold up the army or this infernal war, for goodness' sake. Just make a one-sentence inquiry. I only want to pay respects to my husband's grave."

Reynolds sighed, then patted her shoulder. She took his hand, squeezed it, then released it. Her tears chafed her cheeks in the icy wind.

The last of the regiment filed past them, and the adjutant trotted his horse ahead of the carriage. A short distance down the road, Reynolds reached into a deep inner pocket of his overcoat and pulled out two heavy revolvers. He whispered, "You needn't worry 'tol 'bout no marauders, Miz Cyntha. I got things well in hand."

"Yes, Reynolds, I know you have the guns for our protection, but don't let the soldier see them, or he'll arrest you."

Though Captain Dawes had given her assurances of their safety, the new warning from the colonel left Cyntha anxiously glancing left and right into the shrubs that crowded Telegraph Road. A few snowflakes danced in the wind about them.

⸺◈⸺

A quarter mile outside of Springfield, they were directed by guards through a makeshift gate of a heavy tree trunk laid across two stumps on either side of the road. Six soldiers lifted the log at one end and swung it away. After Captain Corkrell and the carriage passed through, they brought the tree trunk back in place. A company of grim soldiers, perhaps eighty men by Cyntha's quick count, shivered behind shallow bulwarks along Telegraph Road. Stretching for several yards up to the tree lines, the army had prepared a fortification of a wide abatis of felled trees, the treetops facing south from where a potential attack might come, and the trunks extended toward Springfield. Behind that, perhaps another forty men, some whites, some Negroes, labored with picks and shovels tossing up dirt to form earthen ramparts abutted on either side of the road. The walls already reached a steep-sided height of over six feet. Behind the rampart, two forty-feet-wide plank barbette platforms were installed with artillery in place and gunners at the ready, a full battery of six guns, three cannons for each platform. Each barbette was surrounded by sandbag walls and staked pointed logs.

Cyntha wished to ask one of the soldiers nearest the carriage if he knew of the whereabouts of the First Iowa regiment, but the carriage passed too quickly. The sun was setting, and snowflakes whirled about, driven by a sharp north wind. At the outskirts of town, they passed a gristmill, its wheels turning, and several corrals crowded with beeves and others with horses and mules. With Captain Corkrell directing them, Cyntha and Reynolds delivered the carriage and horses to the livery stable, then the captain led them on foot. Springfield was crisscrossed by a handful of roads, and several homes and stores lay in burned rubble, the snow beginning to whiten the charred remains. Most of the intact businesses were well lit with kerosene lanterns burning in the windows, pouring light into the dark streets, while the majority of the homes were dark, their curtains drawn. Above the doors of two homes, large funeral crepes were draped. Cyntha remarked, "The poor souls. I shall pray for them even if they are rebels."

Passing an alley of the main street, the three heard snarling and snapping. A pack of dogs bit and clawed at the innards of a dead mule. Reynolds pulled Cyntha aside and walked between her and the dog pack. She was about to remark about the army's callous disregard for a dead animal left in the street, but, seeing the sour look on Captain Corkrell's face, chose not to.

They passed a small white cupolaed church with one wall charred black and partially collapsed. Cyntha observed the sign dangling from a post. It read, "First Gospel Church—Reverend Edward Felder, Pastor."

On the streets and boardwalks, despite the increasing snowfall and slicing wind, a prodigious number of Union soldiers in heavy coats rambled about in groups, peeking in windows, talking jovially and obscenely, and drinking pungent liquor from all manner of vessels—tin cups to glass goblets. One large fellow standing in the middle of the street, to the amusement of his comrades, poured draughts down his throat from a bucket. Two soldiers not far from him took turns howling like hounds at the sky.

A few soldiers rushed here and there on what appeared to be urgent errands. Not on a few occasions, Captain Corkrell forced an avenue for Cyntha and Reynolds through a group of tilting, stumbling soldiers. The smell of sour mash and vomit filled the air.

The hubbub and lack of proper military comportment that Cyntha observed was so unlike the camp at Keokuk where Joseph had trained. She said to Reynolds, "Why is there not more order maintained?"

Reynolds did not answer but did his best to shield her from the tangle of men carousing along their path.

When they reached the center of town, Captain Corkrell pointed out the blackened remnants of the burned out courthouse. A warehouse, the largest building in the city, sat beside the courthouse remains. Cyntha observed through several wide doorways on the bottom floor of the building groups of soldiers stacking crates, sacks, and barrels. The upper floor had been converted into a hospital. The large, unshaded windows revealed rooms flooded with light in which male and female nurses rushed about among almost a hundred beds, each one with a wounded or ill man.

Across from the warehouse, they entered the boarding house. Captain Corkrell walked to the dining room. On his return he said, "The proprietor has assured me that Captain Sheridan, who maintains his quartermaster headquarters here, procured a room for you."

"Before you leave, may I ask you two questions?" Cyntha said. "First, do you know the whereabouts of the First Iowa Regiment? And second, were those cannon and soldiers on the Telegraph Road heading toward a battle?"

Captain Corkrell paused. "Mrs. Favor, the Army of the West has been fighting a number of skirmishes with the retreating secessionists down the length of the road for several days. That answers your second question. As far as the First Iowans, I am positive they are already deployed, at least to the Arkansas border."

Cyntha's face fell, for Colonel Merritt and the answers to her questions she desired to ask him were beyond reach.

"And let me add," Captain Corkrell said, "in light of Colonel Buescher's orders, your leaving Springfield without permission could land *you* under guard and your companion here on a work detail." Giving a slight bow, he exited into the crush of drunken soldiers.

Cyntha and Reynolds took seats on an overstuffed, floral-patterned sofa in the parlor, lit by numerous kerosene chandeliers. The snowstorm howled outside. On the street, a regiment of Federal soldiers, a few holding torches, marched to a drum cadence out of town. The rabble of drunken soldiers who were milling about stepped aside to let the column pass and shouted encouragements that were often ribald.

Cyntha heard one slurring voice call, "While you're searchin' for them Rebs, be sure to look under the ladies' skirts, and mind you, save some for me!"

Attempting to ignore the hooting and raw language outside, Cyntha tried to read from a tome titled *At Last* by Marion Harland.

Reynolds thumbed a worn Bible. "Look at this passage right here, Miss Cyntha." He pointed to a verse.

She leaned over to look, then read aloud, "And Jesus said, 'he that lives by the sword dies by it.'"

Reynolds's eyes showed mild amazement. "I declare, Jesus done come up with prophesies that tell what this country's goin' through now. Yes, suh."

Before Cyntha could respond, two dowagers threw open the double doors allowing the cutting wind to blow through, sending the chandeliers careening, and causing the lamps to flicker. The two elderly women paraded in, turned, and leaned against the wind-held doors. When the doors snapped shut, they brushed snow from their garments, all the while scowling at Reynolds. On the boardwalk outside the door, their two slaves, being jostled by the passing soldiers, stood shivering, peering through the frosted door windows.

The younger dowager looked straight at Reynolds and remarked with vehemence, "I cannot believe what has become of this country letting niggers into any fine establishment. We must complain to the proprietor. And with General Curtis's Yankees swarming about like rats, we have nowhere to escape their wickedness."

"Let us not think of their depravity, Sister," said the other. "Our glorious Southern armies will soon put an end to any further discussion of freeing the niggers and put them back in their place. Even now, the newspaper from Memphis has announced that General Van Dorn will soon drive the Yankee vermin from our midst."

Cyntha stood to retort. Reynolds touched her elbow. "There's no need, Miss Cyntha. They don't understand. Jesus would say just to forgive them."

She sat, demure, well aware of her need for restraint in this hotbed of Southern resistance. "I do forgive them, Reynolds," she said with her teeth gritted, "but they must also be told they are wrong. Or they will never know. There, I missed my chance. They've gone into the dining room. I guess I'll let it go . . . for you, Reynolds."

A middle-aged woman with lucent, shining skin, deep set eyes, and a hawk nose walked toward them. She wore a black dress with a lace collar up to her chin. Her hair was done up in a chignon. First, looking contemptuously at Reynolds, she smiled at Cyntha. "Hello, I trust that you are Mrs. Favor. I'm Mrs. Schmidt, the proprietor. I apologize for the crass manners of the Yankee army, but we are their captives here. The city has been imprisoned under the whimsical order of General Curtis and his invaders. They have moved into every store, the livery, the barns, and even many homes. This town has been in a troublesome plight ever since the Yankees stole the town from our brave Southern soldiers who had only restored it to us a few months before."

The matron sighed dramatically and pointed out the windows at a gaggle of stumble-drunk soldiers. "Even now, the quartermaster, Captain Sheridan, has bribed their soldiers, whose enlistments had ended, to *reenlist*, luring them with drink and a night of unrestrained carousing. As you can see, an unhealthy number of them have taken him up on the offer. I fear for the young women in town."

"That *is* a shame that those men fight for no greater cause than free liquor and a night of wantonness." Cyntha realized her naiveté had misled her again in that she had imagined that all the Northern soldiers were fighting for the same noble cause for which her husband, Joseph, had enlisted—the freeing of the Negroes. She had difficulty listening to Mrs. Schmidt because of the soldiers' commotion.

"The barbarity of the Yankees," Mrs. Schmidt ranted, "has brought shame to this whole town. We are no more than prisoners. I quite expect them to force us into slavery like the Egyptians did to the Jews."

Perceiving that Cyntha was no longer paying attention, Mrs. Schmidt touched her on the elbow. "Quartermaster Sheridan has ordered that you be given a room," Looking down her nose at Reynolds, she said, "and perhaps a place in the stable for your nigger?"

"I would prefer a room for my friend, if that is possible. He is not my 'nigger.' I don't think the stable is . . ."

"I'm afraid that would not do. The people of this town would never allow that. Oh no." She wagged a finger side to side. "That certainly would not do. And did you say he was your *friend*? This is a decent establishment. We have no room for such dalliances. Indeed!" She crossed her arms, an indignant frown on her face.

"If you'd let me finish, Mrs. Schmidt!" Cyntha's voice rang. "I am a widow. Reynolds is a freeman who has accompanied me here for my safety. He can pay his own way."

Reynolds had gathered the carriage blanket and his bundle of clothing tied with a coarse rope and was headed out the door. "It's all right, Miss Cyntha. I be fine in the stable. I even prefer it there. Soft hay. Look out the door at the stars. I be fine."

Before Cyntha could respond, he was out the door conversing with the two Negroes on the boardwalk.

Cyntha stood with her mouth open. Mrs. Schmidt took hold of her arm and led her to the check-in desk. "Come, dear. I am glad that your slave has earned his freedom. He seems to have much more common sense than most darkies have. Now, come with me. And I'm sorry to hear about the death of your husband. Was he a soldier?"

Cyntha sighed. She knew that there was no point in arguing the principle. She was in slave country. She hated slavery so passionately, but this was not the place to bring war on herself, and more particularly, on her friend. Reynolds was right. She thought, *He has considerable common sense. Far more than you have, madam.*

"I am expecting to meet a Mrs. Grunewald," Cyntha said. "She's a spiritualist. Would you alert me when she arrives, please? She wrote me saying she would meet me at this boarding house."

"Of course, dear." The woman's tone was patronizing. "Mrs. Grunewald is staying at another boarding house here in Springfield. I'll send a boy to request she come here. I would warn you that her demeanor is . . . Actually, I don't quite know what to make of her."

FOURTEEN

Understanding Hard Things

SIX MONTHS PREVIOUS

AUGUST 17, 1861, THE REEDER HOME, 7 AM

Joseph lay in the front bedroom on his back in the bed that Lucas had shared with his wife before she passed away. Despite a slight breeze rustling the curtains, sweat stood on his brow. The morning coolness was fast subsiding. Beside the bed, Sara sat on a rail back chair, slumped and weary, her brow pinched in concern, and her tired eyes held dark circles under them. She would occasionally spoon-feed him chicken broth; the soup trickled into his mouth, and he eventually swallowed. She then dabbed a cloth in a basin of water and lay the cool cloth on his forehead.

Lucas entered and sat next to her. "Sara, I think it's time you let me watch over the wounded. You've been waiting on them for hours. I can see you are exhausted."

Sara shook her head. "I have this feeling that if my brothers were still alive, they would have been fighting in this war and perhaps had been wounded in the battle. Or in another battle laid up in some far-away home. I would hope that for these brothers and sons and husbands lyin' in our home that their families can feel assured we are doing all we can."

"I understand, but you still need rest."

"And doesn't this one that we ourselves saved from the field look like our neighbor boy, Samuel, who died last year? Except for the blond hair, the fuzzy beard. Samuel was such a pleasant boy. And this soldier's face is almost his image."

"I can see a little resemblance, but I'm afraid that if he doesn't wake soon . . ." Lucas stopped when he saw the sorrow spreading across Sara's face. "Well, let's just see what he says when he wakes up."

Joseph shifted in his coma sleep. Sara rose like he had been stabbed with a knife. Lucas reached out his calloused hand and pulled lightly on her apron. "Let him be, darlin'. You *will* go rest a spell. I forbid you to stay any longer."

Sara opened her mouth to speak but relented and nodded her head. She tiptoed into the great room where a dozen wounded soldiers lay on pallets and cots, convalescing. All twelve were Confederates, none of them Union. Most were asleep, some were reading. The ones with amputated stumps of legs and arms were faring the worst, with infections and swelling of their torn limbs. One of the youths, not yet twenty, his stub for a leg oozing blood and pus, moaned in pitiful dreams. The soldier's skin was pale as snow. The Reeder home, like every farm in the vicinity, had been procured as a hospital of sorts for the Confederacy. Most of the Northern army's wounded had been sent north in Union ambulances.

Every day, more ambulances came to pick up those able to travel up Telegraph Road.

A single orderly, the only one left of the original five, sat leaning back in a chair in the great room, asleep and snoring like a muffled trumpet. The others had marched with McCulloch's army west toward the Boston Mountains cantonment.

Blood stained the floor and every piece of furniture. Flies buzzed throughout the darkened room. Blankets and quilts hung on ropes to separate the three most severely wounded from the others. Despite every window being open, a fetid stench stung Sara's nose and eyes. She had taught herself in the past week to take shallow breaths, and when she could, to cover her nose with her wrist.

Sara picked her way around the pallets and cots to her room, closed the door, and fell face-first across her bed, too weary to unlace her shoes. The sun dipped in and out of the clouds, dancing beams through her window. She lay there awhile remembering an easier time when her older brothers played with her and teased her gently. As she drifted to sleep, she was remembering a playhouse in a tree that William had built for her.

Abram entered Lucas's bedroom, a short pile of folded shirts in his arms. He set the clothes in the armoire. He looked at Joseph, then at Lucas with a vexed expression. "That soldier boy done been out for most of a week, Lucas. He ain't swallowed hardly nothin' but water and broth since he been here. What we expectin' him to do?"

Lucas reflected. "We'll wait a while longer. Then we'll turn him over to the army surgeons. I just hope I can convince Sara."

"She outdoes herself takin' care of these boys. A soldier sings her one song, and she's in love with all of them. Shore do beat all." Abram sat on a large wooden chest bound around with huge iron bands. He rubbed his hands together. "My old hands sure are hurtin' more and more. Makes it hard to pick up things."

Lucas looked at Abram's bent, arthritic hands. "Abram, you know I've hinted to you lately that it's about time I gave you your papers and set you free. You should live out your life a free man. Why, you're no more my slave than I'm the king of England."

Abram knit his brow. "I knowed you been thinin' that. I could see it in your eyes and from little things you said now and then. And . . ." He paused. "I been thinin' about that, too, that maybe it would be nice to be free. I mean, I is ready. As ready as I could ever be. But then I think that maybe I ain't ready to be free. Who's gonna hire an old black man like me what can't work a lick and can barely pick up a hoe handle, much less lift it to crack the ground?"

"I have one more idea," Lucas reflected. "I can't live with myself keeping you a slave much longer. And the way this war is sure to work out, I know that the Yankees will come down here and take you anyway. And who knows where they'll take you? There is no way these Secessionists with all their bluster can stop the outcome. The people in the North are too numerous, too powerful, and too haughty to be denied. They will win this war, unless the politicians mess it up."

"Yes, suh."

"That Lincoln. He's to blame for this. He could've stopped the war. He could've negotiated. Been patient. He's a tyrant for bringing on this war."

"I wouldn't know that, Lucas. He seem pretty all right to me, but then I only read some things in the paper."

"Well, you ain't right about Lincoln. And there's another thing. You can *read*. You are no less of a man than me. I propose that as soon as we can, at least before winter sets in, that we travel north to Illinois and find a family who will take you in. I know some folks up there."

"Yes, suh. Illinois is cold, isn't it? Cold makes my old bones hurt. But that be all right."

Lucas sighed. "There's too much work that needs to be done. I'm gonna need a younger man soon. More importantly, the jayhawkers may hit our farm any day. As long as we have some of the Confederate army nearby, they won't chance a raid, but when the army's gone, I hate to hazard a guess at what they'll do. It's not safe for you, nor, for that matter, for Sara and me."

Abram continued to rub his hands. "I see yor point, and I appreciate the offer of freedom, however . . ."

"If you won't take your freedom, then I propose that I sell you to the Dent family over to the east side of the state. If I can't find you freedom with a family up north, I believe Julia will take good care of you and see no harm comes to you."

"Yes. I see. That mistress Dent be from a fine upbringin', and that farm is mighty fair. I remember from when I went there with your wife a'visitin' back many years ago."

"I'm an old friend of Julia Dent's family. She married a clerk. Different last name now. I feel you would be treated well and perhaps be safer. I'm sure Julia would give you a job in the house. Some light work."

"Thank you, Lucas. That be mighty nice. But what about you and Sara? What you gonna do?"

"I haven't quite figured that out yet. Maybe sell the farm. Head west. Start over. I don't know."

"I see. Well, *freedom*. Hmm. Yes, suh."

Abram stood and plodded into the great room, stepping gingerly around the sleeping wounded, and went in to check on Sara. After easing the door open a sliver, he whispered, "You sleep now, chil'. You ain't done nothin' in this life but make me and yor daddy happy and tend to others. You sleep."

He closed her door and made his way back to his room. Lighting a yellow candle, he looked at his visage in the cracked piece of mirror hung on the wall. "I's too old, Lucas," he said in a whisper. "Damn you for wantin to gi' me my freedom now when I is too old. I am fierce angry with you. You and your sweet daughter are the only family I got. Damn you. You be my friend, and you be my enemy." He sat down hard on his bed and rubbed his sore hands.

Lucas sat pensively watching the young man in his bed. The blond soldier never stirred, but breathed as if in a peaceful slumber. *If you don't wake pretty soon, young fella*, Lucas thought, *you're going to starve to death*. He reached to the lamp stand to take up a book he had been reading and bumped the water glass. It toppled to the floor and broke noisily. The young man stirred. Lucas picked up the pieces of glass and carried them back to the kitchen and set them on the drain board.

When he returned to the room, Joseph was sitting up in the bed, looking about rapidly and blinking his eyes. His fingers of one hand pinched at the sheets. The other hand worried the fabric of his nightshirt. He attempted to speak, but no words came out of his parched lips. He tossed off the sheet and stood on wobbly legs.

"Hold on there, young man," Lucas ordered. "You've been out cold for a week. You best rest for a spell."

Joseph went pale and collapsed to the floor, knocking over the washstand.

Sara, awakened by the crash, rushed into the room, her eyes wide.

She and Lucas lifted Joseph and seated him on the bed. Abram arrived at the doorway just as Joseph regained consciousness. "Where . . .?" Joseph coughed, his weakened frame shaking.

"You're awake!" Sara exclaimed. "Praise God." She propped him up with her arm. "I was so afraid . . . *We* were so afraid you would die. I was beginning to give up hope you would ever . . ."

Joseph's eyes fluttered shut, then with a deep sigh, he opened them again. He slumped like a drunken man, his mouth too dry to speak.

Abram hurried to the kitchen and retrieved a ladle of water from the bucket. He handed it to Joseph who slurped the water.

"Where am I?" Joseph asked.

Lucas spoke slowly. "You are in our home. We are the Reeders. This is my daughter, Sara, and my name is Lucas. That man is Abram Reeder. We've been taking care of you. You've been in a battle. Our troops got caught in a wedge, but you all fought bravely and drove the Yankees back. *You* took some blows to your head. Now you need to rest."

Joseph reached up and felt the still tender welt and scab on his forehead "What was I doing? I don't remember a battle!"

"Yes, you were in a battle, and you got knocked out." Lucas

continued, "You haven't had anything to eat, and very little to drink for a week. As best we could, we poured water, broth, and a little brandy down your throat a trickle at a time."

Abram brought another ladle of water. Joseph drank it, slurping.

"What's your name?" Sara asked. "We are so pleased that you have awakened and . . ."

Joseph's eyes grew wide. "Name. What's my name?" His body tensed, and his gaze moved left and right as he searched his mind for answers. He whispered, more to himself, "What *is* my name?"

Sara and Lucas and Abram eyed each other, concerned.

"Do I have a family?" Joseph asked. "Do they know I'm here?"

With his deafness affecting his hearing, Lucas had developed a sense of lip-reading to supplement when people spoke quickly, so he handled the rapid questions well enough. He said, "We don't know about your family. You took a fierce blow to the head, so you might be a little muddled right now. Just relax. Let's get some food in you, and . . ."

Joseph stood again. He wobbled from one end of the room to the other, holding onto the bed frame or wall. He looked out the windows, then turned to peer through the doorway into the great room where the convalescing soldiers, awakened by the noise, stared incredulously at him. He pulled himself along the bottom bed frame up to Lucas. "So, are you a surgeon?"

Lucas said, "No, I'm not a surgeon."

"Can you tell me more about what happened? Is there anyone who would know my name?"

Sara broke in. "You are a soldier in the Confederate army. You are here convalescing with these other wounded, but no one who has come by this week has been able to identify you."

A pall crept over the young man's face. "I can't remember anything. I don't even remember my mama or my papa. I can't remember a face. I don't even know where I live . . ." His voice trailed off.

Sara attempted to help him sit, but he pushed her arms away. At last, he slumped to the floor in a kneeling position. Lucas and Abram took hold of his arms, and though he resisted at first, he allowed them to half carry him to the bed. He looked with remorse and confusion at his well-meaning attendants, then fell face-first into the pillow and wept.

Sara stroked his back. "Don't worry. We'll find out your name. You took a nasty clop on the head. Give it time, you'll get your memory back."

Exhausted, Joseph turned his head toward the wall and in seconds drifted to deep sleep. Lucas lifted his legs onto the bed. Sara said, "At least he has awakened. I hope he has enough strength to wake again."

Lucas and Abram had no answer. The three of them stood by the bed for several minutes until the nurse called them to help with a soldier.

FIFTEEN

Do Not Grow Weary in Doing Good: Thessalonians

Joseph awoke, and, Sara, overjoyed at seeing him awake, coaxed him to eat some cabbage soup and corn bread. He guzzled water, a pitcher full. Even while eating, his quick eye movement indicated he was flipping through mental pages that might hold any image of his past life. After the meal, he slipped in and out of fitful sleep.

Sara sat by his bed and patted his hand when his eyes would flutter open. He attempted to smile at her efforts to console him.

"At least you have your arms and legs and your eyesight," she offered. "And people right here in this house who care about you." She thought better of her comment when she saw his disgusted expression. She was not helping him feel better. She tried to assure him of her unflinching faith that he would recover his memory. "The Lord works miracles every day."

To her continued encouragements he could muster very little response—a mumble or a nod.

"I had three brothers," she at last remarked, "who would have been about your age. They would have made brave soldiers."

He scowled at her, then cursed under his breath.

Exasperated at her inability to offer him solace, she thought that a song might cheer him and ease his suffering as her melodies often had for the other wounded. She began humming "Soldier's Joy."

He interrupted her. "I remember singing . . . in a church, and in a house somewhere. I stood beside a piano." His eyes looked past her at the distant memory. Then, in a whisper, he sang a stanza of "My Old Kentucky Home." The last words came in a whisper.

"Peculiar," he said remorsefully, "I can't remember anything about my life, but I can remember a song." Half humming, half singing, he sang two more stanzas of the song. "I like music," he said. "At least I know that."

For Sara, his acknowledgment of song fueled in her a remembrance of how she had foolishly concluded she could find a sort of passion for the soldier merely because of a well-fashioned tune. Yet, something in this man's face bespoke of a patient, kind nature, and innate benevolence. She remonstrated herself for her earlier folly. Her reckoning, with the tragedies of battle, had hardened her spirit a great amount, and though her idealism was not lost, she factored into her chivalric imaginings that any soldier with whom she may fall in love might be dead on the morrow.

Still, something in his voice made it difficult to assuage her impulses. With candor, she forbade herself from frivolous and ill-conceived notions of love borne of an instant, but with equal frankness she decided not to rein in her feelings too much. "You have a strong, beautiful voice," she said, smiling and hopeful of a considered, positive response from Joseph. The measure of her heartbeats increased. Her cheeks blushed. She saw that he paid no heed to her, though she wished he would. She bit her lip and prayed aloud, "Heavenly Father, please guide this man's memory so that he may recall his life."

"Will you still your tongue? I'm tired of your words."

Sara's face fell.

Joseph looked as though he would speak again, but his eyelids closed. He lolled like a drunken man and laid his head on his pillow and soon fell asleep.

⸺⸺◦《◦》◦⸺⸺

In the early afternoon, the nurse came into Lucas's room where Lucas, Sara, and Abram sat, resting from the heat. He ran fingers through his matted hair. "I'm leavin'," he said. "I done all I could for the wounded today. I gave out the last of the laudanum and colomel. Ain't no more now."

"But how are we to care for all these wounded?" Lucas said. "We don't have the means."

"When I get back to the regiment," the nurse said, "I'll ask 'em to send you some assistance." He took a haversack off a peg in the great room and his rifle from the corner, shouldered it, and shuffled wearily, weaving his way through the pallets and cots toward the back door.

The wounded soldiers called out to him, and they stretched their hands forth to grab at his coat. "Help me!" one of them pled. "I'm in pain."

The nurse walked out the door giving not so much as a glance at the wounded.

"We had five nurses to begin with, then three, then this last one. Now none," Sara said. "How are we to take care of all these men by ourselves?"

"We'll do the best we can for tonight," Lucas replied. "If no one comes by tomorrow, I'll go down to the valley to talk to the cavalry regiment's colonel and ask for help."

Sara, Lucas, and Abram, despite their weariness of spirit and body, began tending the wounded just as they had for a week; warming meals of corn mush in one big pot, and cabbage and onion soup in another. Each man received a bowl of one porridge or the other. Two pickets rode in from their duty beyond the cow meadow and asked for something to eat. So Sara ladled bowls for them as well. They turned the bowls up and slurped down the contents, then tipped their slouch hats in thanks and departed.

Throughout the afternoon, the Reeders cleaned wounds, then rebound them with the last of the bandages. They wiped the sweating brows of those with fever and offered words of encouragement, for there was nothing left to ease the pain, nothing to remedy the diarrhea, no quinine to quell the fever. The smell of rancid, blood-soaked bandages, seeping wounds, sweaty clothing, and vomit permeated the stifling summer air. Flies swarmed about. One of the wounded took it upon himself to limp about as best he could and swat the flies with a rolled up newspaper. Fly carcasses littered the floor.

The three offered what comfort they could for the invalids deep into the sweltering evening. Abram sang spirituals, even while mopping the floor. His deep, sonorous voice was a palliative of sorts for the pain, for the laudanum's effects had worn off. Earlier in the day, he had poured pinto beans, great sacks of which were provided from the army, into the large caldron on a pit fire in the side yard. He threw in pork rinds and handfuls of salt. When the beans were done, well after the sun had retired, and the lanterns and lamps and candles were lit, Sara and he served the soldiers' supper on the family china. They hand-fed four soldiers, mouthful by mouthful.

Using a lap desk, Sara wrote letters to loved ones dictated by each soldier. She used up Lucas's stationery, and then tore cover sheets from her beloved books.

Lucas carried in bucket after bucket of water from the well. After herding the cows from the pasture and doing the evening milking, he gathered up the bandages that were too tattered and blood-soaked, took them outside to a pit, covered them with kindling and pitch, and burned them.

At last, Lucas called Sara and Abram into his room to chairs by

Joseph's bed, and he read from the Bible. Joseph awakened and sat propped up with pillows. He often fell asleep, then would wake, only to drop off again. Most of the soldiers, drained by heat, pain, and fever, settled into a sort of torpor, though several moaned almost without ceasing. The stars filled up the sky, as the waning moon rolled up deep blue and white and cold, like a corpse.

When all the soldiers slept, and Abram had retired to his room, and Lucas slept on the couch like he had every night since the arrival of the wounded, Sara rose from the side of a feverous soldier and slipped into her father's bedroom and sat on the edge of the bed where Joseph snored lightly. She laid her hand on Joseph's. With her other hand, she brushed his blond locks from his tanned face. A tear trickled down her cheek. "I lost three brothers. Though I do not know you, I don't think I can bear losing you." She rose when she heard the creak of a wagon and the whickering of horses, followed by a loud knock at the door.

SIXTEEN

Hope, Withering, Fled, and Mercy Sighed Farewell

Six months later

February 20, 1862, Springfield, Missouri, 7 pm

Despite a crackling fire in the large fireplace, the boarding house parlor had an icy, hostile cold. Blustery wind rattled the windowpanes. Cyntha Favor, sitting erect, blew on her hands to warm them, then folded them in her lap. With a heavy wool shawl gathered tight around her, she perched at the edge of her chair beside a small round table across from an untidy woman with tight, springy, gray curls about her head. Mrs. Grunewald wore a gaudy red cape with a collar of fur from an untellable animal. Her teeth were gray in patches. In her liver-spotted hands she held a set of handmade cards with colorful, bizarre characters painted on them. The cards were smudged with dirt and food. Behind thick spectacles, she blinked constantly like she had grit in her eyes. She lit a stump of a candle on the table and methodically laid the cards down, one by one, pausing after each one.

"You have been in peril and not known it," she said in a hoarse, Southern accent with a hint of Cajun.

Cyntha's eyes widened. "When?"

"Recently," the woman plied her cards on the side table. A lamp with a dusty shade with little cord balls hanging from it provided pitiful light. "You were at a battlefield. Soldiers were close, bad ones—marauders. You did not know." She paused. "There was a river or a stream nearby."

Cyntha again was surprised, this time with the woman's accuracy. "Yes, Reynolds and I were at Wilson Creek. I was listening. I've heard that if you listen just right you can hear the voices of the dead in a place like . . ."

Mrs. Grunewald waved her hand dismissively. "Don't talk. Don't interfere. I must concentrate." She laid down a card with a poorly etched skeleton. Her body went stiff. "I don't know if I should tell this to you."

"Tell me what?"

The frumpy woman settled her frame in the chair. It creaked while she stared past Cyntha's shoulder into nothing for a long moment. Then she turned piercing eyes toward Cyntha. "Very well. Your husband deeply wishes to speak to you from the abode of the dead." Her tone was ominous, not like when, earlier, she had been merely recounting the salient points of Cyntha's life.

"My Joseph wishes to speak to me? What does that mean?" Cyntha was encouraged.

"This is not a good thing, Mrs. Favor. The dead do not wish to speak to their loved ones if they are happy. Your husband is very unhappy. Else he would not desire to talk to you."

Cyntha swallowed hard. She reached her hands up to her flushing cheeks. Then she pulled her shawl tight about her as a chilling wind seeped through the crack under the door. "What . . . What does that mean?"

"Just what I told you. Your husband is unhappy. He needs release from his concerns . . . And only you can help him." She picked up her cards from the table and reshuffled them. The wind moaned and, to

Cyntha, the walls of the boarding house seemed to bend in from each wintery blast. Mrs. Grunewald laid down the cards in neat rows—a black dog, clouds and sunshine, a lamp with curling designs, a jester, a queen, a marionette. "I'm making double sure. Double sure. Yes. There it is."

Cyntha, caught up in the woman's sincerity and apparent skill, looked hard at each card as Mrs. Grunewald continued laying them down, trying to discern a meaning of her own. Her thoughts played with the cards. Did each card hold its own meaning, or were they vocabulary in a sentence of sorts? The seer had not laid down the marionette before. Did it signify a new revelation? Cyntha, biting her lip, hoped for a more encouraging divination at this new sorting of the cards.

At the end of the row of cards, Mrs. Grunewald laid down the skeleton. Grimacing, she said, "Yes, just as I thought. Your husband, Joseph, is longing for peace. Some undone task concerns him a great deal. He is in a place he does not understand. Only you can give his spirit rest."

"How do I do that? Can you help?"

"Oh no, dearie. You must go to someone else. I cannot help with speaking to the dead. I tell of their fates. Nothing more. I am a messenger, not a procurer."

"Please tell me what I should do."

The woman gathered her cards and stuffed them in a torn carpet-bag. She stood abruptly. "Before I depart, I will leave you the name of two sisters who can help. They live in New York in a small town and make contact with the spirits there."

"New York! That is such a far way. And in these times with the war, I don't have the means . . ."

"I will leave their names at the desk. When you leave your payment in an envelope, the owner of this boarding house will hand you the paper with the names."

"Can I not pay you now and receive the names?"

"No, I can take no money at this time. The spirits will see and will never help me again. You must make payment tomorrow when the spirits sleep. Put the dollars in an envelope and leave it with Mrs. Schmidt. I must keep this transaction as secret as possible."

"I understand. I can do that. Did my husband say anything to you? Anything for me?"

"I do not speak to spirits, they simply guide my cards. I hear no voices. You must go to these mediums. They are the best. They will help you, but the journey is long. If you wish to know about your late husband, you must go. Your husband needs you. Go." With that, she bustled away, clutching her carpetbag.

Cyntha rose, watched the decrepit woman climb the stairs to the rooms, then turned to the window, frosted around its edges. She watched a soldier on guard duty, his shoulders hunched against the knife wind, pace back and forth in the glow of a makeshift streetlight, a lantern hung on a shepherd's hook. A layer of ice lay atop his wool hat and across the shoulders of his great coat. A pathetic flame, tortured by the wind, burned a small woodpile in a rock-encircled spot near his feet. He stood and stomped in place while attempting to light a pipe. Cyntha moved closer to the window, so that her breath coated the panes. She thought of Reynolds lying shivering in the stable, perhaps covered only with hay and the single blanket to keep warm.

A tear crept down her cheek. The universe, at this moment, seemed so vast, so cold, and so unfair. She watched sleepy flakes of snow drifting, flickering white in the lantern light, then turning opaque in the shadows. She knew the snow was falling across the Ozark Mountains and hills and, most likely, on the grave of her husband, a grave without a marker, just a forgotten mound of dirt under a blanket of white. Her soul swooned in sorrow as she listened to the wind wailing around the corners of the boarding house. Her first tear was followed by another and another until her face was flooded. "I love you so, Joseph. If what

Mrs. Grunewald says is true, I will find a way to reach you. I will not give up."

The next morning, Cyntha handed an envelope with five dollars Confederate enclosed for Mrs. Grunewald to Mrs. Schmidt who, in exchange, handed her a slip of paper with the names of two sisters who lived in New York. The Fox sisters were in great demand for those wishing to talk to those on the other side.

Cyntha needed cash for the train ride to New York. Her brother, Anthony, was a bank officer and wealthy. She would telegraph him in Minnesota and hope for a speedy reply.

SEVENTEEN

Fortune in Horror

DECEMBER 14, 1861, HYDESVILLE, NEW YORK, 2 PM

"I can see you drinking that whiskey, Maggie Fox," the woman spoke with a vehement tone. She was dressed in matronly attire. Her starched collar rose high on her neck. Her head seemed loose and ready to topple off its foundation. She waggled it and tsked at her younger sister.

Maggie, sixteen years the junior of her sister, swallowed the glass of liquor in a gulp and wiped her mouth with her sleeve. She tottered out from a shadow by the bookshelves. She held up her arm to the brightness of the afternoon sun spilling in the windows of the parlor. "Leah, I know you can see me. I only drank away from you because I knew you didn't like to see me drink, and . . ." Pouring from a crystal decanter, she filled her glass again. "And . . ." She threw back the drink. "And I don't like your calumny toward me, so I sought to savor a few sips whilst—"

"A few sips! Hardly." Leah waved her hand across her face, already aware of the sour, fusty liquor odor. "I can smell you from here."

Maggie plummeted her emaciated body into a fat armchair. She placed the decanter on a side table, almost toppling the table with the bottle on it. Then she placed the glass upside down on her index finger and jiggled it around. "Oops," she said in a delayed reaction to her near mishap with the table. Her eyes crossed. "I feel sleepy. And that's good."

"Yes, you best get some sleep this afternoon." Leah rose and took the glass from Maggie. She bent down, her hooked nose almost touching Maggie's forehead. "You sleep now, for you have your séance tonight. You must be ready. It means money, and heaven knows we need it."

"That's all you ever think about is money," Maggie said, spit dribbling down her chin. "Why can't Kate to do it."

"Your sister is unable right now and you know that."

"I do?" Maggie heaved a sigh. "Oh yes, I do. She's sick."

Leah harrumphed and walked away.

Maggie leaned over on the arm of the chair, her dark brown hair cut to her chin fell over her face. "We mustn't keep the spirits of the dead waiting. Tonight I go rap, rap, rap, cracking the knuckles of my toes, and the people will think . . ." Her words dissolved into a mumble. "Whatever they want to think."

Leah stood before a mirror primping her auburn hair. "Times are hard, little sister. There's a war on, you know. The Union is split apart. Rationing has already hit even here in New York just like Father said. This morning, I went to the baker, stood in line, and he ran out of bread. He told everyone that the army confiscated all his wares. They even took his leavening. Can you imagine?" She returned to stand before her sister, slumped in the chair. "Maggie, wake up. I said, can you imagine."

Maggie rolled her eyes open. "Yes, yes. I can imagine. I can imagine you rotting in hell. Leave me be, or I'll announce to the audience tonight that it's all a fraud."

"You'll do no such thing." Leah frowned. She stroked Maggie's bedraggled black hair. "Spiritualism is an important pastime now. If

Horace Greeley believes it, and the public believes it, then we best give the public what it wants. Yes, I think it best you sleep now. Sleep off your liquor. With this dreadful war on, I'm inclined to imbibe a snifter myself. But I control myself. I'll wake you in time to prepare for tonight's séance. I'm sure you'll be as successful as you always were in the past."

Maggie drifted to sleep, and Leah departed into the hall. Pulling back the front hall window curtain but a little, she spied three young men, gawkers, who each pointed toward the window when her face appeared. A woman holding a wooden placard stood a few feet from them. She was unable to fully read the wording of the sign, but gathered the gist as being "curse the Fox sisters for doing the devil's work." Closing the curtain, she walked down the hall and picked up several already opened letters lying on a table. She thumbed through them, smiling broadly. "And you don't know this yet, Maggie, but you and Kate and I are traveling to Philadelphia on Monday to give a week's worth of presentations. This horrid war is turning out to be a boon to us. We shall soon be able to pay for whatever our hearts desire."

EIGHTEEN

Storm and Darkness

DECEMBER 15, 1861, MISSISSIPPI RIVER, NORTH OF ST. LOUIS, 7 PM

Anthony Atkinson, bank officer at the Minnesota State Bank, pulled his top hat tight upon his head and stepped out of his room into the night onto the upper deck of the steamboat side-wheeler. The winter storm wind howled and stirred up high-arching waves on the Mississippi River. The brown, churning waves lifted the steamboat, then dropped it to fall with a noisy splat, sending deep, rolling shudders through the steamboat, and spraying water skyward to the deck where Anthony walked tenuously. A tremor like an earthquake passed along the walkway, and he almost lost his grasp of the rail.

Anthony's right leg was fitted with a hickory stump below the knee. Despite his awkwardness on the slippery surface, he had regal bearing. He was tall with fierce Saxon features and was strong-bodied with sleek, thick black hair like his sister, Cyntha, high cheekbones, and his brown eyes showed a humble confidence.

His heavy, waxed overcoat served him well against the frigid north wind. Glancing down at the ship's crewmen on the lower deck holding lanterns out into the rain to ascertain any river debris that might hang up the ship, he limped along. Keeping a firm grip on the handrail, he arrived at the captain's quarters. He knocked, and the door was opened by a balding, tanned captain with bloodshot eyes. Captain Bernard Singleterry was rotund, with stout arms and a fat neck. The captain looked relaxed and not in the least vexed by the storm.

"Ah, the banker. Come in, Mr. Atkinson," he said cordially. "It is unusual to have paying civilians on the *Aurelia* these days, and I am glad to have you and the four other guests, or rather, five, counting the young girl. Since the army took charge of the river, all I've generally carried lately have been regiment after regiment of Union soldiers, and horses and cannons, and every assemblage of war imaginable. It makes me shudder to think of all those barrels of gunpowder so close to my boilers. This trip, we be carrying barrels and barrels of salt pork. So much pork, you can hear the squeal." He chuckled at his joke, "Be at your leisure. What can I do for you?"

"Thank you, Captain Singleterry. First of all, I am grateful to have been even granted passage. Everywhere are rumors of Rebel spies. I've heard rumors of Confederate vessels plying the waters even this far north. I almost decided against the journey. I hope we will not encounter a Confederate gunboat that might fire a cannonball in our direction."

"Yes, I've heard the idle chatter, too. Fortunately, I think that most of the rumors have been just that—rumors. I can tell from your accent that you are from the South, so you must be in favor of the Southern states to win this conflagration. Not that it matters to me either way. I keep a path down the middle, just like staying in the middle of this vast, muddy river, away from the sandbars and the entanglements. And if we keep on course despite this damnable weather, we should reach St. Louis by morning."

The boat shook horribly as it rose and pounded down across a wave. Anthony steadied himself against a chair, the legs of which were nailed to the floor. "I worry about this weather. Should we not be at anchor somewhere?"

"Well, it's not been my decision, but the order of the army that keeps us on the river in this storm instead of anchored safe in a cove," said Captain Singleterry, staggering on the shifting surface toward an inset bar shelf above his desk. "May I offer you some brandy? I also have rum that I give to the crew, but it's not very palatable."

"Actually, no, I seldom partake. Makes the senses dull. But in answer to your earlier inquiry, though raised in Tennessee, I am not in favor of the Southern cause. I live in Minnesota and work as a bank officer. I'm on bank business to purchase some land."

"I see." Captain Singleterry harrumphed as he sat in his desk chair. "Isn't that a little odd to send a bank officer into the heart of the war? Why not send a junior clerk to carry the papers?"

"I also plan to look into the whereabouts of my sister's late husband's grave." Anthony ignored his question. "Cyntha's husband has been reported killed in a battle some miles southwest of St. Louis, and she hopes to learn the whereabouts of the grave and to pay respects."

"Excellent." Captain Singleterry was paying little attention to Anthony and was more interested in the liquor bottle in his hand. He poured himself a snifter. "You have the bearing of a military officer. Did you lose your leg in battle, perhaps in the war with Mexico?"

"No. In my earlier days, I earned a living shoveling coal on a steamboat not unlike this one. One day, the boiler blew, ripping off my leg below the knee." Anthony pointed to the wooden stump, decorated with a wide brass ring fastened around the bottom.

The rain smacked in vicious strokes against the cabin walls, and the steamboat again shook, and the engines sputtered. Anthony knew the river well, and he knew the fury of a storm on a riverboat, but the captain seemed nonplused as he poured himself another drink, his cheeks growing rosy.

Anthony said, "The reason for my visit is to ask why we have not heaved to and set anchor. Why are we navigating through this storm at night? I know enough about steamships to believe this is folly."

"Worried we might sink, are you? Well, so am I, but the major in charge is following orders which are that this load cannot wait for a storm. Besides, he's heard of the pirates along this stretch of the Mississippi and wants to be past it. Not that I blame him for that." He poured himself another shot.

"Very well, but I would think an army officer would defer to the ship's captain."

"You're asking the army to be reasonable. If there's anything I've seen a lack of with the army, it is their lack of reasonableness."

"I see." Anthony struggled to stay erect as the steamboat tilted on a large wave. "Before I go, I do have another question. I spoke with the Negro who serves as the cabin attendant."

"Yes, my slave, Owen."

"Your slave? Very well then, your slave. He said you knew all the pilots that worked the riverboats and that you might know of a friend of mine—a Mr. Sam Clements. He's the man who saved my life when the boiler blew. I wanted to say hello if the occasion afforded itself."

Without hesitation, the captain replied, "Yes, I know Sam Clements. Hell of a pilot. He piloted the *Ohio Maiden* as recently as a few months ago. That is until the war broke out."

"I see. Did he transfer to a different vessel?"

"No, he didn't. He signed up with a volunteer company of the Confederacy right here in Missouri. Told me he intended to get in a few blows before it all ended. He said he was yearning to be in a good fight. He's strong. I bet he could have whipped a whole passel of Yankee shopkeepers."

"I see. You say he '*could* have whipped Yanks.' Did you mean to imply he is dead or captured?"

"Hell no." The captain downed his snifter and poured himself another round and swirled the liquid in the glass. "Got a letter from Sam. He's headed out west to California. According to him, his volunteer company disbanded after just a couple of weeks. I'm guessing the army life of drill, drill, drill and beans, beans, beans didn't please any member of the company, so the whole outfit just up and quit, including Sam."

The strained steam engine clanked like a basket of tin plates. Captain Singleterry's eyes indicated concern at this new engine sound. He rose, and, holding a hand up, listened intently. Anthony knew enough about steam engines that he, too, was alerted.

The steamboat rose high on a huge wave, tilting to starboard. Both Anthony and the captain lost footing and slipped toward the wall. Anthony grabbed the end of the bar to keep from falling. The captain held onto his desk. The boat crashed down, and the engine clattered to a stop.

"That does it," said the captain, more angry than worried. "I shouldn't have listened to that harping commissary major. He's in charge of this pork and wanted it rushed to the front." He buttoned a waxed coat about him. "Balls! I should've set anchor in a safe cove. The hell with the army!" He stormed out, leaving Anthony alone. The door to the cabin banged wildly in the gale. Rain blew into the room. Anthony knew that if the crew did not get the engines started again that the steamboat could run aground or crash against the river cliffs and sink. He left the cabin and angled toward his quarters. Hurrying along the walkway, he took note of the longboat suspended on its poles, swinging and twisting in the wind. He knew a second lifeboat hung on the starboard side. He passed the captain's slave, Owen, dressed in a white shirt and white knee-length pants, carrying a long wooden spar used for pushing the steamboat off a sandbar. Owen rushed along, his eyes focused. Another crew member, swarthy and muscled, ran down the walkway in haste to the port side lifeboat and began untying the knots of the securing ropes.

In his cabin, he gathered papers, a capped inkwell and pen, and blotter, then slid them into a valise. He then removed his wooden leg, opened the top of it, revealing an opening. Next, he pulled two cloth bags laden with coins from his suitcase and placed them in the hollow of the prosthesis. He adeptly secured the wooden stump and stood.

The boat moaned like a banshee, but no engine sound could be heard. Anthony left his cabin carrying his heavy satchel, passed through the center walkway to the starboard side, and braced himself, using the wall as a shield against the icy wind and rain. With bare light from the cabins and the lantern running lights, he could see large trees extending out from the side of the cliff, their limbs like giants' arms reaching out, ready to clutch and crush the vessel. The side-wheeler was being hurtled by the wind from the port side toward the craggy bluffs that rose like a castle wall thirty feet higher than the top of the *Aurelia*.

Boulders lined the bottom of the cliff. Anthony decided it best to go to the port side to endeavor to help lower the lifeboat. When he arrived there, he saw the lifeboat dangling from a single rope and banging against the railing. No crewman anywhere. Just then, the boat's hull struck bottom with a deafening crunching screech as wood, iron, and rock met. Anthony fell and slid back down the walkway to the starboard side, nearest the cliffs, stopping finally when he collided with the railing. A wave crashed over the deck. His hat flew away into the night.

Sailors and soldiers and passengers rushed about the heaving walkway. In the storm's darkness, the sailors and soldiers jostled to extend long oak spars out against the rocks. Anthony rose, set down his valise, put a foot on it, and took hold of a section of a spar along with four other men. They pushed mightily, straining to release the boat from the river bottom, but to no avail. Anthony glanced up and saw a lantern burning in the wheelhouse. Shadows of men pulled against the ship's wheel.

Then, as if a great hand threw the riverboat sideways, it elevated on a wave and struck the boulders with a devastating jolt. The paddle-wheels careened off the huge rocks, sending splintered boards flying like missiles through the air, striking the walls of the riverboat and soldiers and sailors. Two sailors and a soldier went down, bloodied.

The handful of passengers crowded against the walls, ducking their heads, despair and anguish upon their faces. Anthony's valise slipped from under his foot and fell into the river with a plunk and disappeared. He felt but a sliver of remorse for its loss, all the while struggling to gain footing himself. Another wave like the last would toss him into the drink as well.

"We're sinking! We're sinking!" a woman wailed as she clung to a small girl. The child's screams of terror echoed about the boat that abruptly tilted toward the boulders. Barrels of pork that had been strapped on the stern deck broke loose and plummeted into the water. The tree branches smashed against the ship, crumbling railings. Passengers, sailors, and soldiers slid, then scrambled to the interior walkway to gain the port side, ducking the tree limbs. The starboard lifeboat hung on its pinions, entangled in branches. Anthony helped a corporal with a sliver of wood the size of a butcher knife stuck in his shoulder to stand. They struggled last up the walkway leading to the port side. Before him, a half-dozen soldiers and sailors and the five other passengers crowded against the railing, sleet and wind slicing at them. Above the dissonance of many voices yelling against the storm, Anthony heard Captain Singleterry bellowing orders from the wheelhouse but could make no sense of the words. The waves continued to throw the paddle wheeler against the cliffs. She was rapidly sinking. The bow rose higher than the stern, the entire boat crashing up and down with each successive wave.

With swinging deck lanterns lending a dancing sort of light, Anthony witnessed passengers and crewmen jumping into the water. Above him, a distress rocket fired. It streaked crimson and gold only for a moment into the pouring rain, then vanished. He clung tight to the railing of the tilting steamboat, his wooden leg slipping.

He looked once more at the lifeboat dangling by a lone rope twisted in the pulley. Anthony eased the wounded corporal down to sit on the walkway.

"I'll be all right," the corporal said, wincing.

Then Anthony saw Owen. He grabbed the big Negro's sleeve. "Come with me!" he yelled. Owen followed Anthony to the railing just beside the dangling lifeboat. "We've got to get it loose!" he yelled into Owen's ear. "Can you climb on the railing and release the rope? I'll hold you here. I would climb the railing, but my leg . . ."

"No need to explain, Mr. Atkinson. Let's get that boat." He reached behind him and yanked a huge, broad-bladed knife, an "Arkansas toothpick," from his belt, gave a toothy grin, and climbed atop the upper rail, clinging to the lifeboat pinion pole. Anthony held tight to the big slave's belt and braced as best he could against the railing. Glancing right, he saw two soldiers jump from the railing into the dark water. The boat swayed with each wave. Owen leaned out, the great knife in one hand, the other hand on the pole. His knife found purchase with the twisting rope, and he sawed at it.

The rope snapped when a jarring wave collided against the port side. Anthony lost his grip on the teetering slave, and Owen plunged into the black water. Lightning flashed, revealing to Anthony that the lifeboat had landed right side up. He saw Owen swim up and grab hold of the lifeboat's stern gunnel. Lightning lit the sky again. Dark figures in the waves were swimming toward the lifeboat.

Scrambling for traction, Anthony arose and pulled himself along the railing toward the wounded corporal. Then the steamboat shuddered and lurched down and forward. Anthony was catapulted overboard like a barrel jettisoned onto the water. He landed hard and sank into utter blackness. Underwater, he heard the amplified grinding of the boat against the rocks and the sucking sound of water rushing into the vessel. His prosthesis weighed him down despite his strong legs and arms. Pulling and kicking in desperation, he struggled to reach above the water, his lungs aching. He broke the plane of the waves and gasped for breath, but his heavy coat, boots, and wooden leg acted like an anchor on him. The sleet, a million tiny knives, sliced his face.

The roar of thunder filled his ears, and the sloshing waves batted him around like he was a ragdoll. He hollered into the night and noise. He could see nothing, save the lantern in the wheelhouse faintly glowing, and, as best he could tell, Captain Singleterry's face pressed against the window glass. His strength was waning, his arms felt like rubber.

Without warning, he felt rough hands on his collar, dragging him upward. In a moment, he was free of the river in the lifeboat. Shadowy persons moved about him. "Grab this oar!" a crass voice hollered in his ear. An oar was thrust in his hand. He immediately began rowing. He felt another man next to him rowing in rhythm with him. "Row with my voice!" the noxious voice called. He hollered over and over in rhythm, "Row!" The rain increased its punishment. Anthony caught glimpses of hands feverishly cupping water from the bottom of the lifeboat and flinging it over the side. It was so dark he could not tell if they were rowing toward shore or not. Suddenly, a huge wave swept over the gunwale. He heard the small child's scream, and all about him, bodies were thrown together.

A moment later, large branches scraped across Anthony's back and shoulders, ripping through his clothes to his flesh. The lifeboat swung wide. The angry voice yelled, "Grab the branches! Grab the damn branches! Pull us to shore!"

Anthony reached up, took hold of a thick tree limb, the bark tearing at his hands. He pulled hard toward the shoreline. In what seemed like an eternity, the boat's bottom began scraping gravel, then it rammed hard against a sandy shore. He and the other survivors clamored out of the lifeboat, wading through reeds and bulrushes, slipping in the river slime.

Anthony slogged forward ahead of the others to solid ground. He extended his hand and found a tiny child's hand in his. A soft, woman's hand followed, and he pulled her ashore. Then a calloused hand. Soon, there were eight people standing somewhere on a gravelly shore. The night shrouded them all so that Anthony could make out no one's face.

"Wish we had a lantern," a smooth Southern voice said. Anthony recognized the voice of Owen. Other voices shouted and cursed. Huddled close together, the survivors struggled away from the shore and eventually to a spot under a rocky overhang that blocked the rain somewhat. Exhausted, Anthony and the others collapsed against the cliff walls.

NINETEEN

Silence Is the Truest Friend

FIVE MONTHS PREVIOUS

AUGUST 18, 1861, THE REEDER HOME, WILSON CREEK, 6 AM

In the early-morning hours of the day after the last nurse had abruptly left the Reeder home, the gray-haired slave, Abram, rose to raucous knocking on the back door and hurried to open it. A soldier six feet tall and three inches more stood in the doorway. "How do, folks. I believe this is the Reeder farm."

Before Abram could answer, Lucas, his trumpet to his ear, said, "It is."

"I been ordered," the soldier announced, "to take care of these here wounded."

"Come in, then," said Lucas. "We can use the help."

Sara, arriving from her room, turned up the kerosene lantern. The new nurse before her ducked his head to avoid hitting the doorjamb. He resembled a scarecrow with a large auburn mustache and moles on his face. He was dressed in a light gray uniform, newly sewn. The trousers were too short for his long legs, the shirt ill-fitted as well. He doffed his slouch hat. "Howdy, sir, ma'am. My name is Dred Workman

. . . Corporal Dred Workman. I am the new orderly, and I'm going to make some sense out of this here melee you been dealin' with."

"What regiment you with?"

"I'm with Colonel Greer's Third Texas Cavalry. The regiment just received its official name, and I just recently enlisted. Since I have experience dealing with battle wounded, they promoted me to corporal and gave me this here task."

"So were you in the battle?" Lucas asked, switching the trumpet to his other hand.

"Yes, sir. Seen a lot of fightin'. Seen too much. Now I'm a nurse." Workman shifted uneasily and adjusted his new uniform, tugging on the too-short sleeves. He had decided to tell as few people as he could get away with that he had switched allegiances from Iowan Union to Texan Confederate, fearing the label of traitor and questions from those who would doubt his authentic change of heart.

"Very well, then. This is my daughter, Sara, my . . ." Lucas could not call Abram his slave. He was too much his friend. "This here is Abram. Best cook in these parts. My name is Lucas Reeder."

"Nice to meet you folks."

"You say you have experience working with battle wounded. Are you old army?"

"Yes, sir. I served in the cavalry out in California and in Iowa, but now I'm fightin' with the Confederacy." He tried to look proud.

Lucas said, "I was in the cavalry, too, but lost my hearing when a cannon blew."

"That's a terrible thing to happen, sir. But, if you'll excuse me, I best get to tending these wounded." He went back out to a wagon, and, with help from Lucas and Abram, pulled out several wood boxes of medicine, bandages, and cotton cloth, jars of pickled beef, sacks of rice, beans and cornmeal, and carried them inside. He handed Sara a handful of blank newsprint paper and a bottle of ink and pens. "In case any of these boys want to pen a letter. All of this is courtesy of the

Union army, spoils of war when we took back Springfield, and them Yanks hightailed it north."

Sara beamed at the stash of stationery, but especially at the news that the Union army had retreated north. Abram unhitched the mules from the wagon and stabled them in the barn.

The last item Workman carried in was a fiddle and bow in a burlap sack. "I was told one of the wounded here might be missing his music-makin' device."

A young Confederate soldier who was well on the mend from a saber wound to his arm raised his good hand. "That'd be mine."

Workman handed the instrument to the brown-haired, soft-eyed soldier. "What's your name, soldier?"

"Robert Giles, sir. Private Giles."

"No need to call me *sir*, Private Giles," Workman said with a snort. "Corporal Workman'll work for me. But you brush up on your playin' tomorrow. I'll expect to hear a song."

"Oh yes, Private Giles," Sara chimed in. "Music would be most welcome."

The young private grinned, took out the violin, and plunked an airy tune on the strings before returning it to the sack.

Then Workman, with Sara at his side holding the last lamp with any kerosene, went around to all the wounded. She informed him of each one's condition. In short order, he set about replacing bloody bandages, administering calomel and quinine, applying an oily tincture to scarred wounds, and chatting cheerily with the men. For their part, most complained bitterly to him of their wounds and sufferings, for he had new ears to listen. At one point, he noticed Joseph lying atop the sheets in the bed in the front room. He could see no evidence of a wound on the prone figure.

In an hour, when all but one of the wounded in the great room were in laudanum-induced sleep, Workman asked Sara, "Who's that fella in the front room? He an officer?"

"No," said Sara, "he's a Confederate soldier who has been unconscious for some days. He's awakened just yesterday and can't remember his name, nor even the battle he fought in. He doesn't remember his mother or father. It's very sad."

"So, is he hurt otherwise?"

"Yes, a head injury that has now mostly healed."

"And he gets the bed?" His tone was sardonic.

Sara frowned. "I'll have you know that that soldier has paid a heavy toll."

Workman nodded. He whistled a low tune as he completed smearing a poultice on an older soldier's ulcerous leg. "You be going home in a day or so," he said to the man. "You got a woman waitin'?"

"Yes, in east Missouri."

"Since you've been wounded so, the grand Army of the West is gonna get you a ride home."

The soldier nodded his appreciation, his eyes glazing over from the laudanum.

Workman stood. "Let's go see about this fellow in the front bedroom." Sara and he walked to Joseph's bed. The sheet partially obscured Joseph's face. "You say, he's a Confederate and don't remember nothin'?"

"Yes," Sara replied. "He can't remember the battle or even his regiment. No one has been able to recognize him. We think he might have been in a Texas or Arkansas regiment. His trousers are gray. When we found him on the battlefield, he was holding that sword that is leaning in the corner, and a revolver that we have hidden away. The saber would indicate he may be in the cavalry. That's all we know."

Workman leaned closer to Joseph's face. "I see. Well, maybe I can help. Hold that lamp a little higher," he said, lifting the sheet. He looked at the tanned face with yellow hair and immediately recognized him. Surprised, he straightened. "I know who this is. I fought right next to him." Workman, having served with Joseph in the Iowa regiment and fearing reprisal or, at least, suspicion from the Reeders if they found out his former allegiance to the Union army, set his mind to planning. He paused a long moment, an idea forging its way forward.

"He's one of the finest Confederate soldiers I ever saw fight," he said at last. "Yes ma'am. He's a shore-enough Confederate. His name's Joseph Favor." Workman smiled to himself. He figured that if Joseph did recall his memory that he would say his ruse was all in jest and would help this Yankee escape to the northern army. He knew that if he told what army Joseph really belonged to, he would betray his own secret, and he did not relish the idea of being called a traitor, even if the Confederates were moderately glad to have him. He encouraged himself, thinking, *I ain't no Benedict Arnold. I'm just fighting for the side I should have been fighting for in the beginning.*

Workman thought back to his own capture during the battle and his imprisonment behind the roped-in space with other Union soldiers clad in blue, unlike him in his Iowa gray uniform. He had looked at his own uniform and the gray clothing of his Confederate captors, and being from Kentucky in a region rife with slaves, decided he would rather fight for keeping slaves in their place. "After all," he had said to himself, "perhaps I'll get to own a slave someday." He had argued his changed allegiance repeatedly with ever-advancing ranked officers until he was brought to General Benjamin McCulloch's tent. He remembered how weary and belligerent the man looked, yet he spoke to Workman in the kindest tones. After hearing Workman's pleas and his reasoning, McCulloch had him recite an oath that must have been engendered of the moment and then sign a paper stating his loyalty to the Southern cause. He sent him with a note to Colonel Greer, who regarded him with caution, but found plenty of work for him—digging latrines, washing other soldiers' clothing, or shucking corn for the cooks.

The day that Workman showed an orderly the correct way to change a bandage, Colonel Greer promoted him to corporal and gave him his new task. New uniforms had arrived that same day, so Workman was handed one.

Sara, jubilant, thanked Workman and left to pinch out the two stubs of candles in the great room as the lamp flame ebbed. She felt a flood of relief that she now knew the amnesiac's name. She tiptoed past Lucas asleep on the sofa, whose one leg lay extended against the back of the sofa, the other foot sat on the floor. Stroking her father's hair, she said, "Your sacrifice is not in vain, my dear papa." Once in her room, she found rest easy.

Workman spread a blanket on the front porch. For a few hours, the first time in a week, everyone slept.

TWENTY

Hope Casts the Shadow of Our Burden Left Behind Us

AUGUST 19, THE NEXT DAY

In the morning when the sky was pearl gray with the sun stretching amber tendrils over the low hills, Lucas awoke with a start. With the loss of much of his hearing, his other senses had become heightened, and he had a feeling that something was amiss, but could not put his finger on what was wrong. His body ached from lying in such a curled position on the short sofa. He pulled on his boots and swept back his sweat-matted hair from his face. The sweltering evening had given way to a cool morning. Rising, he maneuvered past the sleeping soldiers, walking stealthily around the bedpans, pots, and bowls scattered over the floor that were used for vomit or diarrhea or wound washing. Dipping the ladle in the water bucket on the table, he drank and looked about the room, finding no cause for alarm, then he drew a deep breath.

Before stepping into the morning, Lucas listened with his trumpet, thinking perchance that he had awakened some soldier. He could barely perceive the faint ticking of the mantel clock and a soft, even sound that he took to be the snores of the wounded. As his eyes grew accustomed to the predawn light slipping in the slightest beams through the eastern windows, he surveyed the men on their cots and mats. He noticed a couple of mice scuttling about in the waning darkness, in and out under the cots and nibbling on the scraps of food on the floor and pulling threads for their nests from the used bandages tossed in the corner. Despite the fact that his life had been turned upside down, he felt rectified in allowing his home to become an infirmary.

Lucas took the covered hog slop bucket sitting by the door and the last lantern with any oil left and stepped outside. He breathed in the aroma of the dew-wet pine and cedar. Holding his ear trumpet under his arm and strolling along in the first blush of light, he felt refreshed. A mosquito harassed his ear until he swatted it against his cheek. A light fog lay close to the ground. He had only walked a few yards toward the barn when the cows set to mooing, followed in short order by the old sow snorting, and the shoat squealing in their sty behind the barn. Then he saw the cause of his earlier misgivings. Two saddled horses stood outside the open barn door.

He set down the lantern, dropped the slop bucket, and sprinted back to the house. He burst in and went to Abram's room, shaking him from sleep. "Quick! Get the corporal from the porch. Tell him to bring his rifle. Marauders are in the barn."

Abram rushed to the front porch and awakened Workman. Some of the soldiers sat up, yawning. "What's happenin'?" one of them asked. Lucas reached into the back of the cupboard behind a sack of flour and retrieved Joseph's revolver. It contained but one bullet, but he figured the appearance of the gun could be persuasive.

Workman, rifle in hand, came from the porch, and Lucas swiftly explained the situation. They raced out the door, Workman in the lead. Just then, though the sky was scarcely lit, Lucas saw two shadowy figures sneaking out the barn door, one was pulling a cow by a rope. When they saw Lucas and Workman, they left the cow, leapt on the horses, and sped into the woods.

Workman stopped, aimed his rifle, and fired after the retreating figures. Lucas hastened toward the barn while Workman tamped down another rifle load. He stopped outside the barn door. With the pistol cocked, he flung the doors open. The rooster crowed, and the chickens fluttered down from their crannies. The horses whickered and stamped their hooves.

Workman, leading the cow, walked up beside Lucas. "They got away. But I must've winged one. He was screamin' like a stuck hog."

Lucas replied, "Good, but there may be more of them inside."

Abram arrived with Lucas's rifle. He said, "I told the wounded to stay inside. I tol' Miss Sara, too, but you know how she is. She was throwin' on some clothes. Glory be. Here she come now."

Lucas read lips well enough, so he understood Abram's meaning.

Sara jogged up to the three men, carrying Joseph's saber, her face fierce.

"Stay here, Sara!" Lucas commanded.

"In a pig's eye. If someone hurt my horse, I'll splay 'em with this sword."

The four turned when they heard galloping toward them. Two Confederate pickets jumped down from their horses even while the horses were skidding to a stop. A stocky fellow with his rifle in hand said, "We heard a shot and some screaming!"

"Marauders trying to steal the cows," Lucas said. "I think we scared them off. But there may be more."

Together, the six cautiously entered the barn and searched throughout. They found no other marauders. Workman said, "I'd hazard a guess that they were just the first of more to come."

Knowing the depravations of war and how war often changed people's moral compass, Lucas said, "I think it best that we ask Colonel Greer for a guard for the barn." He kept the knowledge to himself that his neighbors had been deprived of their livestock by either the Union or Confederate armies. His farm, alone, had been left the privilege of keeping his animals.

Lucas thanked the pickets for their prompt response, and the two rode back to their posts.

Sara returned to the house. Abram grabbed several handfuls of chicken scratch from the barrel and tossed it about the barn floor and out into the yard. The chickens fluttered out, followed by peeping chicks. Lucas gathered eggs from the nests and placed them in his hat, and gave it to Abram who carried it back to the house. A handful of the wounded had gathered in the yard. Lucas waved at them, indicating that all was fine, and they went back inside the house. He fed and watered the horses and mules and milked the cows while Workman slopped the hogs and turned the horses and mules out into the meadow.

When Lucas finished milking, Workman carried the buckets of milk to the house. Then Lucas drove the cows to the meadow. He closed the gate to the meadow and waved at the two Confederate pickets beyond the far fence. He felt a modicum of relief knowing they were near, but he knew the army would soon be gone. Walking back to the house, Sara met him and began asking rapid-fire questions about the attempted theft, and he answered her until, growing weary, he said, "Sara, go tell the soldiers what I've told you. I'm sure they'll want to know, too." She rushed to inform them, and he thought in jest, *Next time, I think I'll just send her to the fight. She's so fearless, they'll cower from her.* However, his worries mounted when he considered how he might be forced to fend off a much-larger guerrilla band.

About midmorning, having slept through the earlier commotion, Joseph awoke. Slowly, he remembered his predicament, but nothing more. He sat scrutinizing the ebb and flow of tree limb shadows on his sheet as a stout breeze blew. Looking out the window, he observed, past the shade of the porch, the bucolic green grass meadow, the well-trod path, and, beyond that, the drop-off of the hillside into the valley. In the distance, the low hills rose green and gray. Nearer, he heard chirping birds. He raised his hand and stared at it, noting the blue veins just below the skin's surface, the lines in his palm, his nails in need of a trimming and a hangnail. He bit at the hangnail and spit it out. For him, the world was much as he knew it to be, except that his memory of loved ones and his own personal history were lost. He rose on weak legs and viewed himself in Lucas's wall mirror. He stroked his unshaven face and stared deep into his blue eyes, searching for his identity. "Who am I?" he said. "I have blue eyes, and I'm young and . . . that's all. How old am I? Where do I live? Where is my life?" He could appertain no characteristic of himself that recalled any memory.

In the reflection, he saw Sara coming in from the great room carrying a plate of fried eggs and bacon. He turned, and she set the plate in his hands.

"I think you'll be happy to know," she said, smiling, "that the new nurse has recognized you. He is a friend of yours. Your name is Joseph Favor."

Caught off guard, he said aggressively. "What friend? And I'm supposed to believe that's my name just because someone says it?" He set the plate on the bed.

"I'll have you know," Sara retorted, "that I was the one who saved you from the battlefield and stayed by your side all the while you couldn't wake up." Her face grew red. "And I sat right there in that chair," she proclaimed, pointing, "praying you'd come back to the living!"

"Makes no difference," His voice was calm now. "I'm in the land of the living with no life." His teeth gritted. "Maybe you should've just let me die."

"Maybe I should have, you ungrateful man!" The statement flew out of her, but all the while she hated the words as she said them.

Joseph chafed at her strident remarks. His life was bewildering enough as it was without this harpy haranguing him.

The two stood staring at each other, both infuriated, until tears pooled in Sara's eyes and spilled down her cheeks. She put her hand to her forehead. "This is all too much for me. All these men so dreadfully hurt. And you, not behaving like I hoped you would. Not like a gentleman at all." Her expression melted from anger to despair.

Seeing Sara's tears, Joseph relaxed his tone. "I'm sorry. I wasn't expecting to learn my name. I don't even remember my mother and father." He reached out awkwardly to touch her arm, but withdrew his hand and ran it through his hair.

"The new nurse from the Third Texas Cavalry recognized you," Sara choked out, wiping her tears with hands bloodstained from working with the wounded. "He fought beside you in the battle. He knows who you were."

Joseph's face lighted. "And he fought beside me? Perhaps I'll remember him."

"Yes, I'll bring him to you." She hurried into the great room. Joseph grabbed the plate and forked down the breakfast. Sara returned, tugging Workman by the sleeve. "Corporal Workman, tell this soldier his name," she demanded.

Workman and Joseph shook hands. "Good to see you again," the tall nurse said. "Do you recognize me?" He winced, not sure what Joseph's response would be.

Joseph searched the man's face for anything he could recall, but saw nothing familiar.

When Joseph did not answer, Workman said, "Well, we only just met, but you is part of this here Texas outfit that is still positioned here about, foraging, scouting, and such. You told me you hail from Tennessee and Texas. Yor name, boy, is Joseph Favor. You're a corporal. It were a pretty frenzied fight, and smoke and all, too. I lost track of ya."

Joseph did not speak, but his eyes showed he was trying to find a reason to believe the wooly-mustached corporal, yet he found no recollection of the soldier before him. After a long pause, he whispered, "Well, I guess that's who I am, but I don't recall." Listening to his own words, he recognized a strong Southern accent. Despite the story told him, he still felt that something was amiss. His thoughts tumbled like they were falling down a mountain in a landslide of stones and rubble. "Where was the battle?"

"Down the hill yonder."

"Who is the colonel of our regiment?"

"Colonel Greer. Don't tell me you don't remember him." Workman felt more comfortable now with his prevarication. *If, by luck, I can keep this up.*

He attempted to divert Joseph's attention. "At least you ain't forgot how to talk. As soon as you're feelin' regular, I think you'll be able to mosey on back to the regiment. You still know how to ride a horse, don't you?"

"Yes, of course," Joseph said, his thoughts turning in all directions. "Well, I assume I do know how to ride." He turned to Sara. "I'm sorry if I've been unappreciative of all your help. This is all very frustrating."

Sara nodded, but her tone was reserved. "Your memory will return." She bit her lip. She berated herself for showing her anger toward this man whom she barely knew. Her heart felt like wrenching from her chest, for she had not wanted their first words to be rancorous. She looked up at his eyes that looked at her with an expression like a stone idol—vacant and cold.

Workman said to her, "Miss Reeder, I would appreciate your assistance in washing that sergeant's leg wound."

"Surely," she snapped. "And, Corporal Favor, if you have enough energy, get dressed. You should be walking, not sleeping." She turned and followed Workman into the great room.

Watching her walk away Joseph took a deep breath. He noticed the gentle sway of her hips and the energy that seemed to exude from her. He admired that. He smiled and thought, *She is indeed pretty. Too bad she has such a temper. I don't need that kind of fire.*

————)(()(————

Workman kept busy in the morning roving though the woods carrying two haversacks and gathering herbs to use for poultices and treatments for dysentery and fever. He found skunk cabbage, cherry bark, mint, and sassafras. He used a hatchet to chip off the bark of a slippery elm tree and peeled away the inner bark fiber and placed it in the haversack. Upon his return, Abram and he chopped and ground the herbs into powders which Workman placed in patches of cotton cloth, then folded into a bag and tied the top with string. He was surprised when Abram told him, "Yes, suh, I can spell. You tell what to write, and I'll write it."

Workman called out the titles of each herb, and Abram penciled the words on scraps of paper that they then sealed to the bags with beeswax. Finishing up about eighty herb bags, he told Abram, "The dogwood bark does a good job to combat bilious fever, like you would use quinine." They both swatted at flies that buzzed incessantly.

"And you say you are Lucas's slave?" Workman said. "And yet you sleep in the house and sit down to supper with 'em."

"Yes, suh, I am sittin' pretty, for a slave. I . . . am Lucas's friend."

Workman finished tying the last pouch of herbs. "That would never happen with me and a slave. But I'll admit you have a way about you. Maybe I need to learn more about slaves."

In the late afternoon, Lucas and Abram toiled over the cauldron on an outside fire pit making lye soap. Joseph, feeling stronger from the afternoon and evening meals of pork sausage, corn bread, and greens, got dressed. He said to Workman and Sara, "I feel I can take in a walk."

"Then you're coming with me," Sara commanded. She grabbed his sleeve and handed him a bushel basket. "Take this."

"Don't think you're going to order me around. You're not a sergeant."

Sara smirked and gave him a shove out the door. "Get going, Corporal."

The two walked into the forest where the flowing shadows of the trees, driven by gusts of wind, danced against the ebbing light. In a short while, Joseph saw the purpose of their errand, and he hurried to keep up with her, though he sometimes paused to catch his breath. Sara and he sought out the sweet gum trees that were prevalent throughout the hilltop forest, and they gathered the brown, spikey globes into the basket. They did not talk much, but he copied her actions plucking the fruit.

With her back to him, Sara said, "I'm of the opinion that this walk will help you retrieve your strength and, hopefully, your memory." She pointed to a high point in the tree. "Pick those sweet gum berries there. They're too high for me." He did her bidding, plucking the globes and placing them in the basket.

At one point, they both reached toward a branch, and their bare arms brushed. Sara felt such a surge of sensual chills, she turned, blushing. Seeing her reaction, he smiled. With the basket full, they returned home. Sara thought to make amends with a more congenial attitude. She reached out and took one of the handles of the basket. His face remained stolid.

Once in the house, Joseph watched while Sara made candles from the trees' bundled fruit. She placed the globes into bowls of melted lard and allowed them to become saturated. About the time the sun dropped below the hills, she lit the globes. Floating about in the bowls, her fruit globe candles gave off a fairylike light. The glow allowed them to attend the wounded.

"Right pleasant," Workman remarked, "but in the morning, I best go down to the regiment and fetch up some kerosene for the lamps."

When all the work was completed, most of the wounded had fallen asleep on their pallets and cots, and it being the Sabbath, the Reeders, Joseph, and Workman gathered in the front bedroom, where Lucas read from the Bible with a single candle for light. An ebbing moon shone its beams through a window and cast a square of pale, bluish-white light that extended from the floor up onto Lucas's pants and across the Bible. The candlelight flickered like soft moonlight over his face. One soldier, leaning on an elbow, listened to Lucas's reading of the scripture, followed by the murmured prayer. He elbowed a soldier next to him, who nudged another, and soon, several soldiers were attuned to Lucas's pleadings to heaven.

When her father finished, Sara prayed in urgent intonation for the wounded. "Father in heaven, please look down on these wounded and grant them healing and peace. We thank you for the arrival of Corporal Workman and his evidential knowledge of the medical arts and for Corporal Favor waking. Please bless us all."

When her prayer ended, the first soldier called from the darkened great room, "Can you sing us a song, miss?"

"How about a hymn?" she replied.

Her answer brought a chorus of yeses from the soldiers.

Sara, remembering a hymn often sung in Reverend Felder's church, said, "Well enough, but it'll have to be soft for the sleeping ones."

The soldier called back, "There ain't a one of us who won't sleep more sound if you give us a song."

Sara smiled, and in a clear soprano sang into the somber shadows.

What wondrous love is this, oh, my soul. Oh, my soul
What wondrous love is this, oh, my soul. What wondrous love is this
That caused the Lord of bliss to bear the heavy cross for my soul, for my soul
What wondrous love is this
Oh, my soul.

On the last line, several soldiers mumbled attempts at the lyrics.

Sara turned to Abram. "Please do sing another verse. You always sang such beautiful songs ever since I was little." After her mother's death, Abram had done the duties of caring for the young Sara as well as any plantation house maid, reading to her and singing her lullabies.

Abram chose a verse with a purpose in mind. As he sang it in a mellow baritone, many of the convalescents, Joseph and Lucas and Sara, too, hummed or intoned the words.

When we're from slavery free, we'll sing on, we'll sing on
When we're from slavery free, we'll sing on.
When we're from slavery free, we'll sing and joyful be
And through eternity, we'll sing on. We'll sing on.
When we're from slavery free, we'll sing on.

When the last note hung propitiously in the air, all were quiet. The crickets chirped outside, the wounded soldiers lay back to slumber, the Reeders, Joseph, and Workman went to their beds, and each found sleep easy. Abram, the last to retire, doused the fairy lanterns. He stopped to look at the waning quarter moon, smiling amidst the stars. Lying on his back on his cornhusk bed, he gazed for a long while out a window at the cloudless sky. He reflected on his years of hard labor for Lucas's parents with nary a reprieve or even a thank-you, and of the later decades that had become a gentle life with Lucas's family whom he admired as if it were his own.

"Thank you, Lord," he prayed, "for allowing me the blessing of this family in my final years. I do not know why the white man feels he needs to own the black man, but I believe you have a plan, though it be through fire, to save us all."

TWENTY-ONE

The Path of the Wicked

By the time the sun peered its rosy face, flashing its beams on the now-placid Mississippi, storm-tossed debris was spread over the river-banks. The eight survivors from the smashed, half-sunken side-wheel-er slept on a narrow spit of rock-strewn beach at the river's edge that butted up to a steep cliff. Anthony Atkinson awoke first. His leg ached where the stump below his knee met the peg. In the frosty morning, he stood, bumping his head against the cliff's rock overhang which had covered them from the storm. Rubbing his head, he hobbled to a boulder, took off his jacket, and undid the shoulder strap and waist belt that helped hold his prosthesis in place. He undid the buckles of the leather harness around his thigh that secured the peg against the stump. Holding the peg in one hand, he shook out from the hollowed out leg two cotton pouches filled with gold coins. He placed the sacks in his coat side pockets, then squeezed out as much river water as he could from the sheepskin padding of the prosthesis. Then he reat-tached and buckled all the accoutrements.

Rubbing his arms to warm up, he looked about at the sleeping survivors who had escaped with him in the lifeboat. Among those who had made it to the beach were four white men beside himself, Owen, and the woman with a small girl. All of them were soaked, muddy, and shivering in restless sleep.

He looked upriver. About fifty yards away, lodged against the shore, the half-sunk *Aurelia*, its black smokestacks bent forward, looked oddly peaceful in its derelict condition. The riverboat tilted to starboard and had settled into the water past its first deck, the bow shattered. Debris from the wreck—barrels, splintered boards, and an entire section of the bow that looked like the apex of a roof—drifted lazily on the molasses-colored river entangled with branches and entire uprooted trees. The detritus driven by the current ultimately entangled on a sandbar, creating a barricade in the river thirty yards wide. Hung up in the trees and ship wreckage, he perceived the bodies of two Union soldiers.

Beyond the barricade, the river was divided into channels by pods of islands. The nearest and largest island was covered by trees and lay about a hundred yards from where he stood.

Anthony looked back at the dense clay and rocky bluff with various shrubs and trees growing from its side rising fifty feet straight up above the overhang of the cave.

He decided to wake the huddled survivors in order to manage as quick a departure from their predicament as possible. He called out, whistled, and clapped his hands. The weary survivors awakened, stretched, stood, and acknowledged each other with nods and mutterings. They emerged from under the overhang and surveyed their surroundings, especially looking up at the formidable cliff encircling the entire beach. A broad-shouldered man, dressed in a suit, wagged his head as if in despair. The young woman held her whimpering daughter close, stroking the girl's matted hair.

"Fortunately," Anthony said, "the weather has warmed, and the sun is up. Unfortunately, we appear trapped against this bluff with no other exit except back into the water."

"And who was it put you in charge?" an angry crewman growled. He was dressed in an unremarkable blue and white doublet, with white knee britches, muddied to black.

"I didn't say I was in charge. I was merely stating the situation for—"

"Well, why don't you shut your yap and let me decide what we're going to do!" The stocky, balding man with huge jowls and a mustache of mixed brown and gray extending an inch past his chin trudged across the muddy, pebbly soil and looked up at Anthony, closing one eye as he surveyed this tall stranger. Anthony was not intimidated by the squat sailor, but marveled at the man's bluster.

"I'm the first mate of the *Aurelia*," the little man announced, "and she went down through no fault of mine, but I'll be the one in charge. We're still under the laws of the river, and I'll not be thwarted." Spit plumed from under his mustache as he spoke.

Anthony took a step back and said, "I totally concur."

"Concur? What does that mean?" the first mate hammered his words.

"It means I agree with you, First Mate . . ."

"Turnbuckle is the name. And you best follow my orders." Hands on his hips, he swiveled at the waist toward the rest of the shivering group. "And that goes for all of ya!"

No one answered but nodded. He turned again to Anthony. "You there. Since you take yourself to be so high and mighty, take down the names of everyone here. I'm going to make a reconnoiter. Perhaps I can find us a way off of this beach. Wait here." He huffed off, slopping through the sandy mud around a patch of scrub bushes and was soon out of sight.

Anthony looked around at the beach no more than fifty yards across. To one side were boulders and driftwood extending to the river's edge; to the other was the tangled mass of tough-rooted shrubs, cattails, and, gnarled, thorny trees that Turnbuckle had just disappeared into. "Wait here?" he said, wagging his head. "Where would we go?"

The young woman attempted to stifle a laugh. Soon, the whole group was chuckling. With a sigh, she said, "I'm just glad we're alive." She had a narrow, gentle face and brown hair with dark, almost black, eyes. Her muddied dress was a royal blue and of fine wool weave. A black bonnet, smashed and muddy, hung at her neck, the strings tied in a tight knot, and on her hands, dainty gloves that had once been white. "There'll be another steamer along here soon, won't there?" she asked. "What with the war effort and all."

Anthony took her hand and nodded affirmatively, then said to the group, "My name is Anthony Atkinson, and in recognition of all we've been through, I'm very glad to meet you all."

Each man said his name. Owen announced his last. The young woman's name was Jeanette Bennett. Her daughter, a shy five-year-old, was named Clara.

Anthony asked Mrs. Bennett, "Was your husband on board?"

"He passed away but a year ago. Clara and I are traveling to St. Louis to live with relatives."

"My condolences."

She smiled her appreciation with shivering lips.

"What happened to the lifeboat?" a man as thin as a sapling asked. He sneezed and wiped his nose with a soggy kerchief.

"I don't know, Mr. Garner," Anthony replied, pointing to where the lifeboat had been. "It appears it was blown away in the storm."

"I say we grab some of these driftwood logs and throw them in the river," offered the broad-shouldered man named Faribault. He stomped in place attempting to warm himself, "and kick our way to that island. It looks to be a more hospitable spot with possibilities to be seen by approaching riverboats."

"Yes, Mr. Faribault," Anthony remarked. "And the next town downstream may very well be St. Louis."

The drenched, untidy group were cheered by this thought.

Presently, First Mate Turnbuckle marched back around the mott and into the midst of them. "Gather round," he commanded.

Before he could speak, a rotund man in a nightgown and heavy boots and wrapped in a heavy coat, said, "I'm Byron Croft. Are there any more crew members nearby?"

Turnbuckle, as gruff as before, replied, "Not here, Mr. Croft, unless you count the nigger, but I imagine if they didn't drown that they made their way to some spot downriver and are wondering about us as well. Now, for the good news. I found the lifeboat and oars, just around the bend behind these trees. So there is no need to climb out of here up that cliff as many of you were worried about."

Anthony could not remember anyone mentioning climbing the cliff and smiled at the little man's arrogance. Each person of Turnbuckle's audience looked up at the insurmountable cliffs, then back at Turnbuckle.

"So let us be about pulling the boat off the rocks. She was tossed up there after we moored here last night. With this many able-bodied gentlemen, we should have not a single difficulty getting her afloat again." Turnbuckle's voice turned more benevolent. "And begging your pardon, ma'am, you best stay here and tend to your wee one."

The men trudged in behind First Mate Turnbuckle. They found the lifeboat, and the oars were in good condition. The men took hold of the sides of the boat and methodically half-lifted, half-shoved it down to the water's edge.

"There now," Turnbuckle said, "ain't that a pretty sight. We be on our way to St. Louis in no time."

At that moment, Mr. Faribault called out. "There're men on the other side of the river! Look! Just in front of the forest."

Five men stood on a sandy beach before a dense pine forest about one hundred yards downriver on the shore of the long island. The trees extended into the land that sloped gradually upward. The men were jumping up and down and beckoning for Anthony's group to come to them. Anthony and his companions cheered and waved back.

Turnbuckle waded into the river to his waist, waved at the men on the other shore, then returned. "That be Captain Singleterry if ever I knew a man. I recognize his uniform. Him and some sailors apparently managed an escape as well. He's a brave man—the captain. We are indeed in good fortune."

The group pulled the lifeboat into the river and boarded, and with a generous crosscurrent, glided toward the opposite shore. They rowed carefully around the sandbar barricade and across the river. Nearing the island, Anthony noticed four of the men had disappeared, and a single tall sallow fellow with a blue soldier's jacket hung open over a torn brown shirt and patched pants continued motioning to them, urging them forward. "That's it," he called in a croaking voice. "There ya be. Keep a' comin'."

The lifeboat slid onto the sandy beach. The ragged man stood beside a large tree limb that had washed ashore. A musket leaned against the limb. He smiled liberally at them. "Welcome," he called.

As the survivors exited, Anthony assisted Jeanette and Clara, his wooden stump sticking deep in the wet sand. The other men pulled the lifeboat further onto shore.

The welcoming man asked point-blank, "Do any of you have weapons?"

The group shook their heads and looked at each other, surprised at the question. The man had no teeth in the front of his mouth, his beard was scraggly black, and his face and hands were unwashed and smeared gray. Anthony caught sight of several long streaks of blood traced on the sand, as if bodies had been dragged across it. Before he could react, the man pulled a pistol from behind his back and said, "Then I'll be asking you all to get down on your hands and knees."

"What's the meaning of this, soldier?" Turnbuckle called.

The man fired a shot at Turnbuckle grazing him in the arm. Turnbuckle howled, clutched his arm, and fell to his knees. "You're lucky I just winged ya'," the gunman said. "I meant to kill ya'. Now if the rest of ya' would be obligin' to kneel."

The survivors obediently knelt. Clara cried. Anthony was in front, hands and knees in the wet sand. He was nearest the lapping waves of the river. Further ashore and to his left, Mr. Garner knelt, trembling. Directly behind Anthony, Mr. Faribault knelt, with Clara, Jeanette, and Mr. Croft beside him. In the rear, Turnbuckle and Owen knelt, Owen a few feet from the lifeboat.

At this time, four motley dressed men strolled out from the trees. The obvious leader, imperious in his nature, was rotund with bushy muttonchops. He wore the captain's doublet. Under the open jacket, a purple sash adorned his chest from shoulder to waist. In rakish fashion, a wide-brimmed hat sporting an eagle feather adorned his head. The others were dressed in various Union soldier and sailor jackets over ragged shirts. They carried rifles.

The man with his pistol trained on the survivors said to the leader, "Here they are, Captain Harry." He smiled a toothless grin.

Harry replied, "Thank ye' much, Parcher." He clapped his hands, then rubbed them together in the fashion of a man who had found a great treasure. "My, what a lovely lot we got this time. Four stout men, one nigger, one wounded old crust, a pretty little girl . . ." He turned toward his men, rolling his eyes skyward, then turned back, his eyes squinted lustfully at Jeanette. "And one woman. We ain't had one of those in long time, have we, boys?"

Harry's men howled like dogs. One of them sporting tangled, black hair under a satin top hat licked his lips, his eyes showing a cavernous darkness.

"But," Harry said, "before we begin, we're going to see what we have." He strolled confidently around the kneeling group. He lifted the chin of the big man, Faribault. "This man's wearing a suit. Perhaps he'll bring a ransom." He grabbed Faribault's right hand and tugged a gold ring from his finger. He held it up, and tossed it to the dark-eyed man. He then remarked, "The one with the stump leg looks like he might have some money." He walked up to Anthony and kicked him hard in the side. Anthony fell on his back. Harry placed his large boot on Anthony's chest. "Got any money, sweet thing?" Before Anthony could respond, Harry leaned over, searched his coat's interior chest pockets and removed Anthony's wallet. He opened it and pulled out several wet dollars—ones and tens. "Well, lookie here. This fellow might be worth a ransom, too. With that gimp leg, he ain't worth much else." He tossed the wallet and stuffed the wad of cash in his pants pocket. Anthony brushed his hand over his side coat pockets where the gold coins lay. To Anthony, the pouches felt heavy enough to club a man.

Parcher walked over to Anthony, still on his back. He cocked his revolver, aimed it at Anthony's head, then kicked sand in his face. Anthony grimaced but held himself in check. When Parcher walked back to the front of the group, Anthony noted that, in addition to the Colt revolver in his hand, Parcher kept a small pistol stuck in his right boot.

Harry meandered around to Owen and Turnbuckle near the lifeboat. He deliberately stomped on Owen's hand. Owen made not a sound. Then he pinched the First Mate's bleeding arm at the wound. "That hurt?" he asked sarcastically.

"Yes, it hurts, you fool," Turnbuckle said. "You should be ashamed of yourselves. I'll bet you've killed the captain and probably some good soldiers and sailors, too. You're nothing but a bunch of river pirates."

Harry and his men let out such a cacophony of chortles, giggles, and guffaws that would mimic a cage full of tropical birds.

"We are *not* pirates, old man," Harry replied. "We're merely foragers, accepting what the land, and, in this case, the river, provides us. Yes, we were forced to fight against your brave captain . . . and a half-dozen soldiers. They came drifting up here last night on an up-turned boat with a hole in it. They were unwilling to help us in our endeavor and tried to put up, shall we say, a protracted argument. They killed my friend, ol' Billy. Shame. I'll miss 'im. What else could we do but defend ourselves? As for you, old cuss, no man calls me a *fool*. And besides, the chore we need men for, you would be of no use." With that, Harry jerked out a derringer that had been tucked in his vest. He pushed the gun up against Turnbuckle's temple and fired. Turnbuckle's body slumped to the sand, the blood pooling around his head.

Jeanette reached over and held her sobbing daughter. Mr. Garner's narrow body shook. Faribault cursed under his breath. Anthony, who had risen onto one elbow, looked across at Owen kneeling at the rear of the group. Owen raised his head briefly. Their eyes met. Harry's back was turned as he strode to the front of the captives. Owen took the opportunity to lift a hand and thumb toward his backside. Anthony realized that Owen still had his knife.

Harry continued his triumphant march around the kneeling group. "Let me tell you what you men are going to do. You're going to paddle this boat over to the steamboat wreck. Then you're going to do exactly as we say and load up as much of the merchandise as you can load. If there's a suitcase, take the clothes. If you find a dead body, take the jewelry. And be sure to bring any guns and ammunition. Oh, and any liquor you find. We don't have much time, because another steamboat or a Yankee patrol boat could come cruisin' along. But if any of you are thinking of trying to escape . . . or cause a ruckus," he paused and ground out his words, "we'll kill the little girl."

"Harry," the man with black eyes and tangled hair said.

"Yeah, Zeke, what ya' want?"

"I know you said we need to hurry, but could we take a few minutes with the woman? I mean each of us? Won't take long. I'm sure I'd feel better."

The pirates hollered agreements.

"Well, men," Harry said, "since this is a democracy, I don't see why we couldn't have a little fun before work. Take her, Zeke."

The dark-eyed man came forward and dragged Jeanette from her daughter's arms. Clara screamed, "Mama!"

Mr. Croft held the sobbing child close, restraining her as best he could. Harry told Parcher to remain behind while the others dragged Jeanette into the woods. She struck at them and twice broke away, but was then recaptured. Clara bawled. After a moment, her sobs turned to whimpers, and she slumped onto the sand. Anthony knew he had to do something to save Jeanette. He could only guess what the other men thought.

TWENTY-TWO

All We Really Own

On a late afternoon a fortnight after Workman's arrival at the Reeder's home, Joseph, Workman, Sara, Abram, and Lucas found themselves delivered for a short spate of their duties to the wounded. A crisp breeze brushed the canopy of the tall trees that surrounded the home and filled the air with the aroma of cedar. Joseph, Lucas, Abram, and Workman sat in rail back chairs on the porch reveling in the luxuriousness of the respite from so many days of stifling heat. Sara leaned against a porch support post, relaxed and content. Four of the wounded sat amongst them, chewing on cigars, and another three drowsed in the green grass before the porch. The final two were playing Euchre and Faro.

A cardinal sang its flute-chirp in a cedar branch a few yards from the house, and a squirrel darted about in the oak shade, foraging acorns.

For three weeks, the cadre of caregivers had provided with creativity a successful measure of care for the injured soldiers. Through tedious hours of washing, salving, and rebinding of wounds, they had rehabilitated every invalid. Even the hip-shot soldier had mended well.

With no crutches available, Joseph, who had regained his strength quickly, had fashioned workable walking staves, planed and sanded from hickory branches for the leg supports, topped with mended socks, stuffed tight with cotton wading for the underarm pads. Workman had encouraged Sara, already astute at seamstress skills, to turn her hand at restitching torn wounds. Two soldiers had lived initially in agony caused by weeping, inflamed, ragged leg amputations with stitching hastily done by surgeons directly after the battle. She had drawn from her sewing box common cotton thread and sewing delicate, tight stitches, she resutured the surgery-deformed limbs. After Workman's zealous washing of the wounds with bromine and brushing the wounds with a cool mint salve, the soldiers grew healthier. One older ampu-tee, Private Chamberlin, who had lost his leg and half an arm, chided Workman for saving his life. Workman paid him no heed. "An old raga-muffin like you don't get no opinion," he told the man.

Abram, for his part, maintained the cleanliness of the ward by dumping bed pans and mopping the floors. By his efforts, the acrid, sweaty stench abated. When finished with the cleaning, he boiled red beans and cabbage soup, and baked pans of corn bread. Soldiers from the Third Texas regularly brought great sacks of beans and milled corn laid across their saddles. Others brought medicinal powders and bottles of tinctures and quinine acquired from the apothecaries in Springfield. Some friends of the wounded brought sundry items like pocket watches, leather satchels, tobacco, and bars of aromatic soaps, all of which had come from the camps of the defeated Yankees. Lucas always hid the liquor they fetched up.

Each day, Sara wrote to loved ones for those who were illiterate. Lucas read aloud from the Bible and science books, carried in the wa-ter, and washed the bandages. Joseph tended the cows and the milking and provided a support arm for those who could walk to go on brief excursions about the yard.

Abram, who was always singing, on occasion, brought out his

banjo-like gourd instrument strung with horsehair strings, which he called a *banja,* and would strum and sing until he tired. The fiddle player, Private Giles, his arm much improved, would often join in. For many of the betterknown melodies, the soldiers would sing in a rousing fashion of such off-pitch discordance that Lucas once remarked, "Our musicians would frighten off a host of robbers from Bremen."

On this cool afternoon, the porch daydreamers were poised, not speaking at all, but listening to the birdsongs, the rustling of the leaves in the wind, and the somber, faint rumble of a passing storm far away on the edge of the horizon. Each heard, nearer still, the occasional pops of rifles of the Third Texas Cavalry hunting meat for the day— pheasant, rabbit, or deer.

Joseph, sitting off to the side of the others, considered his new-found family—Sara and Lucas, Workman, and Abram. He had developed a fondness for them, and a camaraderie with the other wounded. He wondered why he could remember the name and the trill of a cardinal and the names of plants and trees, but held no memory of his true family or of his soldier career. As he indulged himself in the quiet moment, an impression formed in his mind of a sweet-faced woman playing chase with a child by a house, the scene, devoid of color, a nondescript gray, him seeing it through the child's eyes. But he could not tell if the child was he. His memory was only of the smiling woman. Was the woman his mother? He held the thought to himself.

Workman had fallen asleep and began to snore atrociously, so Abram spoke. "I hope our fall garden comes to fruition. I done cooked up all our greens from the summer garden and all our canned fruits and vegetables feeding these soldiers. I planted pumpkins, tomatoes, and turnips. I hope to be busy in about a month cannin' for winter."

Workman awoke and stretched. "Somebody say something?"

"Nothing important," Abram replied.

Lucas leaned back in his chair and rocked by the raising of his heels so his toes stood on their tips, then letting the heels back down. He remarked. "Well, let's see. We finished the milking. The Texas Cavalry boys came up here and bought the whole can of milk so we didn't have to try to sell it. Joseph drove the cows to the meadow. The soldiers are convalescing fine, and I think they're about ready to go home. The days will seem slow without the wounded here. And right this minute, there ain't much to do."

"Amen," Workman said.

"Lucas," Abram asked, "you up for a checker game? I'm determined to beat you at least once this month."

Lucas smiled. "You're on." Abram went inside and soon brought out a small lamp table and the checker board with checkers. The recuperating soldiers gathered around to watch the old men play and offer advice. In no time, the checkers were clicking on the board, and the two friends were laughing.

Workman said, "I think I'm gonna take a stroll down to my cavalry regiment and see what's up." He stood and meandered away past the garden and family cemetery and through the lush vegetation. He picked up a stick and began brandishing it about like it was a sword, slicing, thrusting, and parrying. At the turn in the path, he vanished.

Sara and Joseph remained, each in their own quietude.

Joseph reflected, "I'd like to read some poetry, Sara. Might I borrow one of your books?"

Sara went inside the house and returned with two tattered books. She marched down the porch steps. "Come with me, Joseph. I know a wonderful spot for reading poetry."

TWENTY-THREE

Live by the Sword, Perish by It

THE MISSISSIPPI RIVER, A FEW MILES NORTH OF ST. LOUIS,
DECEMBER 16, 1861, MIDMORNING

With his pistol held in a lackadaisical fashion, Parcher stared at the island's forest into which his pirate companions had disappeared dragging the woman, Jeanette Bennett.

Anthony noticed Parcher's dejection at being left out of the debauchery, and he formulated a plan. He said, "Parcher, why'd they leave you here?"

"None of your business!" the toothless man responded. He looked pensively toward the forest.

"Well, it seems to me that you're getting the raw end of the deal. Do they leave you out of the fun all the time?"

"I have to watch you 'cause I'm the one that let that soldier slip by me and shoot Billy dead. Now, shut up."

"Was Billy a good friend of yours?"

"Not much. But Captain Harry said I have no choice. Leave it be."

"I understand. Not much I can do about my situation here, either, but I do have something to offer you, if you'll let me go free."

"I said shut up!" Parcher reflected a moment. "What d'ya mean you have something to offer?"

"Well, if we can strike a deal, I know where there's a lot of money, even gold coins. I'm a friend of the *Aurelia*'s captain you killed, and I know where he hid his personal belongings, if you know what I mean." When Parcher again looked at the forest, Anthony turned his head to look back briefly at Faribault, then at Owen, and gave them a knowing look. They both nodded understanding.

"If you'll let me go, Parcher, I'll tell you where the gold is. Leave the others out of this. Let me get away and just tell Harry that I tried to escape, and that you shot me and dumped me in the river, and the current took me downstream. What'd you say?"

Parcher stood with his gun limp in his hand, his eyes rolling up to the sky, then down to his shoes, then back to Anthony.

Anthony said, "It ain't really fair, them treating you like this. Them having all the fun. If I was you, I'd be real mad. As it is, I know where there's a passel of money and gold."

Glancing quickly at the forest, Parcher said, "All right, so the deal is you tell me where the money and the gold's hid, and I let you go free. That right? How do I know you ain't tryin' to trick me?" He aimed his pistol at Anthony.

Anthony dropped his eyes and held up a single hand, open palm. "How can I trick you? You've got the gun."

Faribault joined in the charade. "Don't tell him anything, Atkinson, you traitor."

Parcher trained his gun on Faribault and cocked it. "So, looks like he does know where some gold is." He turned once more to Anthony.

"You better decide quick," Anthony said. "They'll be coming back any second."

"All right. I'll let you tell me where it is . . . and, *maybe* I'll let you go."

"No," Anthony said adamantly. "I need your guarantee before I tell you a thing."

Parcher smirked. "Fair enough. You tell me where it is, and you can jump in the river and swim, and I'll count to ten before I start shooting."

Anthony cautiously stood. "Follow me. It's hid here in a satchel under the seat in the lifeboat." He walked as rapidly as he could toward the lifeboat. His back to Parcher, he immediately looked into Owen's eyes, and Owen nodded, then slipped one hand toward his back and his broad, long, Arkansas toothpick knife.

"Wait a minute!" Parcher raced forward, grabbed Anthony's arm, and pulled past him, leaving Anthony standing behind him. "I ain't gonna let you grab some weapon in the boat. I'll get the money myself."

He paced up to the lifeboat, pointing his gun back at Anthony while facing the boat, then bent into the lifeboat, looking under the seats. That was all Anthony and Owen needed. Anthony yanked a bag of the solid coins from his pocket and clubbed Parcher in the temple. The man stumbled. Owen leaped up, and, in two rapid strides, was at Parcher, plunging the massive blade deep into the pirate's chest. Anthony slapped one hand across the pirate's mouth to muffle the scream. With the other hand, he knocked the pistol away. It clattered into the lifeboat. Parcher struggled and thrashed out at the two, but Owen twisted the knife hard. In a few seconds, Parcher's pupils dilated and fixed. Owen and Anthony released the dead body onto the sand at the water's edge, the blood turning the foam of the sloshing waves on the shore to pink.

Anthony grabbed the revolver from the boat. The other men had scrambled to their feet. Mr. Garner swept up Clara and placed her in the boat. "Get down," he said. He jumped in beside her, lowering his head. Faribault raced across to the tree and grabbed Parcher's rifle. Anthony took the gun from dead man's boot and handed it to Croft. The four men turned toward the pines.

Garner called to them, "What are you doing? Let's get out of here."

Faribault growled, "We got a woman to save and payback to give."

"Forget the woman," Garner wailed. "They'll kill us!"

Anthony said, "We've got to save the woman. I'll not have her death on my conscience."

The four men looked briefly at Garner, then turned and raced across the beach toward the trees. Anthony called back to him, "You keep that little girl safe. Don't you even think of leaving!"

Despite his prosthetic, Anthony's strong leg muscles helped him keep pace with the others. When they reached the tree line, the woman's screams, though faint, and the men's grunts and laughs could be heard some unknown distance into the trees.

In a moment, with Anthony in the lead, they raced along a well-worn, but rocky path. Drawing nearer to the pirates, the voices became clearer, Jeanette's voice trailing into a mournful cry, but now they could hear drumbeats. Anthony thought, *What manner of men are these? What deadly ritual are they performing?*

Turning a corner in the trail, the pirates' camp came into view. Anthony and his companions drew to a quick halt behind a thick clump of bushes. Peering through the branches, they saw a clearing with hardpan soil blackened from many campfires in front of a hillside cave in a rock outcropping. The interior of the cave was furnished with chairs, tables, barrels, and even beds. Flags of both the U.S. and the Confederacy draped around the opening. Clothing was strung on a several rope lines extending from the cave and tied to trees. Elegant dresses, gentlemen's jackets, and fine shirts were draped among sheets and blankets. Guns and rifles lay in piles beside boxes and crates of every size. Against the cave wall, whiskey barrels were stacked.

In the clearing, Harry sat on a rock to the right near a filthy sheet hanging from one of the lines, his pants about his ankles, laughing. Zeke stood in front of Jeanette, laid on her back on a crude table. Her dress was raised, revealing her white legs still with her shoes on. Zeke's pants were below his rump and he was slamming his body against her. The other two men, whisky jugs in hand, stood to the left, leaning on their rifles and laughing mockingly. One of them beat the butt of his rifle on a tom-tom, keeping rhythm with Zeke's thrusts. The drumbeats, the raucous laughter, and Jeanette's screams had covered the noise of Anthony's and his companion's approach.

Anthony whispered, "Owen, go around to the right. Try to get up close to Harry with your blade. Croft and Faribault, get to the left quick, take down the man on the drum. I've got six shots in this revolver. I'll go straight in from here. I'll give you ten seconds."

The three nodded.

"Go, now!" Counting in his mind, he leaned around the tree. The man with the drum abruptly stopped his beating and had gathered up his rifle. Zeke was backing away from Jeanette and attempting to pull up his trousers. Harry raised a hand to quiet his men and leaned to look in the direction of where Croft and Faribault were crashing through the brush.

The hell with counting! Anthony swung around onto the path and raced into the camp, firing as he went. Two shots went wild, but two bullets plugged the drummer's chest. He collapsed. The other pirate flung his rifle and raced into the woods. Anthony heard two shots fired to his left. Harry attempted to stand and reach for his rifle, but Owen appeared from behind the draped sheet directly beside him. Owen sliced the man's neck so deep, the head tilted back like an accordion fold, and for a moment, Harry's face had the most surprised look, before he tumbled in a heap. Zeke stumbled backward, hung up in his own trousers, landing hard on his side. He started crawling toward his Colt revolver that lay on a rock. Anthony shot him twice, once in the shoulder and once in the side, but Zeke reached his gun. He lifted it, turned, and shot Owen through the thigh. Owen fell with a groan. Zeke collapsed on his back, still breathing. Faribault and Croft sprinted into the clearing. Faribault planted his heavy shoe on Zeke's hand and pointed the boot gun at Zeke's head.

Anthony rushed to the aid of Owen. He turned to Harry's lifeless body, yanked the purple sash from Harry's chest, and applied a tourniquet above Owen's wound. The bleeding stopped. Owen grimaced, but appeared calm.

Anthony rose and joined Faribault and Croft standing over Zeke. The prone pirate's breathing was labored. His eyes showed no remorse, only hatred.

"Get out of the way!" Jeanette called.

They turned to see her aiming one of the dead men's rifles at Zeke.

"I mean it." She cocked the gun. "Get out of the way."

Anthony and the others stepped back. Jeanette, her dress and petticoats reset, walked directly between the man's outstretched legs, pointed the gun first at the man's privates, then at his head and squeezed the trigger. The rifle leapt, belching fire, and the bullet embedded between Zeke's eyes. The concussion of the weapon threw her back a few paces. She tossed down the gun and yelled, "My child! My Clara!" Holding her skirt and petticoats up in her arms, she raced toward the beach.

Faribault and Croft lurched after her. Faribault called, "Your daughter's safe."

But Jeanette ran on, and the two men hastened after her. Anthony helped Owen to stand and supported him in following the others. Owen, with his wounded leg, and Anthony, with his wooden leg, struggled toward the beach. Nearing the edge of the woods, they could see their companions on the beach waving their arms and jumping up and down. Then the two heard the unmistakable sound of a steamboat's whistle.

Anthony patted the coin pouches in his coat pocket. He eased Owen down on the beach beside the others, then retraced his steps to the pirate's lair. He had seen something there that he figured he would take with him.

Leah Fox, prim and statuesque, stepped before the heavy curtain of the packed theatre of about two hundred customers. The audience hushed. Before her appearance, the crowd had been espousing loudly about their beliefs, or lack thereof, in the potentiality of contacting the dead through means of a séance. Leah stood like a taut rope, but slowly scanned the audience, a mix of primarily women, though sprinkled with a few men. Her thin face with a high forehead gleamed whitish in the footlights and spotlight. She next took her finger to her lips as though she bore a secret.

"Are you gonna show us the ghosts or what?" a callous male voice rang out in the darkened theatre.

"We shall not hear or see a thing," Leah said brusquely with a dismissive motion of her hand, "if we do not have absolute silence in this hall. I've not known a single spirit who would ever appear if frightened by an unruly crowd." She paused a full minute while the only sounds were a few coughs and light shuffling of feet on the wood floor. *What a drab, sordid lot*, she thought. "In a moment, we shall pull the curtains back and you shall meet my sisters, Maggie and Katy, gentlewomen of the kindest sort who know only to serve. Indeed, they serve as channels for the spirits of those who have passed on to speak to those whom they love."

Again she paused to add gravity to the moment. "Open the curtains." She marched to the center of the stage where Maggie faced the audience, her short hair shining in the wholly lit stage. Her younger and shorter sister, Katy, though in appearance almost a replica of her, stood beside her. Both folded their hands as in prayer. They wore simple black, mourning dresses with a white apron apiece. No hat, no gloves, but soft leather shoes with wooden soles.

A few in the audience attempted to clap, but quickly ceased at Leah's glare. "At this time," Leah announced in a loud voice, "I invite three volunteers to step onto the stage and examine it, the table, and even my sisters, for any sort of hidden accoutrements that would generate false noises or false movement."

Several hands went up, and Leah picked three from the front rows, two of whom were paid accomplices to the sisters. The two male accomplices wandered about the stage, checking under the bare table and chairs and looking up at the theatre curtain riggings. Each shook their head. Leah guided the one true volunteer, an overdressed matron to step up close and examine Maggie and Katy. The woman timidly touched the backs and hairdos of the young mediums as they turned full circle before the audience. She indicated she found nothing out of order. Leah allowed the three to be seated.

"I will now take a volunteer from the audience. Someone who has a dire need to communicate with a departed family member." A great number of hands went up. Leah looked about. She knew just for whom she was looking. She, at last, chose a girl of about ten in the third row. Leah had selected the girl from the Philadelphia orphanage that very day and had paid the orphanage manager a bribe. The girl would be paid two silver dollars if she performed well, and she could keep the new dress Leah had bought for her for the event. Before the séance, Leah, Maggie, and Katy had taken the orphan out to eat and rehearsed her on her role.

Once up the stage steps, Leah asked the girl her name, though she already knew it well. The girl said it loudly, but Leah repeated it. "Her name is June May Hogan." She led the waif to a chair at the table facing the audience. Maggie and Katy then took seats on either side of her, their profiles to the audience. "Do your part well, and we'll take you to breakfast tomorrow," Leah whispered in the orphan's ear. "Remember, don't smile. Look sad."

The orphan took on a morose face. Katy, who had hitherto re-mained silent, spoke aloud, "Let us pray the spirits are willing tonight." She bowed her head and took hold of the little girl's hand.

Maggie struck a match on the bottom of her shoe and lit a candle in the middle of the table. The spotlight narrowed and shone white on the group at the table. Leah stood nearby in the shadows. Maggie grasped the little girl's hand. "Now, June May, tell us who you want to speak to and why."

"I want to speak to my papa who was struck down by a loathsome Rebel at Bull Run this last summer and left me and Mama alone," June May said the oft-rehearsed words piercingly. The audience murmured.

"And what is your papa's name?" Maggie asked.

"His name is Arthur Hogan."

"Very well. Sister Katy, have you readied yourself?"

"I am calm, and I am a channel."

"I, too, am a channel. June May, what do you wish to ask your papa?"

Again, with memorized lines, she said, "I want to know if he is in pain and is he in heaven."

Leah stepped forward into the spotlight and placed a finger to her lips, then retreated into the shadows. The crowd leaned forward al-most in unison.

"Spirit of Arthur Hogan," Maggie and Katy said in unison, "come forth and reply to our urgent call." They closed their eyes.

A stagehand opened a backstage door, and a breeze blew across the stage, creating a discernable drift in the hems of their dresses and caus-ing the candle to flicker. The audience gasped. The stagehand silently closed the door.

"Spirit of Arthur Hogan, are you here in this hall?" Maggie spoke in a loud monotone.

Katy moaned, then said, "He is here."

"Spirit of Arthur Hogan, if you are here, tap twice."

Katy, in a movement she and her sister had developed to an art form, popped her toe knuckles inside her shoe twice. The sound reverberated against the wood floor into the theatre. The crowd again drew a breath. Katy again moaned and began lolling her head left and right.

"Spirit, your daughter, lovely June May, is here," Maggie said. "She wants to know if you are in pain because you died of a bullet wound. Tap once for yes, two for no." This time, Maggie popped her toe knuckle twice, and an inordinately loud sound echoed off the wooden floor, the natural sounding board. "Spirit, your daughter wishes the best for you. Are you in heaven? Rap once for yes, twice for no."

It was Katy's turn, but she was too busy rolling her head around.

Leah held her breath, and Maggie opened her eyes a moment and glowered at her sister. "I ask again, Spirit, are you in heaven?" Her voice sounded strident.

Katy rebounded from her act, snapped her toe knuckle once, and the crowd took a collective sigh of relief.

"Now, Spirit of Arthur Hogan, would you like to give your daughter a hug before you go? One rap for yes, two for no." Maggie snapped a toe knuckle hard. June May, her eyes closed as if in a trance, did her act well. She rose slightly from her chair and hugged herself, rubbing her arms as if receiving a warm embrace. The stagehand opened the door, the light breeze blew through once again.

Leah escorted the child offstage to the arms of a waiting maid of the Fox sisters. "You may now show your appreciation," Leah said. The audience applauded, though a few nonbelievers huffed out the doors.

For the rest of the evening, Leah called up real volunteers, all of whom were, by her estimation of their facial expressions, ready believers. Even if the questions asked did not quite go with the plan, the young mediums were adept at deflecting the incorrect response by having the volunteer ask the question again.

After the performance, Maggie and Katy sat on the edge of the stage getting as drunk as they could while Leah counted the take, paid the stagehands and the actors, gave a bonus to their maid, and a bonus to the theatre owner. The three of them and their maid accompanied June May back to the orphanage in a horse-drawn cab. Exiting the cab at the orphanage, Leah placed four silver dollars in the little hand of June May, who smiled, her face joyous. Leah handed her over to the orphanage matron, turned, and boarded the cab, knowing full well that the matron would take the money from her charge.

In the carriage, Katy had passed out from drink. Maggie looked barely awake.

"Tomorrow is our last night in Philadelphia. I believe we can do the séance without a child from the orphanage. By now, the entire city are believers. What do you think, Maggie?"

Maggie burped and breathed sour mash whiskey breath into Leah's face. "Whatever you say, sister mine."

"When we get home, you two will take a hiatus from drinking."

Maggie was snoring by now.

TWENTY-FOUR

The Wayfarer

FOUR MONTHS EARLIER

REEDER HOME, AUGUST 30, 1861

Joseph rose and joined Sara in her salience to the poetry reading spot. She flounced along, holding the poetry volumes against
her breasts. Joseph hurried behind her. They rounded the house and
were soon out of sight of it. They passed into the forest glade along a
well-used path. Despite the muffling effect of the surrounding trees,
they heard Abram laugh delightedly at some move he had made in the
checker game. They walked through the towering trees a good while
side by side without speaking. Going deeper into the verdant forest,
they passed here a fallen tree with ants and beetles crawling about it,
and there, giant oaks festooned with lichens, and there, a sprinkling
of starlike flowers nestled in a bed of emerald moss. They hopped a
deep but narrow flowing rivulet. Minnows and other tiny fish darted
in the stream's shadows. Continuing on, the only sounds the two made
were the crackling of the mat of leaves under their feet and their bated
breathing.

Joseph cleared his throat. "So where is this delightful poetry spot?"

"You'll see," Sara grinned.

He liked that smile, its warmth. He was enthralled with her, the curve of her hips, her trim waist, and toned arms. He admired her golden hair rippling down her back, her freckles, even the nape of her neck. A short distance into the forest of hackberries, oaks, and pawpaw trees, he wondered why she looked straight-ahead, not giving him so much as a glance in his direction. He searched his mind for a topic on which to speak, but his mouth had gone dry, and though various subjects crossed his mind, he found himself tongue-tied. In an effort to appear relaxed, he attempted to whistle, but a mere pathetic stream of air came forth from his lips.

She slowed her rapid march. "Before we go to my favorite reading place, I'll show you the bee tree." She put a finger to her lips. "Shhhh, we're getting close."

Sara took a less-trodden path under a dark canopy of trees. Deep green grass covered the path, some of the blades as tall as their knees, and, along the path's sides, poison ivy grew in abundance. In a moment, Joseph heard the mellow droning of the hive. Soon, bees darted past them carrying their nectar to the hive that was nestled in a vast oak that had been sundered by lightning in a time long past. The gnarled tree stood in a sort of cove with an outcropping of rock behind it and with a patchwork of hawthorn trees encircling it. Joseph stopped. The wide honeycomb structure was sheltered in a fire-burnt crevice of the oak with dried, blackish wood sap in streaks down the bark. He marveled at its size.

"Some nights," Sara said, "when the wind is calm, Papa and I'll come down here with a lantern and a smoke torch. I hold the lantern low and wave the smoke around. The bees turn real sleepy-like, and Papa reaches in with a jar and a spoon and scoops out some of the honeycomb. I don't think the bees miss it much, because every time we come back, there's more honeycomb than before. Besides, these bees love these hawthorn flowers.

"Not too much farther to the poetry spot," Sara said.

The two retraced their steps to the main path that ran toward Wilson Creek. In a few strides, they had to duck down going through an arbor of overgrown bushes tangled with vines. The vines hung in rows, resembling sets of string curtains. Walking in a crouch to keep the upper branches from thwacking him in the face, Joseph lost sight of Sara. She disappeared beyond a mesh of draping vines.

Plowing ahead, he burst from the tangled arbor. In that moment, a brief vision of a woman with black hair, deep green eyes, and a sweet smile came to his mind. But it vanished as he arrived on a wide, flat, stone ledge. He stepped up beside Sara who stood near the edge of a drop-off, fifty feet above the creek. Together, they gazed upon the panorama of low hills covered with trees of emerald green, gold, and burnt umber, like gems poured out across the entirety of it. A number of puffy gray clouds, like a flotilla of gunboats, drifted along the horizon.

"Here it is! The poetry reading spot," Sara announced and pointed to a fallen log set back in the shade of a row of elms. She sat on it and patted the log beside her, intending for him to sit. He hesitated for a moment. "Can you not sit?" she said. "Or have you forgotten what logs are put here on earth for?"

Her gentle teasing brought him around. "Yes, God put trees on earth for humans to make houses, to cut into firewood for warmth and hearth, to sometimes fall across our path, and, when they fall, for sitting." He joined her on the log.

Sara opened the first book of poetry by Robert Browning. Together, they took turns reading poems aloud and sharing their thoughts. Sara knew the exact pages of the poems she wished to read. Joseph chose to thumb through the second book, *A Collection of American Poetry,* to find a poem, or at least a title, to his liking. As the hours drifted by, they talked about the aspects of their view into the undulating valleys, and the shadows of drifting clouds upon the forest, and imagined the clouds' shapes as ducks or dragons. They shared about the wounded soldiers' conditions and about the events of the week.

Their conversation moved to Sara's life history. She told him of her mother's untimely death when she was two years old, though she knew none of the details, and the deaths of all three of her brothers when she was eight. "My two oldest brothers were tussling out the woods," she said, "when they fell into a nest of rattlesnakes. They both were bit, then they ran back to the house. Of course, that pumped the poison all through their bodies. I watched them die on the front porch. Papa was away on business, and Abram did the best he could. The youngest brother, three years older than me, had been struggling with bilious fever for months and succumbed to it a few weeks after my oldest brothers died." Sara spoke of the deaths matter-of-factly, but then looked wistfully into the sky.

After a moment, she continued. "I knew my brothers, but wish I had known my mother. In a way, I'm like you. Neither of us knows our mother . . . but you do not remember your father either."

"Or for that matter, if I have brothers or sisters," Joseph said.

Sara allowed her fingers to brush Joseph's hand. "You will always have a family here."

"Thank you." Joseph's response was sincere, but, with so much of his memory lost, her offer brought him little consolation. He felt a hollowness inside—that he should miss his family, but could not. He appraised himself as a sort of late-in-years orphan. Abandoned. He forced himself from his melancholy and said, "I am exceedingly grateful for the warmth and kindness you and your father have shown me." His face belied his sorrow.

"I think I have brought down . . . the moment . . . by reminding you of what you've lost," Sara announced. "I know a clever poem." Immediately, Joseph perceived that she thought better of her announcement as she said, "No, maybe not."

Joseph smiled, folded his arms, and leaned back. "Go on. I'd like to hear it."

Sara stood abruptly and paced back and forth a few steps. She stopped and looked at Joseph, who was still smiling generously. She said, "Very well, then." Clearing her throat, she took a few more steps, then turned to face him and began. "Twas the month of May and the birds were a-twitter." She paused.

Joseph leaned forward. "Yes?"

"I ate too many beans and sat all day in the shitter." She buried her reddening face in her hands.

Joseph laughed so hard he fell from his seat on the log. He jumped up and threw his arms around her. "That was the best poem I've ever heard. But then, since I cannot remember very many poems I've ever heard, that may not be saying much."

"Oh, I should not have recited that!" Sara tore herself from his arms. "What will you think of me from now on? I'm ashamed."

Joseph tapped her on the shoulder. "I shall always think of you as a lady . . . and one with a great sense of humor." Standing close to her, her smell enticed him. It was a delicate smell, a blend of soap and lilac and just a hint of sour sweat.

Sara swirled around, still red-faced, and seeing his grin began laughing.

"Come," she said, "sit once more and let me read you a Robert Browning poem."

"It's getting late, won't your father be worried?"

"Yes, he will, because that is his nature. But I want you to hear this."

They sat again on the fallen tree; she thumbed through the book until she found the poem then began. "Life in Love," by Robert Browning.

Escape me? Never . . . Beloved! While I am I, and you are you,
So long as the world contains us both, me the loving and you the loved.
While the one eludes, must the other pursue. My life is a fault at last, I fear.

Joseph watched her lips read the words and listened to the dulcet tone of her voice. He watched the slight breeze caress her hair, sending a few strands floating like gossamer about her face. Try as he might, he had a difficult time paying attention to the poem.

She finished the last lines.

> *To dry one's eyes and laugh at a fall. So the chase takes up one's life, that's all.*
> *No sooner the old hope goes to ground than a new one,*
> *Straight to the self-same mark, I shape me . . . Ever.*

She closed the book and looked at Joseph. He realized that she was searching his eyes for a reaction. He was caught off guard and thought that perhaps he should ask her to read it again. He dropped his eyes from her, sensing he had missed an important message in the poem.

She said, "I was hoping you would see in the poem the same meaning I see—that I will not give up hope for you of finding your memory, and neither should you give up hope."

He looked pensively at her, then to the vista of lush trees, glimmering like prisms in the glancing light of a setting sun. He said, "I admit that the poem has a good message. Thank you."

She handed him the second tome. "Now, you pick one."

"Very well. Where is that poet with the name I like so well? Ah, here he is—Longfellow. I wonder if he is indeed a *long* fellow, or if his name is the nom de plume of a rather short, pudgy creature."

While he flipped the pages, scanning several titles, he said, "I don't know these poems, so I'll find one with a title that catches my eye." He settled on one of a different mettle than hers. He began, "'The Tide Rises, The Tide Falls,' by Henry Wadsworth Longfellow."

> *The tide rises, the tide falls. The twilight darkens, the curlew calls.*
> *Along the sea-sands damp and brown, the traveler hastens toward the town.*

And the tide rises, the tide falls. Darkness settles on roofs and walls,
But the sea, the sea in the darkness calls.
The little waves, with their soft white hands . . .

He paused a long moment, reading the lines to himself, before finishing his oration.

Efface the footprints in the sands, and the tide rises, the tide falls.
The morning breaks, the steeds in their stalls stamp
and neigh as the hostler calls.
The day returns, but nevermore returns the traveler to the shore.
And the tide rises, the tide falls.

Joseph stared long at the page, silently scanning the words again. "I've never seen the sea, not that I can remember. But I remember a lake's shore, where the waves pushed by a storm rose quite high. These words make me feel that I am like the traveler. I'm in a hurry somewhere, but all my steps have been erased. All is washed away."

Joseph looked across the ravine to the upper hillside covered in trees with leaves of gold and rust. Just then, he noticed movement in the poplars across the creek. At first glance, he thought it might be a bear or elk, but it soon became evident to him that a line of men on horseback were traversing a path single file downward toward the water. At one point, the trees grew sparser, and several horses came into view, but foliage obscured a view of the men atop the steeds. He wondered if they were a Third Texas Cavalry scouting party, then considered that they might be marauders. He remembered that several pickets had bruited that marauders had slipped into the area. In a break in the trees, he saw that *none* of dozen-odd men wore any sort of uniform, neither Confederate nor Union, but had rifles out of their scabbards, holding them at the ready. Two of the men were Negro. In a moment, whoever they were would have a clear line of sight at Sara and him. Not knowing their intent or loyalty, he rose, closing the book.

When Sara stood, she saw the line of marauders as well.

Joseph whispered urgently, "I think they may be Jayhawkers."

TWENTY-FIVE

Dancing Is Wordless Poetry

Joseph and Sara had not gone far along the path to home when they heard a happy clamoring coming from the direction of the house. Sara cocked her head, listening. "I hear my father's voice. He often speaks louder when a crowd of people gather. Since his hearing is broken, he feels he must talk loud. He's laughing. And I hear Workman's voice jabbering away, too."

Though evening twilight had barely begun, they saw multiple lanterns flickering through the trees. Many men were conversing and laughing.

They rounded some cedars, and before them, forty soldiers in gray gathered in the yard. They held drinking vessels of varying sorts in their hands. Some dipped their cups into a wooden tub of liquor. The pungent, oversweet odor of a corn mash whiskey and tobacco filled the air. Many soldiers puffed on cigars or pipes.

Along with about thirty Texas cavalrymen, all of the wounded soldiers were there, seated on crates and barrels or in the beds of five wagons. The wagons' mule teams grazed, tethered on a stringer a short distance from the barn. Close to the well, over a generous fire, pheasants and large chunks of venison hung on spits, the aromatic smoke drifting up into the cedar boughs. The smell of the roasting meat made Joseph's mouth water.

Sara located Workman standing with his arms crossed and smiling while listening to a gray-bearded fellow whom she recognized. It was the old sergeant she and her father spoke to on the day before the battle. Not far from him, Lucas stood, a mug in his fist, laughing at some soldier's telling of a joke. Sara walked up to her father and took his arm in hers. The soldiers tipped their hats and offered a profuse number of "good evening, miss" to her.

She smiled demurely. "Good evening, gentlemen."

A tall corporal, his cheeks already rosy from drink and with his jacket unbuttoned, announced, "Gentlemen, and I *call you that very loosely*, we have a lady in our midst, and you best comport yourselves with a measure of dignity." He lightly lifted her hand to his lips, leaving the breath of a kiss. "Ma'am, I am delighted to make your acquaintance. My name is—"

"Who cares what his name is." A jocular, chubby sergeant with slicked-back, carrot-colored hair butted the corporal out of the way, then tipped his hat to Sara. "Ma'am, my name is Coltharp Higgins, sergeant of the . . ."

He barely had the words out before all the men in the circle were vying vigorously for her attention. Joseph made an awkward attempt to intervene, took Sara's arm, and attempted to slide his body between the men and her.

"Gentlemen!" Lucas broke in with a commanding officer's voice. "Would you excuse this old cavalry major for a moment to be with my dear daughter?" When they looked almost ready to begin their entreaties once more, he added, "If you are patient, I think she may honor you all with a song."

"Boys," Sergeant Higgins said, "we wouldn't want to miss the opportunity of a fair, young woman blessing us with a melody. I get tired of listening to you yahoos soundin' more like hounds baying at the moon. Let us retire to allow our host a moment with his daughter." He shooed his comrades away with considerable animated gestures.

The soldiers disbanded their circle and traipsed off to other groups to gab and joke. Lucas took Sara and Joseph aside and lowered his voice. "They just showed up with liquor and meat and all the fixings for a party. They even turned down the side panels of that buckboard to make it into a table." He looked at Joseph's worried face. "I wouldn't worry that these soldiers will get out of hand. General McCulloch himself is here."

"I'm not worried about them, sir," Joseph replied. "I'm concerned about a dozen marauders on the opposite side of the creek."

Lucas reflected a moment. "Since there is nowhere for them to cross the creek to our side except in the middle of the Texan soldiers' encampment, I'll wager we are safe for now. It would be a good idea later to alert the wounded who have their rifles. For now, I am predisposed to enjoy the party. Come, let me introduce you to my friend, General Benjamin McCulloch." He pointed.

Joseph and Sara looked where Lucas directed and saw a sturdy, black-haired man with a short, well-trimmed beard. He wore a white shirt, and his pants were of dark moleskin. His black eyes, the lantern light glimmering in them, surveyed the men under his command, and he appeared stodgy and a bit mysterious. To Sara, he looked like a soothsayer or a tribal chief from some tale of *The Arabian Nights*. Lucas brought Sara and Joseph over to the general and introduced them.

Despite his bleak, taciturn demeanor, and the fact that a smile barely curled the corners of his lips, he spoke in the kindest, most respectful tone. "It is my pleasure to meet y'all, especially the daughter of my good friend. Young lady, you come from strong stock. Your daddy was unmatched in his scouting skills. I am sorry you must live in these troubling times, and I am indebted to you for taking care of the wounded." He made a slow bow.

Sara smiled and held tight to her father's arm. She looked up at him with admiration.

General McCulloch turned to Joseph. "And I am guessing you are the young fella that Lucas said lost his memories. Do you recognize any of these men of the regiment?"

"No, sir, I'm afraid not." Joseph shook his head.

Sara reached over and patted Joseph's arm. "But we are hopeful his memory will return."

"I will keep you in my prayers," General McCulloch said.

"Sir," Joseph asked, "are these all Colonel Greer's men?"

"A few are Colonel Greer's. The rest are my handpicked scouting party. Men who have lived near these parts. As yet, I haven't found a soldier who can adequately scout a terrain or tell me much about the Yankee army. I've sent most of Greer's regiment west to Mount Vernon, Arkansas, to forage while we gather arms and ammunition. Soon, I'll take the whole army south to Fayetteville, Arkansas, to train and prepare for winter. Colonel Greer's two companies of Texans down by Wilson Creek are there to buffer any quick move by the Union commander, Freemont; and should the Yankees try a flanking move, Greer's men would intervene and slow them up. As it is, we can't hold Springfield, especially since that damned fool, Price, has taken off north with the Missouri Guard fighting his own private war."

"Then you expect the Yanks to return?" Lucas said.

"Yes, and in considerably greater numbers. Their army at Rolla is growing every day with new recruits and supplies pouring in on the railroad from St. Louis. That much, the scouts have told me. What I don't know is the strategic situation here and in Northern Arkansas—exact Yankee numbers, armaments. The scouts, or the ones that *call* themselves scouts, have brought back conflicting information. So I'm going to take a look at the Yanks myself. It's just a matter of time before they move south again."

Sara had a question of concern. "I take it, General McCulloch, that you don't have an interest in bringing Missouri into the Confederacy?"

"Makes no difference to me if they come or stay, but I don't have near enough men or guns to defend Texas, Arkansas, northern Louisiana, and the Indian Territory, and establish an alliance with the Cherokee and other tribes. Missouri is not part of the Confederacy, and I have no orders to protect it or secure it. My hands are full as it is. A quarter of my men still don't have rifles. Ammunition is low, and we need more horses."

"I see," Sara said, dejected that her dream for her home state had been turned aside. She worried again that invading Yankees would steal Abram from them.

A loud hurrah broke their conversation. Several soldiers were hoisting the roasted meat from the fire pit and transferring it to the buckboard bed. They laid it on a grease-stained cloth, and two of them began carving the steaming deer and pheasant. The other soldiers queued up, grabbing noisy tin plates and spoons to get their portions. Abram came from the house, carrying a large cookpot. He placed the steaming pot of potatoes, pan fried in bacon grease and onions, on the table. While nighthawks darted about the sky above them, the soldiers stabbed hunks of the meat and loaded them on their plates. The old gray-bearded sergeant stood by the potato pot, serving each soldier, while Sergeant Higgins tossed dry biscuits from a tow sack onto the plates. Sara, Lucas, Workman, and Joseph received their servings and took seats on camp chairs. General McCulloch came last, allowing Abram to go before him.

When finished with their meals, the soldiers grabbed fistfuls of dirt and grass and rubbed the compound around on their plates to wipe up the grease and leavings. Sara, being more fastidious than the soldiers, poured her cup of water into the plate and sloshed it around to clean it.

A private of slight build with a weasel face came by with a tub, and everyone tossed their plates and spoons in it, then the private set it in a wagon bed. When he came back to the gathering, he carried a small guitar. He strummed it with great vigor and shouted, "Who's up for a song?"

The soldiers whooped their approval and pulled the crates and chairs into a wide circle. No sooner had the private taken a position near a lantern hung from a limb than he was joined by Private Giles with his violin. Their first song, "Soldier's Joy," was well received. The soldiers clapped time; and their drunken, slurred voices filled the air. Next, the duo played "Lorena." Then they waded their way through "Red Haired Boy" and "Devil's Dream."

At that point, Sara rose and trotted inside the house. She returned with Abram's "banja" and presented it to him. "I want to hear you play 'The Fisherman's Hornpipe.'"

Before he could demure, the Rebel soldiers, almost to the man, encouraged him to play with cheers and hoots.

"That old man," Private Giles said, "can strum out a tune that'd make a dead man dance." Again, the soldiers yelled for Abram to play.

Sergeant Higgins called out, "Come on, old nigger, give us a tune. Ain't none of us soldiers fit to play even a drum." The sergeant's smile showed support for Abram.

Sara beamed approval for Abram as he rose to join the other musicians, and they began tuning the pitch of their instruments. The impromptu band quickly struck up "The Fisherman's Hornpipe," and the soldiers laughed and stomped their feet, banged a rhythm on any crate or chair, and clinked their tankards together. Workman, inspired by the music or just drunk enough, jumped up and commenced to dancing a clopping, knee-slapping clog that mimicked a scarecrow blowing in a gale wind. He had barely begun to show off his terpsichorean skills before he was joined by one of the leg-amputees hobbling on a crutch. The man dropped the crutch and hopped about opposite Workman. Then they do-si-doed. That was all that was needed for most of the men, drunk and relaxed, to join in the rumpus. They bumped together, kicked their legs up, danced highland jigs, and raised their arms and waved them about like they were at a revival.

When the song ended, they all sat down, winded. The little band began a slow waltz. Workman wasted no time inviting Sara to dance. She placed her right hand in his left, gathered with her left the corner of her dress, and raised it a few inches. Together, the two waltzed about the yard. Sara noted the smiles of approbation on the soldiers' faces. She let go of Workman and, foregoing chivalric protocol, invited a few other soldiers, one by one, to dance. Each one passed on the offer, blushing in their shyness and pretending lameness or left-footedness or some such excuse. One told her, "I got a wife who wouldn't take too kindly."

Then she came to Joseph, extending her hand to him.

He rose a little reluctantly. "I can't remember if I can dance."

In just a few steps, Joseph found the rhythm. Sara felt they were doing very well. She liked the feel of her hand in his and his strong arm around her waist. On one slow turn, she noticed her father and General McCulloch walking off beyond the group into the darkness outside of the lanterns' glow. From her peripheral vision, she saw Joseph smiling at her, and she turned her eyes toward him and smiled back. The song ended too soon for Sara, but she wondered why her father had left the festivities.

"Thank you for the dance," Joseph said. The musicians began another waltz. Joseph stood, caught in the magic of the moment, but became befuddled that Sara did not take his hand to begin another dance.

Sara looked over her shoulder in the direction her father and the general had gone, then turned back to Joseph. She took his hand. "Come with me. I want to know why my father has left the party."

Joseph and Sara walked quickly into the shadows beyond the lanterns' glare. In a moment, they arrived near her father and the general. The waxing moon with a ring around it had rolled up high in the sky and shone brilliant beams that glazed the gray field grasses before the

barn to hoary white. The two men stood amongst white oaks, shrouded in darkness. They were pointing to the forest beyond the barn and
whispering.

General McCulloch and Lucas turned and acknowledged Joseph
and Sara with nods. Lucas whispered to McCulloch. "How'd you know
they were there?"

McCulloch cupped his hand to Lucas's ear. "I saw their glowing
cigars."

Sara peered across the field to the wall of pines just past the barn. She
could just see occasional blinks of orange spots and phantomlike figures of
men and horses, almost opaque, passing leisurely among the trees.

"So, not Yankee scouts?" Lucas said.

"No." McCulloch shook his head.

"They're marauders then. Can you guess how many?"

"Not enough to cause us any trouble."

Sara broke in, "Excuse me. General McCulloch, how do you know
they're not Yankee scouts?"

"We wouldn't know Yankee scouts were near. Scouts would be un-
seen. Those fools out there aren't soldiers. They're just outlaws. Some
are deserters, Yanks and Confederates. They don't care who dies or
who wins, as long they make a profit. They use the war as an excuse to
steal from, harass, or kill anyone they have a gripe with. You can hear
these simpletons' horses stamping and their bridles jingling. Scouts
would've left their mounts well out of earshot. And they would not
light up cigars. They're watchin' for an opportunity."

Sara was worried and puzzled. "An opportunity for what?"

"They want the mules," General McCulloch said. "They'd use them
to haul their gear, their tents, cookpots, loot they've stolen. They can't
use wagons. Slows 'em down. They're always on the run."

"Sara and I saw what I guessed was a group of marauders," Joseph
interjected. "They were on the opposite side of Wilson Creek. Could
they be these men?"

"Unlikely," McCulloch replied. "Probably a different bunch. That's another reason I don't want anything to do with Missouri. The state can't make up its mind. It's as bad as Kansas."

"Should we drive them off?" Lucas asked.

General McCulloch snickered. "If I sent my men after 'em, they'd ride away. They'd come back later and lay much more inconspicuous. Anyway, we don't have any horses to pursue them. We rode here in the wagons. Besides, my soldiers, in their drunken condition, would probably end up shooting each other. No, we'll just keep an eye on them." He pulled a Colt revolver from his holster and held it across his chest. "Y'all go on back to the party. They'll miss your presence. And send my two sergeants out here, please."

Lucas took Sara's arm and, with Joseph, they turned to go. "Papa," Sara asked, "are we in any danger?"

"Not now," he said. "There's not a half dozen of them, and they don't want a fight. They just want to steal and will wait until they think the odds are in their favor. But we'll need to make a plan for what to do if they come back."

When they returned to the party, Lucas found the sergeants, took them aside, and whispered the general's instructions, and the two joined the general.

Private Giles caught sight of Sara. "How about that song you promised?"

Sara looked about at the soldiers. A few had fallen asleep, others were babbling drunken slurs to each other and stumbling about. Workman was helping a drunken soldier who was throwing up.

Sara, though worried about the marauders, kept her composure. "I will keep that promise." She hailed the musicians and hummed a few bars of the tune she wished to sing, a favorite one that she learned at one of Reverend Felder's church socials. They strummed a while, attempting different pitches until the appropriate chords were found, then signaled Sara they were ready.

With the guitarist's gentle, mellifluous strumming, Private Giles played his violin with a hint of melancholy. Sara sang:

When summer's flowers are weaving, their perfume wreaths in air
And the zephyr's wings receiving the love gifts gently hear;
The memory's spirit stealing lifts up the veil she wears.
In all their bright revealing the loved of other years.

She sang two more verses but stopped when she noticed several soldiers tearing up. It had not been her intent to bring the men sad thoughts. She thanked them and curtsied to applause. The band immediately began a sprightly fiddle tune, and the soldiers smiled again. The band played long enough into the evening until most of the soldiers had drifted to sleep in the yard. Sara, Joseph, and Abram then awakened the wounded and assisted them inside. Private Giles, the last soldier still awake, played one last song, "Aura Lee," the haunting melody drifting out across the hills and into the valley and up into the stars. When Sara came outside to listen, Joseph strode up to her, took her hand in his, and proceeded to waltz her across the grass under the ringed moon. She smiled at him and looked up at the myriad stars sparkling in the firmament and thought to herself, *Despite this war, God has given me a glimpse of the heights of heaven.*

⸺⸺◉⸺⸺

When the rising sun, still below the horizon, painted the overcast sky pearl pink, the soldiers lay about on the grass under buzzing mosquitos, sleeping off their liquor, dew wetting their clothes. Smoke from soggy embers of the night's campfire swirled listlessly upward. The wounded slumbered in the great room. Sara slept in her bed. Workman dozed, leaning his upper body against the sofa, his rear end and legs on the floor. Lucas and Joseph sat looking out the back windows toward the barn, rifles across their knees. Beyond the well, General McCulloch and his two sergeants remained on guard.

As the day brightened, General McCulloch came inside. He nodded to Lucas and Joseph, then slumped into a chair and slept for about an hour. When he awoke, he roused his men. The slowly awakening soldiers bemoaned of headaches, belched from the previous night's meal, and scratched at mosquito bites. They ate no breakfast, but used wax paper to wrap up remaining pieces of the venison, then stowed the meat in their haversacks. Lucas and Joseph milked the cows. Sara, Abram, and Workman cared for the wounded and cleaned the yard.

In the light of day, Sara saw the soldiers differently. Whereas, during the night before, they appeared to her to be a hearty and raucous bunch, now there was a haggardness to them. They seemed well fed, but the privations of war and constancy in their saddles on the hunt or, at least, on alert, told in their faces. Their eyes shone out like flickering coals in a fireplace, and their sunburnt faces were raw and flaky, and even the halest ones among them wore drawn, powder-smudged cheeks. Their boots were in shoddy shape and crusted with mud, some missing heels, many with holes in the soles. Their pants legs were raveling and torn, their sleeves at the elbows were threadbare or patched. Yet, they held an unmistakable esprit de corps and hastened to muster for the general's direction.

About midmorning, somber clouds hung close to the hilltops, and a mizzling rain drifted across the farm. General McCulloch sent his troop, save Sergeant Higgins, on ahead of him to Greer's camp to retrieve their horses and provisions. He said to Lucas, "Old friend, I'm leaving Sergeant Higgins and Private Giles with you. The private is well enough to serve now. They'll be guards against the guerillas. I can't spare any more men, and I can't guarantee they'll be enough to stop the Jayhawkers should they return. In a few days, I'll need all the wounded who've recovered and *can* fight to go with Colonel Greer. I'll send horses for the incapacitated ones so they can go home."

"I thank you, Ben. Be careful. Let some of the others do the fighting if you can."

McCulloch bid farewell to the wounded, to Joseph, and Workman. He shook their hands and insisted they not salute this time. He bowed to Sara, then said wistfully, "I think I'll take a stroll on this fine summer day down to the Third Texas."

As he ambled away in the drizzle, dressed in a plain black jacket and bedraggled hat, he looked to Sara like no more than any ordinary peddler, not soldierlike at all. But she appreciated him. She watched him as he stopped for several minutes at their family graveyard with his head bowed. Then he walked on and disappeared around the curve in the path.

TWENTY-SIX

A Wound Heals, but the Scar Remains

REEDER HOME, AUGUST 31, 1861, 8:00 AM

Workman stood outside the Reeder home under the spreading oak looking into a mirror hung from a branch by a wire. He shaved his face with a straight razor, then scissor-trimmed his bountiful mustache. Pleased with his appearance, he smiled a toothy grin, and wiped the remaining lather from his face. "I declare I am a handsome cuss, if I do say so."

Lucas came up behind him. "So, Corporal Workman, it appears that the injured soldiers are repairing under your care. We've sent five of them home or down to Colonel Greer. You seem to have a healing touch." He sat on a tree stump and put his trumpet to his ear.

"Well, thank you, Lucas. I do pride myself on my work. However, I am disappointed in the progress of Corporal Favor. He still has no memory." He thought to himself that if Joseph's personal history did return, he would be hard-pressed to explain his little prevarication and his being a quisling would most likely not be appreciated.

"I knew a man," Lucas said, "that was hit by a fragment of canister in the Mexican war. He lost his faculties for the better half of a month. His memory started returning, but in bits and pieces. I don't know if he ever got all his memory back."

"'Tis a shame," Workman remarked.

"Indeed." Lucas continued. "Favor seems a fine soldier. I was certain with all those Confederate squads passing by here that at least one of them would have recognized him, like you did. Has me puzzled."

Workman dropped his eyes. "So, how was your trip into Springfield?"

"I got the supplies, except not enough salt. I bought a Memphis newspaper." He reached in his back pocket and pulled out the broadsheet. "You're welcome to read it."

Workman took the newspaper, unfolded it, and surveyed the headlines. "Hmm," he said in a philosophical tone, "it appears there has been considerable fighting elsewhere." Workman then announced the headlines, "Battle of Manassas Brings Rejoicing throughout the South. Confederacy Soldiers Victorious at Big Bethel, Virginia." He scanned a short article. "Well, I declare, the nation has come apart like a poor-made pair of pants. It looks as though some folks in the western part of Virginia have done seceded from the state that seceded. If that keeps up, we gonna have us a passel of little bitty states."

They both laughed.

"Here is a drawing what I don't right likely understand," Workman continued. "It shows a map of the states with a big ol' snake plum around it." Workman showed the drawing to Lucas.

"Ah, yes. It took me a while to figure it out, too. That's a political cartoon taken from a Northern paper. That snake represents the plan developed by General Winfield Scott to crush the Southern states by starving us out with a blockade. It's called the Anaconda Plan."

Workman nodded and turned the page. "I have to say I do like this political drawing of that Mr. Lincoln. They made him out to be part dragon and part duck. I think that suits him."

"I would not wish to encounter any sort of fowl as him," Lucas growled. "Fanged and with a serpent's tail. This war is *his* fault. If it weren't for his election, the country would still be united. If he

really cared for this country, he would have declined to take the post."
Lucas's face grew red. "He is a tyrant! What difference does it make to
him what we Southerners do with our slaves? He does not know how
much we . . ." Lucas caught himself. "How much we *care* for the colored race and teach them and give them training in the Lord's Word,
and . . . I wish someone would shoot the man. Then, maybe the Union
could be restored."

Workman stretched his lanky frame, walked a few paces away,
then turned sharply, his hand stroking his chin. "If that ain't a purty
idea. I bet you're right. If Lincoln was dead, this whole war would be
over. I could go back to Kentucky and start up a livery stable like I've
always wanted."

"Years ago, I watched Lincoln work his malice up close," Lucas
chewed on his words. "He's a lawyer, and a damned one, and back in
fifty-seven, he defended the man who killed my friend, James Preston
Metzger—who was a hell of a good man. Metzger introduced me to
my dear wife."

"What happened?"

"I was up in Macon County, Illinois, on family business. I met up
with Metzger and a couple of his buddies, and, in the evening, we went
to a bar for some drinks. Well, Metzger never was one who could hold
his liquor, so outside the bar he gets to shoving and shouting at two of
his drinking chums. I was standing on the steps of the bar watching,
thinking they were just fooling around. But then the two so-called
friends, James Norris and Duff Armstrong, grab some big logs and
commence to beating him on the head 'til they knocked him unconscious. A few days later, he was dead."

"So how does Lincoln figure into this?" Workman asked, taking a
seat on the grass near Lucas.

"I'm getting to that. The first man, James Norris, was tried and
summarily found guilty. There were so many witnesses I didn't even
get called to testify. But Lincoln was a friend of the Armstrong family,

so Duff's ma pleads to him to defend her son. When we get to the trial, I watch Lincoln, and I can see on his face he knows Duff is guilty as sin. That's how I know he's the biggest, silver-tongued liar this side of the Atlantic Ocean."

"What'd he do?" Workman leaned forward, his chin resting on his bony fists.

"Well, I think the prosecuting lawyer thought he had the whole thing sewn up because of the ease that they convicted Norris, so he just called one witness, Charles Allen, who was respected by almost all the folks there about. Mr. Allen testified that he saw the whole thing clearly by the light of a three-quarter moon. But that slippery Lincoln pulled out an almanac that stated that at the time of the murder, the moon was not full up, so, by his reckoning, there was no way enough light shone on the scene to be certain that Duff killed James. Well, the prosecutor was flummoxed, and the jury got confused. Lincoln was so able to obfuscate the matter, the jury let the killer go. My good friend was murdered, and that no-account man who's the president of this divided nation got the murderer off free as a bird." Lucas pounded his fist on his knee, and his face screwed up into a vile expression. "You have seen firsthand the violence *that* man has wrought on us all. Tell me I'm not right!"

Workman stood and put on his slouch hat. "You're right. That Lincoln is a real jewel. The nation'd be better off without him. I'll bet the Southern states would rejoin the Union if he was gone."

The clip-clop of a mule approaching from beyond the barn took their attention. A young figure dressed in baggy pants and a shabby shirt and wearing a huge felt hat rode upon the mule. Workman, seeing the rider jouncing along from a distance in those clothes, guessed the person to be a boy. Three hounds of various shades and hair lengths ambled beside the mule. When the individual rode up and dismounted, Workman saw the *boy* was a young woman.

"Hello, neighbor," said Lucas, allowing his anger to recede. He stood and walked out to greet the woman. "How are you, Miss Carver?"

Constance Carver was a tall, bony, and overtly skinny girl of nineteen years. Her shabby, soiled shirt hung like a tent on her, and her baggy trousers were cinched with a rope with a good portion of the rope ends hanging loose, the trousers cut ragged about her shins. Her skin was tanned dark as a Mexican, and her tiny, pinched face was creased by thin lips that seldom smiled.

"How do, Lucas. How do, sir. I see you are a soldier," she said directly at Workman.

"This," said Lucas, "is Corporal Dred Workman. He serves as the nurse here. Corporal Workman, let me introduce our neighbor, Constance Carver."

"How do, ma'am," said Workman, tipping his hat.

"Our home was a place for the wounded, too," Constance said. "They either died or got well. Ain't no more of 'em now." The mule extended its long neck and began biting Constance's hat. She grabbed the hat and swatted the beast until it trotted away a few paces. Turning to Lucas, she announced, "I'm done. I can't keep the farm."

"That's sad news," Lucas said. "What does your ma have to say about it?"

"Ma's dead. Came down with lockjaw. Me and that Reverend Felder from Springfield buried her two evenings ago. It's just me now on the farm. With my no-account husband Zebedee done jined up with the Missouri Guards, it's too much work. On top of that, someone stole my milk cow a week ago. The thief had the gall to leave a note that said thanks for my donation to the Union cause. He even signed the note—Doc Jennison. Now why would a thievin' Jayhawker do such a thing as leave a note telling who he was? And a doctor, at that?"

Before Lucas could answer, she continued. "At first, I thought I'd come here to borry some milk, but I changed my mind on the way." She took a breath.

"Slow down, Constance. I'm so sorry about your loss of your dear mother," Lucas said. He stepped forward, offering to hug her, but she backed away.

"Best not touch me. I don't know how contagious that lockjaw is."

"It ain't contagious," said Workman.

Constance stared at the corporal a moment. "Well, I guess a medical man ought to know. Anyhow, I'm givin' up on the farm for now. Just let it go fallow. I'm gonna to be a laundress for the Missouri Guard. All my male kin are in the Guard. I'm related to my two worthless brothers, one of which be only thirteen, and I'm damnably related to my double worthless husband, so they gotta let me in. I hear the pay is decent."

Lucas raised his eyebrows. "I'm sorry to hear about your farm and your mother, Constance."

She scratched a bony arm. "Ain't your fault. It was just time for her to go. Her bein' full-blood Cherokee, she never said a word of complaint. As far as the farm is concerned, I probably could manage, but I hear that if you do laundry for the soldiers, then your husband gets to live with you separate-like, away from the rest of them misfits they call an army. And, begging your pardon . . . I do miss the feel of my husband next to me in bed . . . if you get my meanin'."

"I certainly understand your concern, miss," said Workman. He smiled at her and winked.

She caught his wink, stifled a smile, and ducked her head. The dogs gathered around her, stepping on her toes. She slapped them. "Git!" They galloped into the shade of the trees and lay down.

"Constance," said Lucas, "how can I help you? I can't manage your farm. I have enough to do around here."

"No, Lucas. I am just hopin' you'll watch after my hound dogs. I'll go back to my house, pack up a few things, and ride my mule to catch up with the Guard. I hear Price is up north raiding and heading to St. Louis. I ain't never seen St. Louis, and they's saying this war'll be over in a month or so, then I'll come back for the dogs. You can use them all you want. They pretty much take care of feedin' themselves." One of them had trotted back over beside her, and she kicked it with her oversized shoe.

"We heard about Price's plan for raiding up north," Lucas said. "Soldiers passing through here talk a lot. Don't know how much of it is true. But, yes, we'll keep an eye on your dogs."

Sara came out the back door onto the small porch steps, drying her hands on her apron. "I heard what you were sayin', Constance. I wish you well."

"How do, Sara," Constance called. "You're lookin' mighty pretty. I thought by now I'da been invited to a wedding for you and some young gent officer. Ain't you found a husband amongst all these soldiers here about?"

Sara hesitated. "I think maybe I have, but I best leave that for the future. I'm hopin' though."

"Well, damnation, girl!" Constance responded. "You best let that whoever he is know you want to marry him. You don't want to end up like Pap Doogan's widow, all lonesome by herself in that big old house with no man around."

Sara's face flushed. "Yes, well, best wishes to you, Constance. I will pray for the safety of your husband, your brothers, and you. Wait. I have something for you." She went in the house and returned in a moment with a simple calico dress. "Constance," she said, "I want you to have this. It doesn't fit me anymore, and since you are of a smaller frame than me, I think it will suit you fine. You can't go off with the army not dressed like a woman. Here, it's yours."

Constance blushed and walked meekly forward to receive the garment. "I can't remember the last time I wore a dress. But I guess you're right. If I want all them soldier boys to treat me like a lady, I best try to look like one. I'm much obliged, Sara." She held it up to her body to see how it would look, then blushed again realizing she stood before Lucas and Workman.

"You'll look mighty fetchin' in that dress, Miss Constance," Workman said.

Constance could scarcely utter a thank-you. She took the reins of her mule, then turned to Lucas. "Obliged to ye' for watchin' my dogs."

At that moment, Joseph came strolling out of the woods behind the barn, his rifle over one arm and a brace of dead rabbits in his fist. Constance stood for a long moment watching him approach. She turned to Lucas again. "My dogs can help with the huntin' and would love to go out with that young soldier." She paused. Under her breath, she said, "Handsome." Then louder, she said, "Fare thee well."

Workman and Lucas held the dogs by their scruffs while Constance mounted her mule with the dress under her arm and headed out past the cow meadow.

"If a marauder stole the Carver cow," Lucas said with a worried expression on his face, "they may try to steal ours, too. And I feel bad about Constance and her family and her farm. I hope they have a farm to come back to. I am glad, though, that we have these dogs to set as watch. Remind me, Workman, to tie these dogs near the barn."

"They'll be a good addition to our guards, Higgins and Giles."

———=)((O))(=———

Joseph sat on the back porch skinning the rabbits he had shot. After pulling the soft skin from the last one, he laid the rabbit carcass in a pot beside the other one. He held the pelt and stroked it, feeling its texture. An image came to his mind of a rabbit fur collar on a winter coat, and he was helping a young woman don the garment. She turned toward him, her pale, smiling face, and the rabbit fur was up about her chin. He immediately knew that she was important to him. But who was she? "You have a name! What is it?" He closed his eyes trying to concentrate. "What's your name?" The identity of the woman sat somewhere in a crevice of his mind, but could not be dislodged.

The impression began to fade. Dropping the fur, he tried again and again to remember who the woman was. Her cheeks had glowed pink as if she had been outside in the cold. Her hair was dark, her eyes deep green, and she bore a gentle and regal countenance. The image, despite his efforts to maintain it, completely left him. His frustration mounted until he felt his very thoughts would suffocate him. He stood, stumbled, and almost collapsed, dizzy and short of breath. "You are important! Who are you?" he screamed. "Who have I abandoned? Are you the one?" he asked the vision. "Who are you?"

Sara rushed from the house, followed by Abram.

"What's wrong?" Sara asked.

"I've lost her!" he said and tore inside the house, pushing aside one of the injured who had risen at the commotion. The soldier fell. Joseph stopped and helped the man up. Then he stormed out the front door and kept walking.

———— ❊ ————

Well past suppertime, Joseph returned. When Lucas, Sara, and Abram tried to ask about his welfare, he turned a cold eye to them. He lay on his cot and faced the wall. How could he tell them what he was feeling? His loss. His despair. His soul traveling through a void. He could not trust himself with his own thoughts. How could he share this awkward conundrum with them? He chose to wait—wait until he understood it himself.

TWENTY-SEVEN

If You Have Tears, Prepare to Shed Them Now—
Shakespeare

Lucas and Abram stood beside a caldron over a fire pit outside the house. Using a stout pole, they took turns stirring soiled, bloody clothing in scalding water. Their own shirts were soaked with sweat. Abram struggled, his hands cramping.

"Abram," Lucas said when the old slave began to look dizzy, "we can quit now. We've washed the blood out. When the water's cool, we'll take the clothes down to the stream to rinse out the soap." He doused the fire with dirt.

Lucas helped Abram to sit on a boulder. Abram began turning his hands, bent like claws, looking at them intently. Then he looked up with a pleading look.

Lucas said, "Abram, go lie down. You've worked hard enough today." He helped Abram to his feet and let him lean on his arm walking into the house. Once in his room, Abram lay down and in short order, fell asleep. Lucas wet a cloth from the water bucket and laid it across Abram's freckled forehead.

Lucas looked at his friend, a family slave given him by his father.

He loved the old man. He thought back to his youth and how he had been infatuated with Abram's daughter, Shiloh. She was about fifteen and he sixteen. He found himself constantly looking at her, and she often, after weeks of averting her eyes in his presence, gave him timid smiles. He would take evening walks down by the slave shacks in the hopes of seeing her sitting on the porch singing while her father played his banja. He would stop, feigning to listen to Abram play his instrument and giving approbation to the slave's skill, but he always kept Shiloh in his line of sight. When she sang, her tone had the mellowness of her father's voice and a sweet tartness. Lucas was enraptured by her.

When the circuit preacher gave his monthly sermons on the grounds of his father's plantation, his father demanded that the slaves gather to hear the preacher, and thereby be close to the plantation's white family and white neighbors. Lucas took the opportunity to stand as near to the slaves as he deemed acceptable and take quick glances at her, especially when the preacher called for everyone to bow their heads in prayer. She, too, would look up at him with admiration, though a brazen move for any slave. Once, when the service had completed, Lucas deliberately walked near her in the crowd of slaves and allowed his hand to brush hers. She reached out a finger and briefly stroked the back of his wrist. Then they went their separate ways.

His interest in her and anxiety about his role in his family increased when she contracted bilious fever and became quite weak, and Lucas's father had her moved from field work to the house as a maid. With her in his home, Lucas found many opportunities to steal glances at her, and she at him. One late-summer afternoon, he returned from a hard ride on an oppressively hot day, and after entering the house, he tore off his sweaty shirt and tossed it to a maid. He sauntered into the house library in search of a book and found Shiloh there dusting the shelves. He walked up beside her, cleared his throat, and pretended to search for the book, though by then he had forgotten the title. She continued to dust, stepping a few feet away from him, but he could see her breathing increase. He turned and watched her bosom rise and fall and the slight cleavage in her summer blouse that from much wear had become like gauze, allowing her nipples to show through the cloth.

Then, unable to stop himself, he stepped forward, took her in his arms, and kissed her hard on the mouth. At first resisting, she then kissed back. Her warm lips spread softly across his. Her firm bosom pressed hard against his sweaty chest, her arms embracing him. His heart raced. Then she lightly ran her hand on his cheek and ever so gently pushed him away and said, "It cannot be. Not now. Not ever. Please hold me in your heart, and I will always hold you in mine." With that, she walked away through the French doors and out onto the veranda, then farther down the plantation lawn toward the slave shacks. Two weeks later, her fever worsened, and she passed away. When the Reeder family attended her funeral alongside the slaves, it was all Lucas could do to bear it. Later, in his bedroom, he wept bitter tears.

Lucas looked now at the sleeping Abram. *In another world*, he thought, *in another time, this old slave could have been my father-in-law.* He lifted the slave's arthritic hand and kissed it.

Lucas was exhausted. He had shoed the gelding, milked the cows, and repaired a hole in the barn roof. He looked out the front window to the porch and noticed Joseph sitting on the steps. Joseph had been a big help with chores during his time there, herding the cows to and from the pasture, assisting with the care of the wounded, and chopping firewood. Though he had lost weight during his coma, his work around the farm during his recuperation had rebuilt his strong frame. His chest had broadened, his arms regained their tone.

He and Lucas and Sara had spent one afternoon cutting hay for the winter.

During the cutting, the three moved in unison across the tall grass, slicing it down in smooth motions with their scythes. Halfway across the field, Joseph began behaving in a jocular fashion. He teased Sara about her sweep being too narrow, and twice stepped on her blade, holding it to the ground. Then the two set to fencing, holding tight to the wooden snath handles and sweeping the blades near the ground. Each time the blades chimed together, Sara, recalling passages from chivalric novels she had read, called out, "Take that, you knave!" Eventually, Joseph dropped his scythe, and she dropped hers, and he chased her about the field until he caught her and they both collapsed side by side The grass was so tall that they remained hidden from Lucas's view. When he looked up and could not find them, as if they had vanished into some great hole, he called out. When the youths poked their heads above the grass, all three laughed until tears came to their eyes.

Lucas walked onto the front porch. The sun burned, and the shadows hovered in tight circles about the trees. Workman sat smoking a pipe in a rocker. Private Giles, his brown locks falling about his shoulders, stood churning butter. He finished his labor, wiped his brow, and carried the churn inside. He exited and, with his rifle, climbed a ladder to the roof, there to keep an eye open for marauders. On the steps, Joseph sat sharpening his sword against a grindstone.

"Lucas," he said, "I saw you washing the clothes and wound dressings. When they're cool, I'll fetch them to the creek and rinse them."

"That'd be appreciated, Joseph. You've been a big help these many days," Lucas said, sitting down beside him.

"My memory has not returned, yet I feel strong enough that I wonder if I should rejoin the Third Texas regiment and do my obligation." Joseph placed the cutlass into a newly sewn leather scabbard. "I still don't know who I am or what my past is. I remember some of my childhood. My mama's face now, but not her name, nor where she lives. I can remember songs, Bible verses, even some orders told to me about soldiering, but can't see the face who spoke the words. It's like I'm walking through a house of a hundred rooms, each one filled with fog. I know there's a war. That much I knew when I woke up three weeks ago. And reading the papers you brought from town, I've got a reckoning of the war."

"You best let me go along with you to explain things to the officers," Workman said. "There are some who might not believe your story about losing your memory. I'll be there to corroborate."

"Thank you, Dred," said Joseph.

The three looked up when they heard the rattle of Sara's wagon racketing up the cow path. Sara stood in the seat, waving. Sergeant Higgins, who had accompanied her, rode his sway-backed mare by the porch, tipped his hat, and cantered the worn-out mount to the barn. Sara brought the wagon to a halt in front of the porch, tied off the reins, and climbed down.

"Hello, Papa," she said cheerfully. "I sold all the milk." She handed Lucas a wad of Confederate dollars and a few coins. Then she showed him a scarf filled with chicken eggs. "The Sharp family gave us these for their payment. I do believe their generosity to the army, offering their corn crop, has set them back a bit. You know they still have one big hole left in their house wall where one of the cannonballs blew through? Mr. Sharp and his son were cuttin' boards to patch it."

Lucas pocketed the money, then patted the wagon mules. "That was mighty nice of General McCulloch to let us keep these animals. I'll stable them and rinse out the milk can." He climbed aboard the wagon and headed the team to the barn.

Workman rose from his rocker and tapped out the tobacco from his pipe on his big boot. "I best tend to the wounded. We have three left, and most likely they won't be staying much longer." He lightly lifted the scarf of eggs from Sara and stepped inside.

Sara and Joseph found themselves facing each other in the noonday sun. Sara's face glowed under her bonnet, and beads of sweat glistened on her brow. She smiled at Joseph and began to untie her bonnet, but inadvertently turned the tie strings into a knot. Before she could fuss with them long, Joseph reached out, and with gentle motion, undid the knot. Then he lifted the bonnet and tenderly smoothed her tresses.

"Your hair is like the sun," he said.

Sara's cheeks flushed. "How's that so?"

"It's much prettier when it's not hidden."

The two gazed at each other in silence. At last, Joseph said, "I have to go soon, Sara, and I have so appreciated your care for me. I will miss you and your father and Abram, and I'd like to say that when I do get my memory back, my best memory may very well be of you."

"Joseph, I think on you all the time. And I am so sorry you have lost your memory. And . . ."

"But there's something else you need to know. I have this . . . feeling. This confusion . . . that I have other people in my life . . . Relatives to find. I may be . . . married." He at once regretted saying that word and took Sara's hands in his. "I know no one's name, nor even a remembrance of a kind word said. I have glimpses of faces, and the feelings with them are strong. I cannot in conscience build anything with you, only to dash your hopes later. I must search for who I am."

Sara looked down, hiding her crestfallen face. Joseph felt conflicted. He gently lifted her chin with a finger. Their eyes met.

"Dear Joseph," Sara said, "without knowing you that long, I have given my heart to you. I hope you do not think me forward, but whenever I'm with you, my life feels most complete. I don't wish to hold you against your will. I just . . . would like a chance for love to grow."

Joseph stood transfixed, looking out past Sara's pleading eyes into the forest of green with the azure sky, but felt in his soul that he was lost in a cave of grays and shadows, a sort of limbo. He licked his lips and searched for something reassuring to say to Sara, but could think of nothing. Taking a deep breath, he said, "I can make you *no* promise. I have . . . a deep yearning. I know not for whom, but it is there."

A tear traced down Sara's cheek. "Very well. I understand."

Workman walked out onto the porch. "I hate to interrupt this tender moment, but it looks like we got company."

Up the cow path, a dozen Confederate cavalrymen galloped. Some of them held the reins of saddled, yet riderless horses.

Joseph strode forward with Workman into the yard. Sara stepped into the shadow of the porch.

When the force rode up into the yard, the captain, a short, thin man who looked to be swallowed by his uniform, dismounted. Workman and Joseph saluted, and the captain returned the salute. He said, "Which of you is in charge of these wounded here?"

"I is," Workman replied. "Corporal Dred Workman." He saluted again.

"Very well, here are your orders." He handed Workman a written order. Workman scanned it and gave it to Joseph.

Joseph read it aloud, "To all home hospital orderlies, return to camp by evening. All wounded are to be sent home with provisions for their journey. September 7, 1861. Signed, General Benjamin McCulloch, CSA Western Army."

The captain removed his hat and dried the interior with a kerchief. "The general sends his commendation to you for tending to these wounded, but now it's time for them to go home. How many wounded do you have here?"

"We have three," Workman said.

The captain motioned to a soldier who led three saddled horses forward. Each horse had a full haversack and canteen tied to the saddle horn. "You are to help this private get the wounded onto these horses, donated by General McCulloch in gratitude for their service to the Confederacy, and send them home."

"Beggin' the captain's pardon," interjected Workman, "I be the only orderly here. This here young corporal has been one of the injured. He'll be in need of a mount as well." He nodded toward Joseph.

The captain eyed Joseph suspiciously, seeing his obvious robust health.

"He's *not* been conscious for days," Workman continued, "and has just now got his piss and vinegar back. He's in the Third Texas Cavalry and ready to ride now. And I need a horse, too."

"Very well," said the captain, speaking to Joseph. "Get your kits together and be back at the Third Texas camp in the valley by evening. I'm sure they can find both of you either a horse or mule. We need these remaining spare horses for the wounded at two other farms."

"Yes, sir," Joseph said, but remorse sounded in his tone. He had known he needed to return to service, but had not anticipated leaving so soon.

"As for the rest of the injured, Corporal Workman," the captain said, "have them gone by sundown."

"But they's one of 'em," Workman said, "that ain't fit to ride. He done have but one leg and half an arm, and he's still doing pretty poorly."

"That is no longer your concern, Corporal. The army has done all it can be expected to do for these wounded. We are giving them each a horse, ones captured from the Yanks." The captain took the paper orders from Joseph's hand. Abram and Lucas arrived on the front porch. The captain, seeing Abram, said, "If I were you, I'd be mighty careful around that nigger now that Union General Freemont has taken it upon himself to order that all the slaves in Missouri are free. That slave may try to run or, worse yet, kill you in your sleep." He mounted his horse. "Afternoon, miss," he said, doffing his hat to Sara. Turning once more to Joseph, he asked, "Is that woman your wife?"

"No, sir," Joseph replied.

"Your sister?"

"No, sir."

"Pity. If she were related we could use her as a laundress. Women related to a soldier can be a laundress. Pay's good, but we can't find any women to take the job. With their husbands and sons joined up, all the women are busy tending the farms and stores."

"She lives here with her father," Joseph said. "He needs her to help run the place." In that moment, he imagined the joy he would feel if he were married to her. He turned toward her, his longing and ambivalence tearing at his heart.

"Pity." The officer shook his head. "I've got three more farms to reach this afternoon. Then we catch up with the rest of the Third Texas. They're moving out tomorrow." The troop turned to ride away.

"Are we marching out to fight?" Joseph called as the captain and his squad trotted off to the east.

The captain halted and shouted back, "Hell no! We're going west to Arkansas to join up with the rest of the army. With Price taking his Missouri Guard raiding further north, General McCulloch wants every regiment with him." In a moment, the squad was gone from sight.

"Retreating?!" Workman said with alarm. "That do put a different stroke on it."

Lucas came out from the house. "I heard the whole thing. You two were ordered to the regiment, but until I get an order from General McCulloch himself, Higgins and Giles stay."

Joseph turned to Sara. "I'll stay here long enough to rinse and dry the clothes. Some shirts and pants belong to the wounded as it is. Then I must leave."

Sara tenderly touched his arm. "I'll help you with rinsing the clothes. I'm going to prepare the noon meal now. The clothes should be cool enough later this afternoon."

Sara and Abram prepared a sumptuous dinner of venison stew, corn bread, and collard greens. Afterward, Lucas brought out a jar of honey, and each person sweetened the corn bread for dessert.

When the dishes were done, Joseph and Sara walked out to the caldron. She averted her eyes, unable to bring herself to look at the face she had grown to love. The caldron sat on the dying embers in the pit, smoke still drifting upward. Joseph stuck an elbow into the water and felt that it had cooled.

Sara looked down at the embers and then at the white smoke that rose between her and Joseph. "These embers are your love for an unknown woman, and this smoke is hiding me from you."

"My whole life is clouded with smoke," Joseph responded. "I need your patience and time."

Sara nodded and lowered her eyes.

Joseph looked admiringly at her, then began to pull the wet clothes out of the caldron and loaded them into a handcart. His sleeves were rolled up, but he still got his shirt wet. Sara, too, gathered the bulky clothing, also soaking her blouse. She wiped a wisp of hair from her forehead with her wrist. Joseph watched her. Though he felt confusion about the woman in his flashes of memories, he felt an overpowering attraction to this petite, tough-minded girl. He was grateful for her benevolence toward him. He would miss her singing and her smiles. He felt conflicted, bound both to the woman of his dream and to Sara.

He grabbed the handles of the barrow and forced it forward toward Wilson Creek. Not speaking, they cut to the south through the trees on a meandering path, Sara walking a few feet behind him. The hot sun bore down on them, riffling in and out of wisps of clouds. At length, they reached the clear stream, flowing steadily, the bed filled with large, round, smooth rocks protruding above the waterline. The sunlight danced and shimmered on the water. Bright yellow, curled elm tree leaves floated on the water like tiny golden boats. More leaves tumbled from the trees with each breeze gust. Turtles basked on the sun-drenched rocks.

Sara picked a daisy by the water's edge. She twirled it, ran it briefly under her nose, kissed the petals, then handed the flower to Joseph. He took it, smelled it, and placed it on a shelf rock near the stream. Sara pulled her skirt hem up and tucked the front and back into the waistband, revealing her pale, strong legs from halfway up her thigh and down. "I don't know any other way to do this without ruining my skirt," she said, blushing. "I hope you don't find me untoward."

Joseph rolled his pants legs up to his knees. "Not at all. We've got to get these clothes done for the soldiers. I hope the glare of the sun off my white legs doesn't blind you."

Sara giggled.

They removed their footwear and socks and rolled up their sleeves to the shoulder. Sara tied her hair back with a pink ribbon from her skirt pocket.

Together, they unloaded the soapy clothes on the rocks, then, taking a piece at a time, they dragged the clothes through the flowing stream until the suds were washed free. After that, they wrung the water out and spread each garment and bandage cloth on a sun-blanched rock to dry. Whenever Sara was bent, rinsing a piece, Joseph watched her. When she raised up, he ducked his head, working with his own shirt or cloth, at which time, he noticed out of the corner of his eye, Sara sneaking a look at him. Neither said anything to the other. Joseph struggled to think of a clever or uplifting thing to say, but his mind was crisscrossed. *I wish she'd sing*, he thought. Occasionally, Sara splashed some of the cool water on her sunburned cheeks.

The water was cold despite the late-summer heat. Goose bumps rose on their legs and arms. By the time they were finishing, the fronts of their own clothes were again soaked. Sara's white shirt pressed against the corset of her full breasts, following their contour. A ribbon of water trickled down her neck.

When she laid out the last pair of trousers, she turned to Joseph. He had quit his awkward glances and now stared at her with complete admiration. He walked carefully to her, for the flat rock bottom of the stream was smooth and slippery with algae. He placed one hand around her waist and pulled the two together, their feet sliding on the glasslike surface of the stream bed. With his other hand, retraced the outline of her chin, then softly touched her cheek.

Her heart racing, Sara raised her arms, placing one about his waist, the other at his shoulder. She glided that hand up and down his neck in a slow, deliberate, and affectionate manner.

He then stroked her wet arms, feeling the suppleness and the tightness of her muscles. Her skin shivered with pleasure under his touch. With his forefinger, he brushed her full lips. She closed her eyes and ran her fingers into his blond locks and gently tilted his head toward hers till their foreheads touched. They held each other in that manner, her with eyes closed, deep in his embrace, while he gazed at the loveliest face he knew.

From above them, they heard Workman call, "Hey, Favor. You need to be hot-footin' it. Colonel Greer ain't gonna look too kindly on us showin' up late. Where you at, anyway?"

Joseph, little by little dropped his arms from around Sara. In turning, his lips lightly brushed hers, and Sara yearned for more, the touch of his mouth like a mellow, warming fire.

"Coming up now, Dred!" Joseph called. "We'll be to the house in a few minutes!" He hung his head, unable to look at the woman he desired and knew he could not have. Not yet.

They put on their shoes. Joseph unrolled his pants legs, and Sara reset her skirt, then they gathered the wash into the cart. Joseph placed the dandelion in a button hole of his shirt. Together, they pushed the cart up the path, each holding a handle. By the time they reached the house, the torrid heat had dried their clothes.

"There you are," said Workman, watching their approach from the porch. "You best get your kit together. I'm sendin' two of them repaired soldiers with that private on their way back to Arkansas as soon as we can divvy up their clothes. That Private Chamberlin lives in deep eastern Missouri, and there's no way he can ride with only one leg and one arm. I'm going to ask if I can accompany him home, catch up with our regiment later. I still need to ensure you're allowed into the regiment graciously, so we need to leave soon." He noticed then the uncomfortable demeanor of the two clothes-washers, shifting from foot to foot. Joseph bit his lip and looked up at the treetops. Sara held her head down, blushing. "I see," Workman said. "Well, I've got plenty to do myself. Favor, I'll see you later." He departed into the house.

"Thank you, Workman," Joseph called.

That evening at the good-byes, Sara sensed Joseph's conflicted attitude while he cleared his throat repeatedly and nudged the floor with his boot. She felt a quavering in the pit of her stomach and could not stop her hands from shaking, even when she clumsily embraced him. She then hugged Workman.

Workman harrumphed and smiled. Joseph and he waved good-bye to Higgins and Giles who were standing to the side of the porch, rifles in the crooks of their arms. They each nodded.

Lucas shook hands with Workman and Joseph and bid them, "Safe passage against the storms of war."

"We done sent two of them wounded off with that private," Workman said, "I hope I can convince Colonel Greer to let me escort that Private Chamberlin back to east Missouri. He's in no shape to travel alone. If I ain't back here by tomorrow morning, I guess you'll just have to send him along to do the best he can by hisself."

Workman and Joseph took up their rifles and hung their haversacks and bedrolls over their shoulders. Joseph handed the Colt revolver to Lucas, then thrust his saber into the new-made sheath. The two soldiers walked out the door and down the hill toward the regiment that was lighting campfires for the evening. To Sara, watching from the porch, the two men looked to be walking into the stars of the deepening night.

Sara said to Joseph in her mind, *Turn around. Turn around.* Joseph kept walking, and the two soldiers slipped deeper into the shadows. *Turn around!* Sara shouted in her mind. "Turn around," she pleaded in a whisper. "I love you."

At the curve in the cow path, a sliver of moonlight revealed

Workman and Joseph. Workman kept going, but Joseph stopped and turned fully toward the house. Sara could not see his face, only the outline of his shadowed form. He stood there for a minute, then gave a brief wave and walked around the bend and out of sight.

Sara's tears burst forth. Lucas put his arm around her and held her tight as she buried her face against his chest.

TWENTY-EIGHT

That Which Is Coarse

Cyntha awoke deep under her blankets in her room in Mrs. Schmidt's boarding house. A bugle was blaring discordantly just outside her window. In a moment, different bugle tunes sounded from every quarter, some nearby, others far away. The army camped in and around Springfield was waking.

Easing out of bed, when her feet touched the icy floor, she recoiled. The plight of Reynolds, sleeping for a second night in a livery, came immediately to her mind. This was their second night in Springfield, and the temperature had grown more frigid. *Reynolds forced to sleep in a barn because of the color of his skin*, she thought. *If I feel so wretchedly cold in this room, he must have suffered dreadfully through the night.*

Crawling back under the blankets, her thoughts flew to finding a means to travel to New York State to obtain a spiritual session with the Fox sisters. She had a sinking feeling in her stomach. She *felt compelled* to meet them and gain their help to speak to the soul of Joseph. Perhaps she could appease Joseph's sorrow and loneliness, lost in the cosmos because his life was cut short. She had read the evidence provided in numerous books and scholarly journals and had become convinced that a handful of people possessed the capacity to break through this earth's plane and speak with the dead. The Fox sisters were the premier seers anywhere in the states and were much sought after. She had read that even Horace Greeley hailed their skills in contacting loved ones from beyond the grave.

Finding a way to escape the town consumed most of her waking thoughts. She had spent the entire previous day looking for unguarded roads, but to no avail.

She lit the lamp by her bed and rose, noting the umbral clouds that hung outside her window. A hard line of ice had formed along the bottom of the window, freezing it shut. The clouds shrouded the sun which she guessed lay just above the horizon. She drew out the bed pan and squatted on it. Finishing, she knelt at the bed, her teeth chattering while she whispered prayers. *Dear Lord, I thank you for many blessings. Thank you especially for the wonderful four years you gave me with my husband, Joseph. But I ask you now for a way to escape Springfield. I am a prisoner here, having done no wrong. My heart is tearing in two for sorrow for Joseph. Mrs. Grunewald said he's in torment and has not yet ascended to your heavenly home. Please help me to reach the Fox sisters so that I might set his soul to rest. I ask this in your holy name. Amen. Oh, and please look after dear Reynolds. He loves you so. Amen.*

She stood and opened her trunk and took out a heavy wool dress and undergarments, woolen socks and a crocheted scarf, and dressed.

Cyntha became aware of the steadily increasing clomp and clatter of hundreds of men walking and running as the army moved out of tents and Springfield's buildings into the streets for roll call. Soon, she heard horses trotting, officers shouting orders, and a band blaring out an ill-tuned melody.

She again thought of Reynolds' well-being. Looping the laces around the hooks of her shoes, she smelled bacon frying and the noises of Mrs. Schmidt's kitchen maids preparing the breakfast. She grabbed her coat, mittens, and hat, exited the room, and collided with a black

maid holding a large metal triangle in her hand. The woman ignored
Cyntha's presence and commenced ringing the triangle with a bar and
calling, "Breakfast!"

Cyntha held her palms to her ears until the torment ended, and
the maid trounced down the stairs. While trying to regain her composure, the door across the hall opened, and a small, skinny man with
close-trimmed dark hair emerged. He had a pencil-thin mustache over
a mouth that sneered like he was about to tell a sordid joke. He spoke
in a voice that was almost feminine in tone. "Good morning, Mrs.
Favor. Yes, I know your name. I saw you speaking to that soothsayer,
Mrs. Grunewald, in the parlor last night. A maid told me your name.
Welcome to Springfield." He tugged at his collar, then bent to adjust
his pants at his boot top.

"Good morning." Cyntha looked down at the little man's hat, surprised at his surly attitude toward her, and managed to say, "And I
know you are Quartermaster Philip Sheridan. I am pleased to meet
you. Thank you so very much for securing a room for me. I have a few
questions for you. First—"

"So do many others, ma'am," he interrupted condescendingly.
"You have a room here as a favor and because you're about the only
woman in this city who's not secesh garbage. I have a busy day answer-
ing other people's questions about feeding and supplying this army.
Your questions will have to wait. Good day." Quartermaster Philip
Sheridan straightened, tipped his hat and loped down the stairs.

Cyntha raised her hand in an attempt to stop him. "But I only
wished to ask if I might be allowed to go north out of the city instead
of south, and . . ." But he was gone too quickly. She watched him vanish
around the end of the staircase, and a short moment later, he emerged
from the dining room with a biscuit in one hand and a handful of bacon
in the other. He shoved the entire biscuit in his mouth, grabbed a great
coat from the hall tree, flung it over his shoulders, then exited. In the
brief time the door was open, Cyntha witnessed what looked like a

wall of blue uniforms packed tight in the streets. "And I also wished to ask if anyone could tell me where my husband was buried," she said to the thin air.

Cyntha descended to the dining room and nodded at the other guests—two army staff officers, three salesmen in ditto suits, Mrs. Schmidt, and Mrs. Grunewald sitting at the long table. The soothsayer wore a profligate number of necklaces, some with rough-cut gems, others with shells, one with a small bone, and she was staring goggle-eyed at the ceiling, her under eyelids red as rouge like she had been drinking.

"Good morning, Mrs. Grunewald, I trust you slept well," Cyntha said cheerily.

Mrs. Grunewald raised her hand at Cyntha. "Didn't sleep a wink. My boarding house ran out of food feeding the Yankee officers. So I must purchase a meal here. Now, hush. The spirits are giving me a message."

"Is it for me?"

"No, dear child. It is for me about my own husband. Now hush."

Cyntha looked about at the others at the table who seemed intent upon sipping coffee or talking with each other. She felt uneasy and unwelcome. She thought, *A rude maid bursting my ears, an arrogant officer with no time for a single question, a rude acquaintance and . . .Well, I'll not let it bother me. I must get Reynolds some breakfast.*

Pulling her woolen hat over her head and picking up a plate and fork from the table, Cyntha slipped into the kitchen. She did not care that the black cook and maids looked surprised when she gathered up several biscuits and thrust them into her coat pocket, took a spoon, and scooped scrambled eggs and bacon from the pans onto the plate, dipped preserves from a jar and slapped it on the plate, and poured a cup of coffee. "Thank you," she said to the cook. "The army's not the only ones who've got a busy day ahead of them."

She stepped out the back door onto a slippery wooden porch,

cautiously negotiating down the steps onto the snow. The coffee and food smelled good, but her concern was at this moment for Reynolds. She rounded the corner of the house and hurried past a sentry blowing on his hands. He watched her wide-eyed, but made no attempt to stop her. She backtracked and handed the sentry a warm biscuit, then trod across the crunching snow, the icy wind cutting at her cheeks. The flag on the pole outside the boarding house snapped with noisy pops in the sharp breeze.

She hopped onto the boardwalk, hurrying to the livery barn. A regiment stood in parallel lines in the street, the soldiers' breaths pouring into the air like smoke from a foundry. Officers on horseback danced their steeds up and down in front of the lines. Looking at the rosy cheeks of the soldiers she thought to herself, *Red cheeks, white skin, blue uniforms. How patriotic.*

Arriving at the barn as the sun was sending sterling beams through the breaking clouds, she nudged a side door open. It was dark inside, and the crisp air made the smell of hay more evident. Horses and mules whickered and snorted. She witnessed their breath rising in little plumes from their nostrils. Men were stirring in the loft, followed by a few whispers.

"Reynolds!" she called.

After a moment, "Yes'm."

"Get down here right away before your breakfast gets cold."

Reynolds scrambled down the ladder and stood before her, shivering. She handed him the coffee first. He took the hot mug in his shaking hands and sipped it. His eyes were red, and tiny icicles clung to his eyebrows and the tips of his bangs and beard. "Thank you, Miss Cyntha."

She handed him the plate and touched his coat at the elbow. Even through her mitten, his coat felt stiff, like it had been dipped in a river and frozen. She then held his coffee cup while he held the plate with one hand and used the fork to wolf down the breakfast. He tried to smile at her while he savored every bite. Little bits of egg stuck to his scrubby beard. When he finished, she handed him the coffee which he guzzled down. Wiping his face with his sleeve, he looked more robust. "'Scuse my manners, Miz Cyntha."

She took the plate from him. "Oh, I almost forgot." Reaching into her deep pockets she pulled out the still-warm biscuits.

Reynolds took them and shoved one in his mouth. After chewing and swallowing, he said, "Hold on a minute, Miz Cyntha." He strode over to the ladder, holding the remaining biscuits in one big hand, and called up into the loft. "Hey, Lothorio, Andrew. Come here."

In a moment, two black faces appeared in the floor opening. "Take these." He extended his hand filled with the biscuits up into the opening to the two Negroes. They grabbed the biscuits eagerly and offered several thank-yous.

When Reynolds returned to Cyntha, she said, "I want to send a telegram to my brother in Minnesota today. I need him to send funds to pay for us to take a train from St. Louis to New York to meet the Fox sisters. So go do your morning business and meet me in front of the boarding house in half an hour." She patted his shoulder and strode away. *How can anyone survive in this weather? I must pray more for our soldiers and find a warmer place for Reynolds and his companions.*

Cyntha returned to the boarding house and found the table empty of boarders. Four black maids were clearing the dirty plates and silverware. At second look, she saw that one of the maids was a young white woman in her late teens, but dark-skinned like few white persons she had ever seen. Though the Negroes wore standard denim blue skirts with a white blouse, the white woman wore a heavily starched apron over a solid black dress that seemed to swallow her narrow frame. Her long, black hair was tied back in a ponytail, and her face was brown enough to have been taken for a Mexican. She was not clearing the table, but stood to the side watching the other maids work. She held a ceramic coffeepot in one hand.

"Good morning, everyone," Cyntha said to the maids. The three Negro maids looked up, their eyes wide, then ducked their heads and mumbled a good morning while continuing their work.

"They ain't supposed to talk much to the boarders or soldiers. Mrs. Schmidt's orders." The white maid spoke with unhesitating authority. "Did ya eat yet?" she asked Cyntha.

"Why no, I haven't. I didn't realize I was gone so long. I'll just have a cup of coffee."

"Won't hear of any such thing. You paid good money to stay here," the woman said. "You sit yourself down here right now." She directed Cyntha to a chair.

Cyntha removed her hat, mittens, and coat and sat, glad that food was forthcoming.

"Abigail, go right now and have cook stir up some more breakfast," the dark-skinned woman spoke directly but kindly. "Right now, Honey. Hurry up."

One of the Negro maids hurried into the kitchen. As Cyntha watched the maids finish clearing the table, the skinny woman in charge set a cup before her and poured coffee. "There ya be. Enjoy your breakfast . . . and if ya care to talk awhile, I'd be much obliged. There ain't been nothin' but soldiers and drummers selling all kinds of wares to the army since January. I been around soldiers so long, I done forgot what it's like to talk with a woman."

"Well, how do you do." Cyntha was a little astonished at the brash comments of the maid. She extended her hand. "My name is Cyntha Favor."

The woman shook Cyntha's hand, "I'm Constance Carver, late of south of Springfield and late of working as a laundress for Guvnor Price's Missouri volunteers. Pleased to meet ya."

"And I assume you now work here at the boarding house."

"Yes, ma'am. Mrs. Schmidt needed someone to keep an eye on her niggers. She's afraid, with the Yanks here, that they'd all run off. So she hired me to keep 'em busy and to lock 'em up at night."

"You lock them up?"

"Sure do. Got 'em a big old cellar room with beds and bedpans and a lantern and all, but no windows. When the rest of us is freezin' up here in this old boarding house, they's as cozy as bedbugs on an old tinker. At nighttime, I herd 'em all in there like I used to herd my hogs."

Cyntha was speechless.

"So, anyhow," Constance continued, "I tried talkin' to that Miz Grunewald, you know, the fortune-teller. Tried to ask her if she knew the whereabouts of the Missouri Guard army and my husband. But that lady is buggy as a rotten apple. Weren't no use tryin' to have a general conversation with her. She started gazin' off into space and talkin' to the air. Gave me a nervous tic."

When Constance stopped to take a breath, Cyntha asked, "How is it that you came upon this position as overseer?"

"Oh, I ain't no overseer. I ain't got the cotton, if'n you know what I mean."

"I'm afraid I don't."

"You know. A man's things, his critical parts. The toughness to take a lash to some nigger. Ain't no way I'd ever lay a hand on these lovely ladies. I couldn't no more whip them than whip my own flesh and blood. We're good friends."

Cyntha again found no words.

"Besides, I'm only here 'cause I got left behind by the army."

"How is that?"

"Well . . ." Constance paused awhile formulating her answer. "You see, before I jined up with the Guard to be a laundress, I helped my husband on the farm. Since he jined the Guard, the army let me be with him some and earn pay for washin' all them dirty boys' clothes."

Cyntha nodded. A black maid entered from the kitchen and placed a steaming plate of eggs, bacon, and biscuits before Cyntha, who began eating while listening to her new garrulous acquaintance.

"Well, before I jined the army, I ain't never drunk anything stronger

than coffee my whole life," Constance said, "even though corn squeez-
in's was always around the house. Anyway, when the other laundresses
finished each day, they commenced to drinkin' some corn liquor. I
didn't want to be unsociable, so I drank some, too. I found I like it. I
liked it too much."

She paused to see if Cyntha was still paying attention. Cyntha nodded for Constance to continue, so she did. "Two weeks ago, I got myself soused, and I paid the consequences. The Guard, including my
husband, marched off and left me, and first thing I knew when I was
decent sober enough to tell, the Yanks had taken the whole town. They
wouldn't let me leave. Said I might be a spy. When I went to the boarding house offering to pay for a place to stay, ol' lady Schmidt hired me
for this job. Gave me this fine dress and apron. She was plumb scared
she was going to lose her niggers. So I've set her mind at ease."

Constance waited while Cyntha finished eating.

Abigail came to the doorway. "Is there anything you want done
now, Miz Constance?"

"I want all you to scrub that kitchen floor and the front hallway.
Get every inch. Them soldier boys done tracked mud everywhere.
Then be ready for a whole passel more to do later."

"Yes'm." Abigail left.

When a consistent scrubbing and clattering noise could be heard
from the kitchen, Constance leaned close to Cyntha. "Mind if I ask you
a question?"

"Surely," Cyntha said.

"You kinda suddenly showed up here . . . and I was wonderin' . . .
Do you have a way out of this town? 'Cause if you do, I'd like to join
you. I'll pay."

"In Confederate money? I wouldn't touch it."

"Why? You a Yank? You sound like you're from the South."

"I am . . . originally. I grew up in the South. I came here to find the
grave of my husband. He died at Wilson Creek."

"So, you're a Yank?"

"I support the Union. Yes."

Constance shook her head, set the coffeepot she had been holding the whole time on the sideboard, and sat beside Cyntha. "Makes no never mind to me if you're a Yank or a Confederate. I just want out of here. I ain't never had no slaves, and that's basically what I do here, is, like you say, be the overseer. I got two silver dollars hid away that I'll give you. That's good money no matter what side you're on. I just want to get back home to my farm."

Cyntha stared long at her conundrum of an acquaintance. She felt herself in the same boat of sorts as Constance. She, too, wanted to escape the town, most importantly, to go to New York to meet and confer with the Fox sisters about her husband. "I'm afraid I'm trapped here like you and . . ."

"I knows a secret way out. I just ain't got no transportation. And these Yanks look like they'll be here forever."

"No. I'm afraid I can't help you. I must go now. I'm meeting someone." Cyntha rose. "It's been nice meeting you, Constance Carver. I'm relieved that you take no pleasure in overseeing the Negroes. They are no different than us whites in the eyes of God." She turned sharply and headed to the door while putting on her coat.

"I believe you are right, Miz Favor!" Constance called after her.

⇒»《◊》«⇐

At the telegraph office, Cyntha dictated her message to a stuffy sergeant with nubs for fingers on one hand. She told him to send it to the Minnesota State Bank in St. Paul. The message read, *To Anthony Atkinson: Dear brother, I find myself in need of cash. Stop. I will explain later. Stop. Your loving sister, Cyntha.* The sergeant handed the message to a sallow lieutenant who read and gave approval for it to be sent. Reynolds and she sat near the potbellied stove on a bench, each reading a book. In an hour, she received her reply.

Dear Mrs. Favor. Stop. Anthony Atkinson is not present. Stop. Left on riverboat to St. Louis in December. Stop. We know he arrived there and the police urgently need to know his whereabouts for important bank reasons, namely his theft of funds. Stop. Elikia Borden, President Minnesota State Bank.

"This is dreadful news," Cyntha said. "That does not sound like my brother, Anthony, at all. Now I must escape this town *and* find my brother. I am sure he is falsely accused." Turning to Reynolds, she whispered, "I know someone who knows a secret way out of Springfield. We can head north and seek out my brother. I hope he is still in St. Louis. It's a few days' journey to Rolla, then we'll take the train to St. Louis."

TWENTY-NINE

A Modicum of Dying

On the morning after the night he had departed the Reeder home, Dred Workman stood smiling his toothy grin on the Reeder's front porch. Lucas opened the door. "Did you forget something, Corporal Workman?"

"No, sir, I'm back for a day or two, then I'm to escort Private Chamberlin to his home in eastern Missouri. Orders."

"So you were able to convince Colonel Greer to let you stay and care for him."

"It weren't no effort at all to convince him, but I think it had more to do with him not wanting the private dying on the trip by himself that weighed on his conscience."

The two walked into the kitchen where Private Chamberlin sat with his one full leg propped on a chair. The stump leg had been sawed off almost to his hip. He was about thirty years old with a copious beard and bushy brows over mournful brown eyes. His expression regularly appeared sorrowful, like he was ready to burst into tears.

"How do, Private?" Workman said.

"Fair enough," the private responded. "I keep feeling my leg below the sawbone's cut. I know it's not there, but I keep feeling it itch, and I want to scratch it. It's like I have a family of them gray back bugs livin' there."

"I've heard tell of that," Workman said. "Phantom pain. Like the ghost of your leg is trying to come back from the dead."

"Well, I'll just have to keep scratchin' the air and hope I get some relief." The sad-faced private garnered a weak smile.

"You're in luck, Private," Lucas said. "Soon, Corporal Workman will escort you home."

"Colonel Greer's orders," Workman said, "They gave me that bay horse I hitched out front so I can ride along with you. This afternoon, I'm gonna see what I can do to modify yor saddle to keep you strapped onto it, so you don't topple off."

"I'm obliged," Private Chamberlin said. Using his crutch, he struggled to rise. Once upon his single leg, he shook hands with Workman.

Chamberlin sat wearily, and Workman pulled Lucas aside. "You know," Workman said, "it's just a matter of time before the gangrene kills him."

Lucas nodded understanding.

"I give him a week before the whole body gives up. I don't know how he's fought it so long. Anyway, I convinced Colonel Greer that Chamberlin deserved some hope. At least we can start toward his home. Maybe he'll make it."

"I hope and pray," Lucas said.

Sara came in the door carrying a basket of eggs, and immediately upon seeing Workman, smiled. "Hello, Corporal Workman. Is Joseph here, too?"

"He's not here, Miss Sara. He's heading west with the last two companies of the regiment. They pulled out two hours ago."

Sara's momentary joy plummeted into melancholia. She gave the eggs to Lucas and went in her room and closed the door.

Workman had lied to Sara. Joseph was still in the camp. The two companies had not marched. For Workman, the opportunity to put distance between himself and Joseph was more important than helping out Chamberlin. He had begun to regret his ruse about Joseph being a Confederate. He thought, *I don't want to be anywhere around him when his memory returns.*

———))(((O))((———

The Third Texas Cavalry camp was clothed in a dewy fog. Joseph sat on a tree stump near Wilson Creek amidst parterres of wildflowers. He watched some crayfish on a slab of rock with their tiny pincers raised in battle. He pulled on new cavalry boots given him by a sergeant just that morning, then he stood. "These are right nice." He strode about, kicking the rattling leaves, happy with the boots' feel and appearance. His thoughts wandered to a vision of himself spurring a horse into a battle line of the enemy. He swept his arm about as if he was slashing a saber. Then, considering that soldiers nearby might have seen him, he turned shamefaced toward the camp. No one was watching. Some soldiers were washing the morning dishes, some pushed their clothes across scrub boards, and a handful of others cavorted at a sort of leapfrog game. Most either sat playing cards or stood around jawing at each other and drinking coffee. One older soldier with waxy, pale skin sat staring contemplatively at the fog-laden vista. At the camp's edge, a handful of men played a game of bowls using cannonballs and rough-hewn cedar pins. Nearer still, a single soldier sat tied on a fence rail with his legs dangling, a punishment meted out to him for some infraction of the rules. Joseph could only guess at the man's contravention.

Then he heard the sergeant barking, "Rouse, rouse, rouse! Roll call."

Joseph rushed toward a sort of parade ground. He passed a tent he had not observed the night of his arrival. A sign on a pole read in rough letters, "Quarantine." A private whose face was splotched with beet red spots sat by a fire stirring a pot of boiling peanuts with a carved pine spurtle. Joseph glanced back at the man who had commenced a deep hacking cough. Standing beside the private, a rawboned young man of almost fragile dimensions and with the pallor of a cadaver prayed. He was dressed in black from hat to shoes and held a worn Bible.

Joseph joined the two companies of men arrayed in four parallel lines and listened for his name to be called. When the sergeant read one name, no soldier answered, and he remarked, "Ah, yes. I forgot. Got to mark that one out." He wrote a note on his paper. At the end of the roll call, Colonel Greer exited his tent. He wore a plumed hat and an elegant waistcoat with embroidered gold filigree on the sleeves. "Attention!" the sergeant shouted.

The men, including Joseph, snapped to attention.

"All present, sir," the sergeant said, "except the two we lost to the measles last night."

"Yes, I see. It's a sad loss." Colonel Greer removed his hat and bowed his head. Replacing his hat, he asked, "Have you set a burial detail?"

"Not yet, sir," the sergeant replied in a Scottish brogue. "It is to be done following your comments."

"Thank you, Sergeant. I see that the good Reverend Felder is here from Springfield to offer the last rites." Joseph now knew who the black-clad Bible reader was.

Colonel Greer waved his gloved hand high with a flourish. "At ease. Men of the Third Texas Cavalry, I know you are disappointed that we have not departed for the Boston Mountains in Arkansas. We were scheduled to leave today, but it seems the two extra wagons in which we were to load our supplies have been stolen. Though we have a surfeit of food and ammunition, we still maintain a mere six wagons. I have it on good account that a band of Jayhawkers have absconded with the other two. Lieutenant Jordan will select a half-dozen men to go in search of them. In the meantime, I have sent an emissary to some farmers a few miles south to allocate two wagons."

Joseph, his first time to lay eyes on the colonel, thought him a handsome man. He was clean-shaven, tall, and robust. He bore himself with confidence. The colonel's resounding voice sounded much like a politician's Joseph had once heard. His mind searched for a reference to his memory. Then an image swept into his mind of two men standing on a platform, one of them short and stocky, the other tall, lean, and ill-fitted to his clothes. Both had honest faces and were involved in a debate. The shorter one charged the tall one with erroneous arguments about the value of slaves to the republic. Douglas was the short man's name. Stephen Douglas.

The taller man with dark stringy hair seemed nonplussed by his opponent's harangue, though Douglas's argument seemed well-formed in Joseph's mind. *Who is the other man, the one with deep set, thoughtful eyes?*

Joseph could not maintain his attention to the memory and forced himself to focus on his new commanding officer. Colonel Greer had been marching up and down the line admonishing his men to be diligent in their watchfulness against the "loathsome Yankee dogs who ply their way by stealing and plundering."

Colonel Greer stepped up on a tree stump and spoke in a more subdued tone. "Now, as many of you know, I am the Texas state commander of the Knights of the Golden Circle, and once this travesty of justice which has been thrust upon our Southern dignity and sovereignty is averted by brave men such as yourselves, and through the generosity of liberty-loving individuals who give of their wealth and hearth for the cause . . ." He paused to take a breath. "I will raise an army to bring the Northern Mexico counties of Tamaulipas and Coahuila into the fold of this great Confederacy. Indeed, the noble state of Texas deems as much a necessity. I am close friends, as you know, with President Jefferson Davis and have recently appraised him regarding this endeavor. He finds the goal worthwhile." His next words rolled out like thunder. "I would be remiss if I did not convey to you the importance of your maintaining your rigor in support of our cause. Can I count on y'all?"

The soldiers cheered.

"All right. All right. Quiet down, my hearty lads," said Colonel Greer with his hands outstretched. "As soon as the wagons are procured, we will depart to join the rest of the regiment in the Boston Mountains, there to recoup and train for yet another imminent victory." He pulled his sword and hoisted it above his head. His voice fairly rang, sending a flock of crows flying from the trees. "Let the Yankee rats think they can invade. We'll drive the vermin back into their burrows!" To more cheers, he stepped from the stump and made his way with a triumphant stride back to his tent.

Before dismissing the company, the sergeant selected some men for the lieutenant to chase after the Jayhawkers who had stolen the wagons. They departed for their horses. He chose two men for latrine duty, four to hunt for game, and then selected the burial detail. The last man he pointed at was Joseph. The group of men gathered shovels reticently, then tied kerchiefs over their mouths and noses. Joseph followed their lead. He had never buried anyone before. When the detail arrived beside the stiffened corpses lying on a tarp by the Quarantine tent, Joseph marveled at the inert flesh of the dead. Four men came up carrying rough-hewn coffins. At the burial, while Reverend Felder read the last rites, Joseph recalled the name of the other debater—Lincoln. *His name was Lincoln.* Despite his recognition of the name, he had no further remembrance about the man. *Whoever he is, he reminds me of Dred Workman.*

The next morning, Joseph rode on his new mount, a roan mare, with the two companies of the Third Texas Cavalry toward the cantonment in the Boston Mountains. Though he tried to feel the exuberance the rest of the company seemed to feel, his thoughts fled always to Sara.

That very morning, two events occurred not far from where he rode. Sara, not knowing Joseph was in the column, stood on the escarpment watching the last of McCulloch's Confederate army leave Missouri. She had come to the grassy spot on the hill to lay flowers at the graves of two Union soldiers who had died there. She had not known them but felt that someone should remember them. She thought of Joseph and the possibility that he might die. Her longing for Joseph was both a wellspring of tender love and a tearing at her soul.

In the trees below her, and out of sight of the Confederates, a lone individual whose face had a scar running from his forehead across his nose, observed with interest the departure of the remaining army from the valley. His smile was never a real smile, but that smear of lust and greed curled his lips, and he looked a long while up at Sara on the hill's edge, then turned his horse and crossed the creek.

THIRTY

Malice in the World Comes from No Good Place

Abram, leaning back in a chair in the backyard, strummed his arthritic hand lightly on his banjo, creating a tune of his own making. Private Giles sawed an accompaniment on his violin in long strokes. Sergeant Higgins, a thoughtful expression on his gray-bearded face, used his bayonet to tap a rhythm on an upturned wooden bucket. Twilight settled about them, the day crisp, the trees painted autumnal red and gold. Heavy drapes of rain clouds gathered to the north. Constance's mutts trotted about, heads down, sniffing, and occasionally snapping at the chirping crickets that flitted in the tall grasses beyond the yard. Sara exited the house carrying a tray of glasses of lemonade. "This is the last of the lemons," she said. "Soon it will be time for hot cider."

Following her, Lucas brought his telescope and tripod. "Tonight, if the rain holds off," he announced, "we'll all take a look at Saturn and Jupiter."

The little band ceased their melody making, and each took a glass of lemonade. While Lucas set up the telescope, Sara sat down next to Abram on a tree stump. "Play 'Billy Boy,' Abram," she said. "I love when you play."

He commenced the lively melody, and Giles joined in while

Higgins blew on a mouth harp. Corporal Workman came out the back door helping Private Chamberlin descend the steps. The tall, one-legged soldier's face was as pale as a cloud, his hair hung straggly from his head. He leaned on his crutch, and each step he took brought pained expressions to his face. Workman helped the private gain a chair. "Well," Workman said, "I'll be taking you back to your home tomorrow, Chamberlin. It took me a lot longer to rig up your saddle than I thought it would, but it's ready now. Won't your family be pleased to see you? This is our send-off party."

Private Chamberlin offered a weak smile but clinched a fist and pressed it into his upper thigh. Sara, sitting some distance from the man with the gangrenous leg, could smell the fetidness, and it was all she could do not to put her hand to her nose. She knew, like Lucas, Workman, and the others, that the man was not long for the world. Workman had taken three weeks to rig a sort of wood-braced and leather-strapped saddle in which the man in his wretched state could stay seated on the horse given him by the Confederate army. Workman on the morrow would escort him home in eastern Missouri, if he made it that far, to die in the arms of his family.

For the Reeders, their work of tending the wounded was over. Sara listened to Abram play, and the tune swept her thoughts to Joseph. The creases of loss in her heart seemed to expand more every day since he left. She pursed her full lips and imagined herself kissing him.

The song ended, and the group sat quiet listening to the thrumming of the crickets. Then Lucas looked up and saw the orange glow and smoke beyond the trees to the southeast. He bolted from his stool. "Fire!" he called, pointing. Everyone, save Chamberlin, stood. "It's in the direction of Constance Carver's place. Quick, Workman, gather guns and meet me at the barn. We'll ride over and try to put it out before it spreads to the whole forest. Giles, you come, too. Abram, you and Higgins stay here. Guard the house. I'll bet my life it's some Jayhawkers started it."

Sara grabbed Lucas's arm. "Let me come, too. Constance is my friend. She followed after her husband with the Missouri Guard, but I know she'd appreciate it if I tried to save her home. And—"

"No, darlin' daughter. Stay here. Be safe. Mind after Chamberlin." Lucas ignored her exasperated sigh and rushed after Giles already heading to the barn. Workman came from the house with two rifles and a pistol and sprinted to catch up. Abram came from the house, checking the load in his rifle while Higgins leaned a ladder against the house and scrambled up it. Sara helped Chamberlin into the house. She stopped at the doorway and watched her father, Workman, and Giles race away on their steeds toward the Carver home. She caught whiffs of the charred effluence now billowing out above the trees.

Some many minutes after they went inside, a moonless night shrouded the farm. Distant thunder timpani-drummed in an approaching storm. Sara lit a lantern in the east bedroom where Private Chamberlin lay, weary and fretful. She tried to take his mind from his pain by reading from a poetry book. Chamberlin fell into a restless sleep. She closed the book, sitting quietly in the room.

Of a sudden, Constance's hounds began howling, then snarling, then angry barking. Looking out the window into the dividing darkness, she made out both of the shadowy dogs lunging and retreating at the grove to the south of the house. She immediately heard Higgins climbing down the ladder, then watched him dart behind the rain barrel beside the back door. She hastened to the remaining rifle leaning against the bookcase.

No sooner had she set the firing cap in place than she heard the cracks of rifle and pistol. The thuds of horse hooves, too. She heard one of the dogs yelp in pain. Bullets plugged the house. One bullet shattered a windowpane, glass spraying across the floor. Creeping to the back door, she inched it open. Dark forms of men on horses darted across the yard, their guns flashing. Two shadowy figures, torches in hand, raced toward the barn. She caught site of Higgins by the water barrel, his revolvers spilling bursts of flame. She watched him turn and shoot two shadows who were almost upon him. They dropped, dark mounds, lifeless. Higgins swirled to his right, but he was too late. A shotgun blast plowed into his chest. He crumpled against the water barrel. A figure, opalescent in the torchlight's glimmer, strode up beside him. She just caught the glint of a saber as it crashed down on Higgins's neck. She screamed. The saber man suddenly collapsed with a groan. Sara realized Abram must have shot him, but she knew not where Abram hid. "Stay safe, Abram!" she whispered.

Looking again toward the barn, she saw the dark figures pulling the cows and mules from it. Then the men tossed torches into the barn. In a minute, the barn was ablaze, flames licking the night sky. In the holocaust of light, she made out about a dozen men, three of them Negro, the rest white.

The shooting stopped. She closed the door. Attempting to secure the crossbar, her hands shook so much, she dropped the board. It clattered to the floor. She stepped back into the gloom of the great room. She heard the calls of men herding the mules and cattle away, and the retreating sounds of hooves. Something crashed through a front window. She turned to see in her father's bedroom, a torch bleeding flame against the wall. The fire caught the curtains and spread lightning fast. She heard more torches thump against the roof, then the crackle of the burning cedar shingles. She glanced back and saw the fire engulfing the bedroom wall. Smoke drifted into the great room. Flames of the barn fire glimmered on the window glass.

Sara stood with her eyes focused on the back door, her rifle cocked, her finger trembling on the trigger.

Out in the yard, she heard a voice call, "Come on, Richards. We got the cattle and mules. Let's go before that major comes back."

Outside the door, a voice like train wheels grinding called out. "Naw. I got sumpin' else to do first. I won't be that long."

More horses galloped away. In interminable time, Sara poised with her gun pointed at the back door. A glimmer of lantern light shone along the door's seams. Smoke billowed vigorously from her father's bedroom. She coughed.

Suddenly, the door sprang open, and a mass of darkness framed in lantern light crouched there. Sara fired. The lantern fell, crashing to the floor, but was still lit and flooding the lower half of the room in light. The man howled. "Damn, girl. You done shot my hand." He held a revolver in his other hand. The man's face was in shadow; his eyes were dark slits, like a snake's.

The man—the creature—strode into the house, confident, waving his hand like he was trying to sling water from it. "Damn, you little whore. That stings." He stopped his forward motion and sucked at the wound, then he licked his lips like he savored the taste.

He moved forward again, the revolver aimed at Sara's belly. Sara dropped the rifle and backed up against the bookcase. Smoke was now drifting through the windows and doorway and filling the room. She inched her hand up to the books to grab one to throw.

"I wouldn't do that, lady." He stepped back and gathered the lantern from the floorboard with his injured hand, then held it up to shine on Sara. "Let me introduce myself. I am B. Franks Richards." He paused and clucked his tongue. "I'm your new master. And you are now my slave. You Southern Secesh shit know what slaves are, don't you. Now, why don't you come closer? I want to see that pretty dress." His voice with an accent not of the South sounded sharp and callous, as if it had never once said a kind word in his life. Sara perceived a long scar across his nose.

Of a sudden, a different form appeared just behind Richards, a tall man using a crutch. Private Chamberlin punched a revolver to the back of Richard's head. "Now, you bastard, that little lady is not going to do any such thing, but you're going to drop that gun."

Richard's revolver fell from his hand. He backed away from Chamberlin who still held a bead on him. The man held up his hands. "Don't shoot," he said. "I was just funnin'."

Smoke abruptly swelled into the room like a dense, opaque sheet. Chamberlin coughed. Richards dived out the door, tumbling on the earth like a boulder. Chamberlin fired at the Jayhawker again and again, but the smoke covered him. Sara ran up beside Chamberlin, and they watched the man vault onto a horse and race away into the darkness.

Sara dashed to her bookcases and began tossing books out the windows. Chamberlin called after her. "No, Miss Sara. The roof's gonna cave. Get outside now."

Sara looked at the encroaching flames and realized the pointlessness of trying to save the home's contents. She rushed to Chamberlin and helped him negotiate the steps out into the yard. Once outside, Sara spotted Abram's body on the ground near the house. While Chamberlin limped away from the fire and smoke, she grabbed Abram's arms and pulled him far from the flames. Placing a hand on his chest, she felt a heartbeat. She ran around the house and did the same with Higgins's inert body. Higgins had no pulse. She left the dead bodies of the Jayhawkers where they lay.

While Chamberlin watched the barn collapse into charred rubble, Sara rushed to the unconscious Abram and held his head in her lap. "Don't die, Abram, oh, don't die!" she sobbed. The storm that had built to the north now began bleeding a steady rain, halting the spread of the fire.

Workman, Giles, and Lucas galloped into the yard. They leapt from their horses and formed a bucket line from the well to the house and worked for an hour, and, with the help of the rain, succeeded in dousing the blaze. Half of the great room, the kitchen, and the easternmost bedroom were saved. For the rest of the house, its joists and support boards stood twisted like the deformed skeleton of a dragon.

Finally, the rain subsided.

Abram at last awoke from unconsciousness, bleary and frail. Sara helped him sit up, then she crept inside the still-smoking house and found blankets in the east bedroom for Abram and Chamberlin. She wrapped the blankets around them both.

When morning light trickled across the sky, Sara, Abram, Giles, and Workman awoke where they had collapsed to sleep in the wet yard. A fog shrouded the once-vibrant farm. Chamberlin sat up last, his face pallid. "I should've shot him."

"It's all right, Aaron," Sara said. "You saved me." Tears perched on her eyelids. She stood and wrung water from her dress, and pulled her bedraggled hair from her face.

"I just couldn't let the last thing I do before I die . . . be killin' a man." Chamberlin hung his head.

Lucas, who had not slept, walked up from the remains of the barn. His face was black with soot. He retrieved the banja and handed it to Abram. He found Giles's fiddle crushed, but picked it up and tossed it away. Then he picked up the remnants of his shattered telescope. He held the broken pieces a long while looking at the charred home, smoke still drifting up. "President Polk gave me this telescope," he said, more to the sky than to anyone.

Sara stepped up beside him. Putting her arm around him, they stood looking at the rear of the house. With half the roof still in place, and the outside wall only grayed from smoke, the house from that perspective appeared as it always had. Yet, when they stepped a few paces to either side, the charred, wrecked half of their home came into view. She moaned, "Why us, O Lord? Why now? Did we not do your will to help those wounded for so long? Why this chastisement?"

Abram went up the back steps of the home first and into the kitchen. He made his way into the east bedroom, untouched by flame, and gathered the bed coverlet and another blanket. He came out and placed the coverlet tenderly around Sara's shoulders. She smiled a half smile and pulled the coverlet about her, for the foggy morning was chilled. Abram helped Chamberlin up from the ground, found him a chair, and wrapped the additional blanket around him.

Workman was kicking through the burned rubble of the barn. After a few moments, he dug out two spades, their handles still workable, and strode back. "I guess we best be about burying these dead." He picked up Lucas's ear trumpet from where Lucas had dropped it and raised it gently to Lucas's ear. He spoke again.

Lucas looked at Workman like he did not know him, took hold of the trumpet, and pitched it a distance from him. He turned toward the sun, faint in a dismal, smudged sky. He dropped the telescope pieces and shook his fist. "Damn you, Lincoln. This is what you brought to us. You destroyed the peace. You broke the nation in half. You may be half a continent away in Washington, but, somehow, you will pay."

THIRTY-ONE

The Parting

Lucas chose to be last to enter his burned-out home. Sara had gone in and gathered a handful of unburned books. She brought them out, set them down, still clutching a partially scorched Bible close to her chest. Workman had helped Abram bring out sundry cookware, crockery, buckets, and silverware. Last, he brought out two blackened wooden chairs. Lucas waited to enter until they had buried their friend, Higgins. He helped Workman dump the four dead Jayhawkers and the dead dogs in a shallow trench.

Then he allowed himself to enter the house. He went to where his room had been. The walls and floors after the rain were a muddy porridge of black and white ash. The iron bedstead was black and twisted from the heat. From the ashes he picked up the charred frame that had once held a photograph of his wife and his children. He dropped it and stared out across the meadows where his cows had grazed and at the low hills to the north. Silently, he trudged back to the east bedroom, untouched by the fire, where he opened a trunk at the foot of the bed and lifted out his major's uniform. He held it up, breathed in the mustiness of it. He checked it for moth holes and found little wear at all, then he smoothed the wrinkles. In an epiphany of sorts, he saw his future and the path he felt he must take. The notion raced with great urgency into his mind from a long buried desire. This new impulse burned within him.

Laying the uniform back in the trunk, he went outside, gathered up his trumpet, and walked up to the little distraught group. He wiped the tears from Sara's reddened cheeks. "We'll go."

He turned to Workman. "In the morning, we . . . all of us, will go east to take Chamberlin home. He won't have to ride in that confounded saddle you made, but in the wagon. After we deliver him to his family, I plan to visit an old friend, a Miss Julia Dent."

When Abram heard the last words of Lucas, he hung his head. He knew well Lucas's plan. He felt shaken from his moorings, like an oak toppled in a storm blast, for he knew that Lucas intended to either give or sell him to the woman. He usually could hide his feelings, but now, as Lucas continued to explain, he looked down at his arthritic hands and fought off tears.

"After our visit," Lucas continued, "we go further east to see if I can offer my services to the cause. I would hate it, but maybe a job at a desk, helping with army supply requisitions. After we take Chamberlin home, Workman, you can return to Arkansas and join your regiment. Sara and I will find residence perhaps in Richmond. I know people there."

"No, Papa."

Lucas turned to face his strong-willed daughter. The fog had dissipated, and a new breeze blew her long, blond hair. His face now bore a grizzled beard, and his heart beat like thunder, for he had watched her mood careen into darker places ever since Joseph had departed, and he had guessed her thoughts and her will. He could almost speak her words for her.

"Papa," Sara said, "I'm not going with you."

Lucas's face grew fierce for an infinitesimally small moment, then

softened. This was his last child. He had raised her to be too impetu-
ous. But she was seventeen and could plot her own destiny. "And why
is that, darling daughter?"

"I feel I must . . ." She paused, choosing her words carefully. "I must
follow after Joseph. My heart is with him and for him, and perhaps
I'm ready to die for him. I don't completely know why, but I must find
him. I will marry him and make him a good wife. I will work for the
army like Constance Carver and be a laundress."

"But, Sara," Lucas replied, "how do you know he cares to marry
you? Perhaps his memory is still lost. What kind of life would you lead
with a man with no past?"

"Our life together will be in our future."

"What if he says no to your entreaty?"

"You don't know him as I do. We read poetry together." She took a
long breath. "We kissed."

"And do you plan to chase after this love of yours even though you
can't be sure that he'll return your love?"

"I do, indeed! Papa, consider this. I have walked and ridden amid
the terror of a battlefield and came out unscathed. I have nursed dying
men back to health. I have helped you farm this land. I am determined,
and I will not be dissuaded from my future. Not by you, nor anyone."

Lucas thought for a moment of slapping his daughter, something he
had never done, as a chastisement for her tone in speaking to him, but the
very thought pained him. He did not want the last interaction with his
daughter to be one of anger and remorse. Instead, he looked back at his
destroyed home and barn, the life he had built—snuffed out like a candle.
"Well, there's nothing for us here anymore. I have hated the advent of this
day when I would lose you, my dear child. But I raised you the way you
are, not too unlike myself, though you mostly take after your mother."

"Yes, and, Papa, I know this land. If I go now before the winter sets
in, I will find the Confederate camp. If it is not to be, I will wait out
the winter in Fayetteville, and I will follow you to Richmond in the

spring." Sara knew she had to give her father some reassurance, and, in a way, reassure herself. If her father did indeed find work in faraway Virginia, she may not see him ever again.

Not see him ever again in my life, she thought. The impact of the words flooded her heart and spilled into her whole being. At this moment, her life was shattered. Ripped apart. She remembered her father's words those several weeks ago on the battlefield. The nation was cleaved in two by this inglorious war. And a thousand hearts were like so much wheat on the threshing room floor. She knew in her core that she would never see her father or Abram again. Her tears became a torrent down her face. Lucas hugged her tight. They stood in their embrace in the warm afternoon sun for a long time.

The next morning, Private Giles was gone. They called for him for an hour, but he never appeared. At length, the family began the journey. Workman rode beside the wagon, loaded with many of the salvaged household—pots, chairs, a few books. In the back sat the trunk with Lucas's uniform. On the wagon seat, Private Chamberlin, weak and shivering from a fever, slumped between Abram and Lucas. They were headed first to Springfield, then into eastern Missouri to Chamberlin's home, then to the Dent family farm.

Sara, riding Esther loaded with several haversacks of vegetables and dried meat spared from the fire, waved a forlorn good-bye and rode alone and silent down the path, then across Wilson Creek and onto Telegraph Road, heading west toward the Boston Mountains and the Confederate cantonment of General McCulloch's troops. She could not help looking back over and over again. She passed beside the poplar trees with their shredded limbs. At that moment, she remembered the day of the battle and, afterward, hearing the odd comments of the captured, tall Yankee soldier, and a bit of bewilderment settled in her brain. Why did that fellow seem familiar? Later, she crossed the stream in the shady glen where she had tended to the blue-coated, wounded cavalry and the young Confederate who had once held her fancy. Numerous grave mounds dotted the entire valley. On the road, she passed the Rays' house where the Negro slave woman sat with her daughter on the front porch, snapping peas. Sara waved at them. Only the little girl waved back. The woman scowled, threw down the pot of beans, and stormed inside.

She remembered her father's words like a recurring echo in her mind. *Asunder.* The word plunged deep into her soul.

AFTERWORD

Thank you for reading *Asunder*. I hoped you enjoyed the first in the Asunder Trilogy. Your opinion means a great deal to me. Be sure to leave a comment about the book on my website: curtlocklearauthor.com and sign up for regular, but occasional e-mails keeping you informed of the progress of Book Two of the trilogy.

The adventure continues with lightning speed. Your opinion matters to me. Please leave a review on Amazon and Barnes and Noble. com and send me an email -curt@curtlocklearauthor.com

CPSIA information can be obtained
at www.ICGtesting.com
Printed in the USA
FSOW02n1751151116
27417FS